The Grraf-Comn[...] Locklear's shoulder.

"That is pure torture," Locklear said, wincing, and saw the navigator stiffen as the furry orange arm dropped. If only he had recalled the kzinti disdain for torture earlier! "I am told you are an honorable race. May I be treated properly as a captive?"

"By all means," the commander said, almost in a purr. "We eat captives."

Locklear, slyly: "Even important ones?"

"If it pleases me," the commander replied. "More likely you could turn your coat in the service of the Patriarchy. I say you could; I would not suggest such an obscenity. But that is probably the one chance your sort has for personal survival."

"My sort?"

The commander looked Locklear up and down, at the slender body, lightly muscled with only the deep chest to suggest stamina. "One of the most vulnerable specimens of monkeydom I have ever seen," he said.

That was the moment when Locklear decided he was at war. Vulnerable, and important, and captive. "Eat me," he said, wondering if that final phrase was as insulting in kzin as it was in Interworld. Evidently not . . .

CATHOUSE

DEAN ING

BAEN
BOOKS

The Man-Kzin Wars is created by Larry Niven.

A Baen Books Original

Baen Publishing Enterprises
260 Fifth Avenue
New York, N.Y. 10001

ISBN: 0-671-69872-9

Cover art by Larry Elmore

First printing, May 1990

Distributed by
SIMON & SCHUSTER
1230 Avenue of the Americas
New York, N.Y. 10020

Printed in the United States of America

CATHOUSE

Sampling war's minor ironies: Locklear knew so little about the *Weasel* or wartime alarms, he thought the klaxon was hooting for planetfall. That is why, when the *Weasel* winked into normal space near that lurking kzin warship, little Locklear would soon be her only survivor. The second irony was that, while the Interworld Commission's last bulletin had announced sporadic new outbursts of kzin hostility, Locklear was the only civilian on the *Weasel* who had never thought of himself as a warrior and did not intend to become one.

Moments after the *Weasel*'s intercom announced completion of their jump, Locklear was steadying himself next to his berth, waiting for the ship's gravity-polarizer to kick in and swallowing hard because, like ancient French wines, he traveled poorly. He watched with envy as Herrera, the hairless, whipcord-muscled Belter in the other bunk, swung out with one foot planted on the deck and the other against the wall. "Like a cat," Locklear said admiringly.

"That's no compliment anymore, flatlander," Herrera said. "It looks like the goddam tabbies want a fourth war. You'd think they'd learn," he added with a grim headshake.

Locklear sighed. As a student of animal psychol-

3

ogy in general, he'd known a few kzinti well enough
to admire the way they learned. He also knew
Herrera was on his way to enlist if, as seemed
likely, the kzinti were spoiling for another war.
And in that case, Locklear's career was about to
be turned upside down. Instead of a scholarly life
puzzling out the meanings of Grog forepaw gestures and kzin ear-twitches, he would probably be
conscripted into some warren full of psych warfare
pundits, for the duration. These days, an ethologist had to be part historian, too—Locklear remembered more than he liked about the three
previous man-kzin wars.

And Herrera was ready to fight the kzinti already, and Locklear had called *him* a cat. Locklear
opened his mouth to apologize but the klaxon
drowned him out. Herrera slammed the door open,
vaulted into the passageway reaching for handholds.

"What's the matter," Locklear shouted. "Where
are you—?"

Herrera's answer, half-lost between the door-
slam and the klaxon, sounded like 'atta nation' to
Locklear, who did not even know the drill for a
deadheading passenger during battle stations.
Locklear was still waiting for a familiar tug of
gravity when that door sighed, the hermetic seal
swelling as always during a battle alert, and he
had time to wonder why Herrera was in such a
hurry before the *Weasel* took her fatal hit amidships.

An energy beam does not always sound like a
thunderclap from inside the stricken vessel. This
one sent a faint crackling down the length of the
Weasel's hull, like the rustle of pre-space parch-
ment crushed in a man's hand. Sequestered alone
in a two-man cabin near the ship's aft galley,
Locklear saw his bunk leap toward him, the iner-

tia of his own body wrenching his grip from his handhold near the door. He did not have time to consider the implications of a blow powerful enough to send a twelve-hundred-ton Privateer-class patrol ship tumbling like a pinwheel, nor the fact that the blow itself was the reaction from most of the *Weasel*'s air, exhausting to space in explosive decompression. And because his cabin had no external viewport, he could not see the scatter of human bodies into the void. The last thing he saw was the underside of his bunk, and the metal brace that caught him above the left cheekbone. Then he knew only a mild curiosity: wondering why he heard something like the steady sound of a thin whistle underwater, and why that yellow flash in his head was followed by an infrared darkness crammed with pain.

It was the pain that brought him awake; that, and the sound of loud static. No, more like the zaps of an arc welder in the hands of a novice—or like a catfight. And then he turned a blurred mental page and *knew* it, the way a Rorschach blot suddenly becomes a face half-forgotten but always feared. So it did not surprise him, when he opened his eyes, to see two huge kzinti standing over him.

To a man like Herrera they would merely have been massive. To Locklear, a man of less than average height, they were enormous; nearly half again his height. The broadest kzin, with the notched right ear and the black horizontal fur-mark like a frown over his eyes, opened his mouth in what, to humans, might be a smile. But kzinti smiles showed dagger teeth and always meant immediate threat. This one was saying something that sounded like, "Clash-rowll whuff, rurr fitz."

Locklear needed a few seconds to translate it, and by that time the second kzin was saying it in Interworld: "Grraf-Commander says, 'Speak when you are spoken to.' For myself, I would prefer that you remained silent. I have eaten no monkey-meat for too long."

While Locklear composed a reply, the big one—the Grraf-Commander, evidently—spoke again to his fellow. Something about whether the monkey knew his posture was deliberately obscene. Locklear, lying on his back on a padded table as big as a Belter's honeymoon bed, realized his arms and legs were flung wide. "I am not very fluent in the Hero's tongue," he said in passable Kzin, struggling to a sitting position as he spoke.

As he did, some of that pain localized at his right collarbone. Locklear moved very slowly thereafter. Then, recognizing the dot-and-comma-rich labels that graced much of the equipment in that room, he decided not to ask where he was. He could be nowhere but an emergency surgical room for kzin warriors. That meant he was on a kzin ship.

A faint slitting of the smaller kzin's eyes might have meant determination, a grasping for patience, or—if Locklear recalled the texts, and if they were right, a small 'if' followed by a very large one—a pause for relatively cold calculation. The smaller kzin said, in his own tongue, "If the monkey speaks the Hero's tongue, it is probably as a spy."

"My presence here was not my idea," Locklear pointed out, surprised to find his memory of the language returning so quickly. "I boarded the *Weasel* on command to leave a dangerous region, not to enter one. Ask the ship's quartermaster, or check her records."

The commander spat and sizzled again: "The crew are all carrion. As you will soon be, unless you tell us why, of all the monkeys on that ship, you were the only one so specially protected."

Locklear moaned. This huge kzin's partial name and his scars implied the kind of warrior whose valor and honor forbade lies to a captive. All dead but himself? Locklear shrugged before he thought, and the shrug sent a stab of agony across his upper chest. "Sonofabitch," he gasped in agony. The navigator kzin translated. The larger one grinned, the kind of grin that might fasten on his throat.

Locklear said in Kzin, very fast, "Not you! I was cursing the pain."

"A telepath could verify your meanings very quickly," said the smaller kzin.

"An excellent idea," said Locklear. "He will verify that I am no spy, and not a combatant, but only an ethologist from Earth. A kzin acquaintance once told me it was important to know your forms of address. I do not wish to give offense."

"Call me Tzak-Navigator," said the smaller kzin abruptly, and grasped Locklear by the shoulder, talons sinking into the human flesh. Locklear moaned again, gritting his teeth. "You would attack? Good," the navigator went on, mistaking the grimace, maintaining his grip, the formidable kzin body trembling with intent.

"I cannot speak well with such pain," Locklear managed to grunt. "Not as well-protected as you think."

"We found you well-protected and sealed alone in that ship," said the commander, motioning for the navigator to slacken his hold. "I warn you, we must rendezvous the *Raptor* with another Ripping-Fang class cruiser to pick up a full crew before we hit the Eridani worlds. I have no time to waste on such a scrawny monkey as you, which we have caught nearer our home worlds than to your own."

Locklear grasped his right elbow as support for that aching collarbone. "I was surveying life-forms on purely academic study—in peacetime, so far as I knew," he said. "The old patrol craft I leased didn't have a weapon on it."

"You lie," the navigator hissed. "We saw them."

"The *Weasel* was not my ship, Tzak-Navigator. Its commander brought me back under protest; said the Interworld Commission wanted noncombatants out of harm's way—and here I am in its cloaca."

"Then it was already well-known on that ship that we are at war. I feel better about killing it," said the commander. "Now, as to the ludicrous cargo it was carrying: what is your title and importance?"

"I am scholar Carroll Locklear. I was probably the least important man on the *Weasel*—except to myself. Since I have nothing to hide, bring a telepath."

"Now it gives orders," snarled the navigator.

"Please," Locklear said quickly.

"Better," the commander said.

"It knows," the navigator muttered. "That is why it issues such a challenge."

"Perhaps," the commander rumbled. To Locklear he said, "A skeleton crew of four rarely includes a telepath. That statement will either satisfy your challenge, or I can satisfy it in more—conventional ways." That grin again, feral, willing.

"I meant no challenge, Grraf-Commander. I only want to satisfy you of who I am, and who I'm not."

"We know *what* you are," said the navigator. "You are our prisoner, an important one, fleeing the Patriarchy rim in hopes that the monkeyship could get you to safety." He reached again for Locklear's shoulder.

"That is pure torture," Locklear said, wincing, and saw the navigator stiffen as the furry orange arm dropped. If only he had recalled the kzinti disdain for torture earlier! "I am told you are an honorable race. May I be treated properly as a captive?"

"By all means," the commander said, almost in a purr. "We eat captives."

Locklear, slyly: "Even important ones?"

"If it pleases me," the commander replied. "More likely you could turn your coat in the service of the Patriarchy. I say you could; I would not suggest such an obscenity. But that is probably the one chance your sort has for personal survival."

"My sort?"

The commander looked Locklear up and down, at the slender body, lightly muscled with only the deep chest to suggest stamina. "One of the most vulnerable specimens of monkeydom I have ever seen," he said.

That was the moment when Locklear decided he was at war. "Vulnerable, and important, and captive. Eat me," he said, wondering if that final phrase was as insulting in Kzin as it was in Interworld. Evidently not . . .

"Gunner! Apprentice Engineer," the commander called suddenly, and Locklear heard two responses through the ship's intercom. "Lock this monkey in a wiper's quarters." He turned to his navigator.

"Perhaps Fleet Commander Skrull-Rrit will want this one alive. We shall know in an eight-squared of duty watches." With that, the huge kzin commander strode out.

After his second sleep, Locklear found himself roughly hustled forward in the low-polarity ship's gravity of the *Raptor* by the nameless Apprentice Engineer. This smallest of the crew had been a kitten not long before and, at two-meter height, was still filling out. The transverse mustard-tinted band across his abdominal fur identified Apprentice Engineer down the full length of the hull passageway.

Locklear, his right arm in a sling of bandages, tried to remember all the mental notes he had made since being tossed into that cell. He kept his eyes downcast to avoid a challenging look—and because he did not want his cold fury to show. These orange-furred monstrosities had killed a ship and crew with every semblance of pride in the act. They treated a civilian captive at best like playground bullies treat an urchin, and at worst like food. It was all very well to study animal behavior as a detached ethologist. It was something else when the toughest warriors in the galaxy attached you to their food chain.

He slouched because that was as far from a military posture as a man could get—and Locklear's personal war could hardly be declared if he valued his own pelt. He would try to learn where hand weapons were kept, but would try to seem stupid. He would . . . he found the last vow impossible to keep with the Grraf-Commander's first question.

Wheeling in his command chair on the *Raptor*'s bridge, the commander faced the captive. "If you

piloted your own monkeyship, then you have some
menial skills." It was not a question; more like an
accusation. "Can you learn to read meters if it will
lengthen your pathetic life?"

Ah, there *was* a question! Locklear was on the
point of lying, but it took a worried kzin to sing a
worried song. If they needed him to read meters, he
might learn much in a short time. Besides,
they'd know bloody well if he lied on this matter.
"I can try," he said. "What's the problem?"

"Tell him," spat Grraf-Commander, spinning
about again to the holo screen.

Tzak-Navigator made a gesture of agreement,
standing beside Locklear and gazing toward the
vast humped shoulders of the fourth kzin. This
nameless one was of truly gigantic size. He turned,
growling, and Locklear noted the nose scar that
seemed very appropriate for a flash-tempered gunner. Tzak-Navigator met his gaze and paused, with
the characteristic tremor of a kzin who prided
himself on physical control. "Ship's Gunner, you
are relieved. Adequately done."

With the final phrase, Ship's Gunner relaxed
his ear umbrellas and stalked off with a barely
creditable salute. Tzak-Navigator pointed to the
vacated seat, and Locklear took it. "He has got us
lost," muttered the navigator.

"But you were the navigator," Locklear said.

"Watch your tongue!"

"I'm just trying to understand crew duties. I
asked what the problem was, and Grraf-Commander
said to tell me."

The tremor became more obvious, but Tzak-
Navigator knew when he was boxed. "With a four-
kzin crew, our titles and our duties tend to vary.
When I accept duties of executive officer and com-

munications officer as well, another member may
prove his mettle at some simple tasks of astrogation."

"I would think Apprentice Engineer might be
good at reading meters," Locklear said carefully.

"He has enough of them to read in the engine
room. Besides, Ship's Gunner has superior time
in grade; to pass him over would have been a
deadly insult."

"Um. And I don't count?"

"Exactly. As a captive, you are a nonperson—
even if you have skills that a gunner might lack."

"You said it was adequately done," Locklear
pointed out.

"For a gunner," spat the navigator, and Locklear
smiled. A kzin, too proud to lie, could still speak
with mental reservations to an underling. The navigator went on: "We drew first blood with our
chance sortie to the galactic West, but Ship's Gunner must verify gravitational blips as we pass in
hyperdrive."

Locklear listened, and asked, and learned. What
he learned initially was fast mental translation of
octal numbers to decimal. What he learned eventually was that, counting on the gunner to verify
likely blips of known star masses, Grraf-Commander
had finally realized that they were monumentally
lost, light-years from their intended rendezvous
on the rim of known space. *And that rendezvous
is on the way to the Eridani worlds*, Locklear
thought. He said, as if to himself but in Kzin, "Out
Eridani way, I· hear they're always on guard for
you guys. You really expect to get out of this
alive?"

"No," said the navigator easily. "Your life may
be extended a little, but you will die with heroes.
Soon."

"Sounds like a suicide run," Locklear said.

"We are volunteers," the navigator said with lofty arrogance, making no attempt to argue the point, and then continued his instructions.

Presently, studying the screen, Locklear said, "That gunner has us forty parsecs from anyplace. Jump into normal space long enough for an astrogation fix and you've got it."

"Do not abuse my patience, monkey. Our last Fleet Command message on hyperwave forbade us to make unnecessary jumps."

After a moment, Locklear grinned. "And your commander doesn't want to have to tell Fleet Command you're lost."

"What was that thing you did with your face?"

"Uh,—just stretching the muscles," Locklear lied, and pointed at one of the meters. "There; um, that was a field strength of, oh hell, three eights and four, right?"

Tzak-Navigator did not have to tremble because his four-fingered hand was in motion as a blur, punching buttons. "Yes. I have a star mass and," the small screen stuttered its chicken-droppings in Kzinti, "here are the known candidates."

Locklear nodded. In this little-known region, some star masses, especially the larger ones, would have been recorded. With several fixes in hyperdrive, he could make a strong guess at their direction with respect to the galactic core. But by the time he had his second group of candidate stars, Locklear also had a scheme.

Locklear asked for his wristcomp, to help him translate octal numbers—his chief motive was less direct—and got it after Apprentice Engineer satisfied himself that it was no energy weapon. The engineer, a suspicious churl quick with his hands and clearly on the make for status, displayed disappointment at his own findings by throwing the instrument in Locklear's face. Locklear decided that the kzin lowest on the scrotum pole was most anxious to advance by any means available. And that, he decided, just might be common in all sentient behavior.

Two hours later by his wristcomp, when Locklear tried to speak to the commander without prior permission, the navigator backhanded him for his trouble and then explained the proper channels. "I will decide whether your message is worth Grraf-Commander's notice," he snarled.

Trying to stop his nosebleed, Locklear told him.

"A transparent ruse," the navigator accused, "to save your own hairless pelt."

"It would have that effect," Locklear agreed. "Maybe. But it would also let you locate your position."

The navigator looked him up and down. "Which will aid us in our mission against your own kind. You truly disgust me."

In answer, Locklear only shrugged. Tzak-Navigator wheeled and crossed to the commander's vicinity, stiff and proper, and spoke rapidly for a few moments. Presently, Grraf-Commander motioned for Locklear to approach.

Locklear decided that a military posture might help this time, and tried to hold his body straight despite his pains. The commander eyed him silently, then said, "You offer me a motive to justify jumping into normal space?"

"Yes, Grraf-Commander: to deposit an important captive in a lifeboat around some stellar body."

"And why in the name of the Patriarchy would I want to?"

"Because it is almost within the reach of plausibility that the occupants of this ship might not survive this mission," Locklear said with irony that went unnoticed. "But en route to your final glory, you can inform Fleet Command where you have placed a vitally important captive, to be retrieved later."

"You admit your status at last."

"I have a certain status," Locklear admitted. *It's damned low, and that's certain enough.* "And while you were doing that in normal space, a navigator might just happen to determine exactly where you are."

"You do not deceive me in your motive. If I did not locate that spot," Tzak-Navigator said, "no Patriarchy ship could find you—and you would soon run out of food and air."

"And you would miss the Eridani mission," Locklear reminded him, "because we aren't getting any blips and you may be getting farther from your rendezvous with every breath."

"At the least, you are a traitor to monkeydom," the navigator said. "No kzin worthy of the name would assist an enemy mission."

Locklear favored him with a level gaze. "You've decided to waste all nine lives for glory. Count on me for help."

"Monkeys are clever where their pelts are concerned," rumbled the commander. "I do not intend to miss rendezvous, and this monkey must be placed in a safe cage. Have the crew provision a lifeboat but disable its drive, Tzak-Navigator. When we locate a stellar mass, I want all in readiness for the jump."

The navigator saluted and moved off the bridge. Locklear received permission to return to his console, moving slowly, trying to watch the commander's furry digits in preparation for a jump that might be required at any time. Locklear punched several notes into the wristcomp's memory; you could never tell when a scholar's notes might come in handy.

Locklear was chewing on kzin rations, reconstituted meat which met human teeth like a leather brick and tasted of last week's oysters, when the long-range meter began to register. It was not much of a blip but it got stronger fast, the vernier meter registering by the time Locklear called out. He watched the commander, alone while the rest of the crew were arranging that lifeboat, and used his wristcomp a few more times before Grraf-Commander's announcement.

Tzak-Navigator, eyeing his console moments after the jump and still light-minutes from that small stellar mass, was at first too intent on his astrogation to notice that there was no nearby solar blaze. But Locklear noticed, and felt a surge of panic.

"You will not perish in solar radiation, at least," said Grraf-Commander in evident pleasure. "You have found yourself a black dwarf, monkey!"

Locklear punched a query. He found no candidate stars to match this phenomenon. "Permission to speak, Tzak-Navigator?"

The navigator punched in a final instruction and, while his screen flickered, turned to the local viewscreen. "Wait until you have something worth saying," he ordered, and paused, staring at what that screen told him. Then, as if arguing with his screen, he complained, "But known space is not old enough for a completely burnt-out star."

"Nevertheless," the commander replied, waving toward the screens, "if not a black dwarf, a very, very brown one. Thank that lucky star, Tzak-Navigator; it might have been a neutron star."

"And a planet," the navigator exclaimed. "Impossible! Before its final collapse, this star would have converted any nearby planet into a gas shell. But there it lies!" He pointed to a luminous dot on the screen.

"That might make it easy to find again," Locklear said with something akin to faint hope. He knew, watching the navigator's split concentration between screens, that the kzin would soon know the *Raptor*'s position. No chance beyond this brown dwarf now, an unheard-of anomaly, to escape this suicide ship.

The navigator ignored him. "Permission for proximal orbit," he requested.

"Denied," the commander said. "You know better than that. Close orbit around a dwarf could rip us asunder with angular acceleration. That dwarf may be only the size of a single dreadnaught, but its mass is enormous enough to bend distant starlight."

While Locklear considered what little he knew of collapsed star matter, a cupful of which would exceed the mass of the greatest warship in known space, the navigator consulted his astrogation screen again. "I have our position," he said at last. "We were on the way to the galactic rim, thanks to that untrained—well, at least he is a fine gunner. Grraf-Commander, I meant to ask permission for orbit around the planet. We can discard this offal in the lifeboat there."

"Granted," said the commander. Locklear took more notes as the two kzinti piloted their ship nearer. If lifeboats were piloted with the same systems as cruisers, and if he could study the ways in which that lifeboat drive could be energized, he might yet take a hand in his fate.

The maneuvers took so much time that Locklear feared the kzin would drop the whole idea, but, "Let it be recorded that I keep my bargains, even with monkeys," the commander grouched as the planet began to grow in the viewport.

"Tiny suns, orbiting the planet? Stranger and stranger," the navigator mused. "Grraf-Commander, this is—not natural."

"Exactly so. It is artificial," said the commander. Brightening, he added, "Perhaps a special project, though I do not know how we could move a full-sized planet into orbit around a dwarf. Tzak-Navigator, see if this tallies with anything the Patriarchy may have on file." No sound passed between them when the navigator looked up from his screen, but their shared glance did not improve the commander's mood. "No? Well, backup records in triplicate," he snapped. "Survey sensors to full gain."

Locklear took more notes, his heart pounding anew with every added strangeness of this singular discovery. The planet orbited several light-minutes from the dead star, with numerous satellites in synchronous orbits, blazing like tiny suns—or rather, like spotlights in imitation of tiny suns, for the radiation from those satellites blazed only downward, toward the planet's surface. Those satellites, according to the navigator, seemed to be moving a bit in complex patterns, not all of them in the same ways—and one of them dimmed even as they watched.

The commander brought the ship nearer, and now Tzak-Navigator gasped with a fresh astonishment. "Grraf-Commander, this planet is dotted with force-cylinder generators. Not complete shells, but open to space at orbital height. And the beamspread of each satellite's light flux coincides with the edge of each force cylinder. No, not all of them; several of those circular areas are not bathed in any light at all. Fallow areas?"

"Or unfinished areas," the commander grunted. "Perhaps we have discovered a project in the making."

Locklear saw blazes of blue, white, red, and yellow impinging in vast circular patterns on the planet's surface. *Almost as if someone had placed small models of Sirius, Sol, Fomalhaut, and other suns out here,* he thought. He said nothing. If he orbited this bizarre mystery long enough, he might probe its secrets. If he orbited it too long, he would damned well die of starvation.

Then, "Homeworld," blurted the astonished navigator, as the ship continued its close pass around this planet that was at least half the mass of Earth.

Locklear saw it too, a circular region that seemed to be hundreds of kilometers in diameter, rich in colors that reminded him of a kzin's fur. The green expanse of a big lake, too, as well as dark masses that might have been mountain crags. And then he noticed that one of the nearby circular patterns seemed achingly familiar in its colors, and before he thought, he said it in Interworld: "Earth!"

The commander leaped to a mind-numbing conclusion the moment before Locklear did. "This can only be a galactic prison—or a zoo," he said in a choked voice. "The planet was evidently moved here, after the brown dwarf was discovered. There seems to be no atmosphere outside the force walls, and the planetary surface between those circular regions is almost as cold as interstellar deeps, according to the sensors. If it is a prison, each compound is well-isolated from the others. Nothing could live in the interstices."

Locklear knew that the commander had overlooked something that could live there very comfortably, but held his tongue awhile. Then, "Permission to speak," he said.

"Granted," said the commander. "What do you know of this—this thing?"

"Only this: whether it is a zoo or a prison, one of those compounds seems very Earthlike. If you left me there, I might find air and food to last me indefinitely."

"And other monkeys to help in Patriarch-knows-what," the navigator put in quickly. "No one is answering my all-band queries, and we do not know who runs this prison. The Patriarchy has no prison on record that is even faintly like this."

"If they are keeping heroes in a kzinti compound," grated the commander, "this could be a planet-sized trap."

Tzak-Navigator: "But whose?"

Grraf-Commander, with arrogant satisfaction: "It will not matter whose it is, if they set a vermin-sized trap and catch an armed lifeboat. There is no shell over these circular walls, and if there were, I would try to blast through it. Re-enable the lifeboat's drive. Tzak-Navigator, as Executive Officer you will remain on alert in the *Raptor*. For the rest of us: sound planetfall!"

* * *

Caught between fright and amazement, Locklear could only hang on and wait, painfully buffeted during reentry because the kzin-sized seat harness would not retract to fit his human frame. The lifeboat, the size of a flatlander's racing yacht, descended in a broad spiral, keeping well inside those invisible force-walls that might have damaged the craft on contact. At last the commander set his ship on a search pattern that spiraled inward while maintaining perhaps a kilometer's height above the yellow grassy plains, the kzin-colored steaming jungle, the placid lake, the dark mountain peaks of this tiny, synthesized piece of the kzin homeworld.

Presently, the craft settled near a promontory overlooking that lake and partially protected by the rise of a stone escarpment—the landfall of a good military mind, Locklear admitted to himself. "Apprentice-Engineer: report on environmental conditions," the commander ordered. Turning to Locklear, he added, "If this is a zoo, the zookeepers have not yet learned to capture heroes—nor any of our food animals, according to our survey. Since your metabolism is so near ours, I think this is where we shall deposit you for safekeeping."

"But without prey, Grraf-Commander, he will soon starve," said Apprentice Engineer.

The heavy look of the commander seemed full of ironic amusement. "No, he will not. Humans eat monkeyfood, remember? This specimen is a *kshat*."

Locklear colored but tried to ignore the insult. Any creature willing to eat vegetation was, to the kzinti, *kshat*, a herbivore capable of eating offal. And capable of little else. "You might leave me some rations anyway," he grumbled. "I'm in no condition to be climbing trees for food."

"But you soon may be, and a single monkey in this place could hide very well from a search party."

Apprentice-Engineer, performing his extra duties proudly, waved a digit toward the screen. "Grraf-Commander, the gravity constant is exactly home normal. The temperature, too; solar flux, the same; atmosphere and microorganisms as well. I suspect that the builders of this zoo planet have buried gravity polarizers with the force cylinder generators."

"No doubt those other compounds are equally equipped to surrogate certain worlds," the commander said. "I think, whoever they are—or were—the builders work very, very slowly."

Locklear, entertaining his own scenario, suspected the builders worked very slowly, all right—and in ways, with motives, beyond the understanding of man or kzin. But why tell his suspicions to Scarface? Locklear had by now given his own private labels to thees infuriating kzinti, after noting the commander's face-mark, the navigator's tremors of intent, the gunner's brutal stupidity and the engineer's abdominal patch: to Locklear, they had become Scarface, Brick-shitter, Goon, and Yellowbelly. Those labels gave him an emotional lift, but he knew better than to use them aloud.

Scarface made his intent clear to everyone, glancing at Locklear from time to time, as he gave his orders. Water and rations for eight duty watches were to be offloaded. Because every kzin craft has special equipment to pacify those kzinti who displayed criminal behavior, especially the Kdaptists with their treasonous leanings toward humankind,

Scarface had prepared a *zzrou* for their human captive. The *zzrou* could be charged with a powerful soporific drug, or—as the commander said in this case—a poison. Affixed to a host and tuned to a transmitter, the *zzrou* could be set to inject its material into the host at regular intervals—or to meter it out whenever the host moved too far from that transmitter.

Scarface held the implant device, no larger than a biscuit with vicious prongs, in his hand, facing the captive. "If you try to extract this, it will kill you instantly. If you somehow found the transmitter and smashed it—again you would die instantly. Whenever you stray two steps too far from it, you will suffer. I shall set it so that you can move about far enough to feed yourself, but not far enough to make finding you a difficulty."

Locklear chewed his lip for a moment, thinking. "Is the poison cumulative?"

"Yes. And if you do not know that honor forbids me to lie, you will soon find out to your sorrow." He turned and handed a small device to Yellowbelly. "Take this transmitter and place it where no monkey might stumble across it. Do not wander more than eight-cubed paces from here in the process—and take a sidearm and a transceiver with you. I am not absolutely certain the place is uninhabited. Captive! Bare your back."

Locklear, dry-mouthed, removed his jacket and shirt. He watched Yellowbelly bound back down the short passageway and, soon afterward, heard the sigh of an air lock. He turned casually, trying to catch sight of him as Goon was peering through the viewport, and then he felt a paralyzing agony as Scarface impacted the prongs of the *zzrou* into his back just below the left shoulder blade.

*   *   *

His first sensation was a chill, and his second
was a painful reminder of those *zzrou* prongs sunk
into the muscles of his back. Locklear eased to a
sitting position and looked around him. Except for
depressions in the yellowish grass, and a terrify-
ingly small pile of provisions piled atop his shirt
and jacket, he could see no evidence that a kzin
lifeboat had ever landed here. "For all you know,
they'll never come back," he told himself aloud,
shivering as he donned his garments. Talking to
himself was an old habit born of solitary researches,
and made him feel less alone.

But now that he thought on it, he couldn't
decide which he dreaded most, their return or
permanent solitude. "So let's take stock," he said,
squatting next to the provisions. A kzin's rations
would last three times as long for him, but the
numbers were depressing: within three flatlander
weeks he'd either find water and food, or he would
starve—if he did not freeze first.

If this was really a compound designed for kzin,
it would be chilly for Locklear—and it was. The
water would be drinkable, and no doubt he could
eat kzin game animals if he found any that did not
eat him first. He had already decided to head for
the edge of that lake, which lay shining at a distance that was hard to judge, when he realized
that local animals might destroy what food he had.

Wincing with the effort, he removed his light
jacket again. They had taken his small utility knife
but Yellowbelly had not checked his grooming
tool very well. He deployed its shaving blade
instead of the nail pincers and used it to slit away
the jacket's epaulets, then cut carefully at the
triple-folds of cloth, grateful for his accidental choice

of a woven fabric. He found that when trying to break a thread, he would cut his hand before the thread parted. Good; a single thread would support all of those rations but the water bulbs.

His wristcomp told him the kzin had been gone an hour, and the position of that ersatz 61 Ursa Majoris hanging in the sky said he should have several more hours of light, unless the builders of this zoo had fudged on their timing. "Numbers," he said. "You need better numbers." He couldn't eat a number, but knowing the right ones might feed his belly.

In the landing pad depressions lay several stones, some crushed by the cruel weight of the kzin lifeboat. He pocketed a few fragments, two with sharp edges, tied a third stone to a twenty-meter length of thread and tossed it clumsily over a branch of a vine-choked tree. But when he tried to pull those rations up to suspend them out of harm's way, that thread sawed the pulpy branch in two. Sighing, he began collecting and stripping vines. Favoring his right shoulder, ignoring the pain of the *zzrou* as he used his left arm, he finally managed to suspend the plastic-encased bricks of leathery meat five meters above the grass. It was easier to cache the water, running slender vines through the carrying handles and suspending the water in two bundles. He kept one brick and one water bulb, which contained perhaps two gallons of the precious stuff.

And then he made his first crucial discovery, when a trickle of moisture issued from the severed end of a vine. It felt cool, and it didn't sting his hands, and taking the inevitable plunge he licked at a droplet, and then sucked at the end of that vine. Good clean water, faintly sweet; but with

what subtle poisons? He decided to wait a day
before trying it again, but he was smiling a ferocious little smile.

Somewhere within an eight-cubed of kzin paces
lay the transmitter for that damned thing stuck
into his back. No telling exactly how far he could
stray from it. "Damned right there's some telling," he announced to the breeze. "Numbers,
numbers," he muttered. And straight lines. If that
misbegotten son of a hairball was telling the truth—
and a kzin always did—then Locklear would know
within a step or so when he'd gone too far. The
safe distance from that transmitter would probably
be the same in all directions, a hemisphere of
space to roam in. Would it let him get as far as the
lake?

He found out after sighting toward the nearest
edge of the lake and setting out for it, slashing at
the trunks of jungle trees with a sharp stone to
blaze a straight-line trail. Not exactly straight, but
nearly so. He listened hard at every step, moving
steadily downhill, wondering what might have a
menu with his name on it.

That careful pace saved him a great deal of pain,
but not enough of it to suit him. Once, studying
the heat-sensors that guided a captive rattlesnake
to its prey back on Earth, Locklear had been
bitten on the hand. It was like that now behind
and below his left shoulder, a sudden burning
ache that kept aching as he fell forward, writhing,
hurting his right collarbone again. Locklear scrambled backward five paces or so and the sting was
suddenly, shockingly, absent. That part wasn't like
a rattler bite, for sure. He cursed, but knew he
had to do it: moved forward again, very slowly,
until he felt the lancing bite of the *zzrou*. He

moved back a pace and the sting was gone. "But it's cumulative," he said aloud. "Can't do this for a hobby."

He felled a small tree at that point, sawing it with a thread tied to stones until the pulpy trunk fell, held at an angle by vines. Its sap was milky. It stung his finger. Damned if he would let it sting his tongue. He couldn't wash the stuff off in lake water because the lake was perhaps a klick beyond his limit. He wondered if Yellowbelly had thought about that when he hid the transmitter.

Locklear had intended to pace off the distance he had moved from his food cache, but kzin gravity seemed to drag at his heels and he knew that he needed numbers more exact than the paces of a tiring man. He unwound all of the thread on the ball, then sat down and opened his grooming tool. Whatever forgotten genius had stamped a five-centimeter rule along the length of the pincer lever, Locklear owed him. He measured twenty of those lengths and then tied a knot. He then used that first one-meter length to judge his second knot; used it again for the third; and with fingers that stung from tiny cuts, tied two knots at the five-meter point. He tied three knots at the ten-meter point, then continued until he had fifteen meters of surveying line, ignoring the last meter or so.

He needed another half-hour to measure the distance, as straight as he could make it, back to the food cache: 437 meters. He punched the datum into his wristcomp and rested, drinking too much from that water bulb, noting that the sunlight was making longer shadows now. The sundown direction was "West" by definition. And after sundown, what? Nocturnal predators? He was already exhausted, cold, and in need of shelter. Locklear managed to pile palmlike fronds as his bed in a narrow cleft of the promontory, made the best weapon he could by tying fist-sized stones two meters apart with a thread, grasped one stone and whirled the other experimentally. It made a satisfying whirr—and for all he knew, it might even be marginally useful.

The sunblaze fooled him, dying slowly while it was still halfway to his horizon. He punched the time into his wristcomp, and realized that the builders of this zoo might be limited in the degree to which they could surrogate a planetary surface, when other vast circular cages were adjacent to this one. It was too much to ask that any zoo cage be, for its specimens, the best of all possible worlds.

Locklear slept badly, but he slept. During the times when he lay awake, he felt the silence like a hermetic seal around him, broken only by the rasp and slither of distant tree fronds in vagrant breezes. Kzin-normal microorganisms, the navigator had said; maybe, but Locklear had seen no sign of animal life. Almost, he would have preferred stealthy footfalls or screams of nocturnal prowlers.

The next morning he noted on his wristcomp when the ersatz kzinti sun began to blaze—not on the horizon, but seeming to kindle when halfway to its zenith—rigged a better sling for his right arm, then sat scratching in the dirt for a time. The night had lasted thirteen hours and forty-eight minutes. If succeeding nights were longer, he was in for a tooth-chattering winter. But first: FIND THAT DAMNED TRANSMITTER.

Because it was small enough to fit in a pocket. And then, ah then, he would not be held like a

lapdog on a leash. He pounded some kzin meat
to soften it and took his first sightings while swill-
ing from a water bulb.

The extension of that measured line, this time
in the opposite direction, went more quickly except when he had to clamber on rocky inclines or
cut one of those pulpy trees down to keep his
sightings near-perfect. He had no spirit level, but
estimated the inclines as well as he could, as he
had done before, and used the wristcomp's trigo-
nometric functions to adjust the numbers he took
from his surveying thread. That damned kzin engineer was the kind who would be half-running to
do his master's bidding, and an eight-cubed of his
paces might be anywhere from six hundred meters to a kilometer. Or the hidden transmitter
might be almost underfoot at the cache; but no
more than a klick at most. Locklear was pondering
that when the *zzrou* zapped him again.

He stiffened, yelped, and whirled back several
paces, then advanced very slowly until he felt its
first half-hearted bite, and moved back, punching
in the datum, working backward using the same
system to make doubly sure of his numbers. At
the cache, he found his two new numbers varied
by five meters and split the difference. His southwest limit had been 437 meters away, his northeast limit 529; which meant the total length of that
line was 966 meters. It probably wasn't the full
diameter of his circle, but those points lay on its
circumference. He halved the number: 483. That
number, minus the 437, was 46 meters. He measured off forty-six meters toward the northeast and
piled pulpy branches in a pyramid higher than his
head. This point, by God, *was* one point on the
full diameter of that circle perpendicular to his

first line! Next he had to survey a line at a right
angle to the line he'd already surveyed, a line
passing through that pyramid of branches.

It took him all morning and then some, length-
ening his thread to be more certain of that crucial
right-angle before he set off into the jungle, and
he measured almost seven hundred meters before
that bloody damned *zzrou* bit him again, this time
not so painfully because by that time he was moving very slowly. He returned to the pyramid of
branches and struck off in the opposite direction,
just to be sure of the numbers he scratched in the
dirt using the wristcomp. He was filled with joy
when the *zzrou* faithfully poisoned him a bit over
300 meters away, within ten meters of his expec-
tation.

Those first three limit points had been enough
to rough out the circle; the fourth was confirma-
tion. Locklear knew that he had passed the transmitter on that long northwest leg; calculated
quickly, because he knew the exact length of that
diameter, that it was a bit over two hundred meters from his pyramid; and measured off the distance after lunch.

"Just like that fur-licking bastard," he said, looking around him at the tangle of orange, green and
yellow jungle growth. "Probably shit on it before
he buried it."

Locklear spent a fruitless hour clearing punky
shrubs and man-high ferns from the soft turf before he saw it, and of course it was not where he
had been looking at all. "It" was not a telltale
mound of dirt, nor a kzin footprint. It was a group
of three globes of milky sap, no larger than water
droplets, just about knee-high on the biggest palm

in the clearing. And just about the right pattern
for a kzin's toe-claws.

He moved around the trunk, as thick as his
body, staring up the tree, now picking out other
sets of milky puncture marks spaced up the trunk.
More kzin clawmarks. Softly, feeling the gooseflesh move down his arms, he called, "Ollee-ollee-
all's-in-free," just for the hell of it. And then he
cut the damned tree down, carefully, letting the
breeze do part of the work so that the tree sagged,
buckled, and came down at a leisurely pace.

The transmitter, which looked rather like a
wristcomp without a bracelet, lay in a hole scooped
out by Yellowbelly's claws in the tender young top
of the tree. It was sticky with sap, and Locklear
hoped it had stung the kzin as it was stinging his
own fingers. He wiped it off with vine leaves,
rinsed it with dribbles of water from severed vines,
wiped it off again, and then returned to his food
cache.

"Yep, the shoulder hurts, and the damned gravity doesn't help but," he said, and yelled it at the
sky, "Now I'm loose, you rat-tailed sons of bitches!"

He spent another night at the first cache, now
with little concern about things that went boomp
in the ersatz night. The sunblaze dimmed thirteen
hours and forty-eight minutes after it began, and
Locklear guessed that the days and nights of this
synthetic arena never changed. "It'd be tough to
develop a cosmology here," he said aloud, shivering because his right shoulder simply would not
let him generate a fire by friction. "Maybe that
was deliberate." If he wanted to study the behavior of intelligent species without risking their learning too much, and had not the faintest kind of

ethics about it, Locklear decided he might imagine just such a vast enclosure for the kzinti. Only they were already a spacefaring race, and so was humankind, and he could have *sworn* the adjacent area on this impossible zoo planet was a ringer for one of the wild areas back on Earth. He cudgeled his memory until he recalled the lozenge shape of that lake seen from orbit, and the earthlike area.

"Right—about—there," he said, nodding to the southwest, across the lake. "If I don't starve first."

He knew that any kzinti searching for him could simply home in on the transmitter. Or maybe not so simply, if the signal was balked by stone or dirt. A cave with a kink in it could complicate their search nicely. He could test the idea—at the risk of absorbing one zap too many from that infuriating *zzrou* clinging to his back.

"Well, second things second," he said. He'd attended to the first things first. He slept poorly again, but the collarbone seemed to be mending.

Locklear admitted an instant's panic the next morning (he had counted down to the moment when the ersatz sun began to shine, missing it by a few seconds) as he moved beyond his old limit toward the lake. But the *zzrou* might have been a hockey puck for its inertness. The lake had small regular wavelets—*easy enough to generate if you have a timer on your gravity polarizer,* he mused to the builders—and a narrow beach that alternated between sand and pebbles. No prints of any kind, not even birds or molluscs. If this huge arena did not have extremes of weather, a single footprint on that sand might last a geologic era.

The food cache was within a stone's throw of the kzin landing, good enough reason to find a better place. Locklear found one, where a stream trickled to the lake (pumps, or rainfall? Time enough to find out), after cutting its passage down through basalt that was half-hidden by foliage. Locklear found a hollow beneath a low waterfall and, in three trips, portaged all his meagre stores to that hideyhole with its stone shelf. The water tasted good, and again he tested the trickle from slashed vines because he did not intend to stay tied to that lakeside forever.

The channel cut through basalt by water told him that the stream had once been a torrent and might be again. The channel also hinted that the stream had been cutting its patient way for tens of centuries, perhaps far longer. "Zoo has been here a long time," he said, startled at the tinny echo behind to think of this planet as "Zoo." It might be begun to think of this planet as "Zoo". It might be untenanted, like that sad remnant of a capitalist's dream that still drew tourists to San Simeon on the coast of Earth's California. Cages for exotic fauna, but the animals long since gone. *Or never introduced?* One more puzzle to be shelved until more pieces could be studied.

During his fourth day on Zoo, Locklear realized that the water was almost certainly safe, and that he must begin testing the tubers, spiny nuts, and poisonous-looking fruit that he had been eyeing with mistrust. Might as well test the stuff while circumnavigating the lake, he decided, vowing to try one new plant a day. Nothing had nibbled at anything beyond mosslike growths on some soft-surfaced fruit. He guessed that the growths meant that the fruit was overripe, and judged ripeness that way. He did not need much time deciding about plants that stank horribly, or that stung his hands. On the seventh day on Zoo, while using a brown plant juice to draw a map on plastic food wrap (a pathetic left-handed effort), he began to feel distinct localized pains in his stomach. He put a finger down his throat, bringing up bits of kzin rations and pieces of the nutmeats he had swallowed after trying to chew them during breakfast. They had gone into his mouth like soft rubber capsules, and down his throat the same way.

But they had grown tiny hair-roots in his belly, and while he watched the nasty stuff he had splashed on stone, those roots continued to grow, waving blindly. He applied himself to the task again and finally coughed up another. How many had he swallowed? Three, or four? He thought four, but saw only three, and only after smashing a dozen more of the nutshells was he satisfied that each shell held three, and only three, of the loathsome things. Not animals, perhaps, but they would eat you nonetheless. Maybe he should've named the place "Herbarium." The hell with it: "Zoo" it remained.

On the ninth day, carrying the meat in his jacket, he began to use his right arm sparingly. That was the day he realized that he had rounded the broad curve of the lake and, if his brief memory of it from orbit was accurate, the placid lake was perhaps three times as long as it was wide. He found it possible to run, one of his few athletic specialties, and despite the wear of kzin gravity he put fourteen thousand running paces behind him before exhaustion made him gather high grasses for a bed.

At a meter and a half per step, he had covered twenty-one klicks, give or take a bit, that day. Not bad in this gravity, he decided, even if the collarbone was aching again. On his abominable map, that placed him about midway down the long side of the lake. The following morning he turned west, following another stream through an open grassy plain, jogging, resting, jogging. He gathered tubers floating downstream and ate one, fearing that it would surely be deadly because it tasted like a wild strawberry.

He followed the stream for three more days, living mostly on those delicious tubers and water, nesting warmly in thick sheaves of grass. On the next day he spied a dark mass of basalt rising to the northwest, captured two litres of water in an empty plastic bag, and risked all. It was well that he did for, late in the following day with heaving chest, he saw clouds sweeping in from the north, dragging a gray downpour as a bride drags her train. That stream far below and klicks distant was soon a broad river which would have swept him to the lake. But now he stood on a rocky escarpment, seeing the glisten of water from those crags in the distance, and knew that he would not die of thirst in the highlands. He also suspected, judging from the shredded-cotton roiling of cloud beyond those crags, that he was very near the walls of his cage.

Even for a runner, the two-kilometer rise of those crags was daunting in high gravity. Locklear aimed for a saddleback only a thousand meters high where sheets of rain had fallen not long before, hiking beside a swollen stream until he found its source. It wasn't much as glaciers went, but he found green depths of ice filling the saddleback, shouldering up against a force wall that beggared anything he had ever seen up close.

The wall was transparent, apparent to the eye

only by its effects and by the eldritch blackness just beyond it. The thing was horrendously cold, seeming to cut straight across hills and crags with an inner border of ice to define this kzin compound. Locklear knew it only seemed straight because the curvature was so gradual. When he tossed a stone at it, the stone slowed abruptly and soundlessly as if encountering a meters-deep cushion, then slid downward and back to clatter onto the minuscule glacier. Uphill and down, for as far as he could see, ice rimmed the inside of the force wall. He moved nearer, staring through that invisible sponge, and saw another line of ice a klick distant. Between those ice rims lay bare basalt, as uncompromisingly primitive as the surface of an asteroid. Most of that raw surface was so dark as to seem featureless, but reflections from ice lenses on each side dappled the dark basalt here and there. The dapples of light were crystal clear, without the usual fuzziness of objects a thousand meters away, and Locklear realized he was staring into a vacuum.

"So visitors to Zoo can wander comfortably around with gravity polarizer platforms between the cages," he said aloud, angrily because he could see the towering masses of conifers in the next compound. It was an Earth compound, all right— but he could see no evidence of animals across that distance, and that made him fiercely glad for some reason. He ached to cross those impenetrable barriers, and his vision of lofty conifers blurred with his tears.

His feet were freezing, now, and no vegetation grew as near as the frost that lined the ice rim. "You're good, but you're not perfect," he said to the builders. "You can't keep the heat in these

compounds from leaking away at the rims." Hence
frozen moisture and the lack of vegetation along
the rim, and higher rainfall where clouds skirted
that cold force wall.

Scanning the vast panoramic arc of that ice rim,
Locklear noted that his prison compound had a
gentle bowl shape, though some hills and crags
surged up in the lowlands. *Maybe using the natural contours of old craters? Or maybe you made
those craters.* It was an engineering project that
held tremendous secrets for humankind, and it
had been there for one hell of a long time. Widely
spaced across that enormous bowl were spots of
dramatic color, perhaps flowers. *But they won't
scatter much without animal vectors to help the
wind disperse seeds and such. Dammit, this place
wasn't finished!*

He retraced his steps downward. There was no
point in making a camp in this inclement place,
and with every sudden whistle of breeze now he
was starting to look up, scanning for the kzin ship
he knew might come at any time. He needed to
find a cave, or to make one, and that would require construction tools.

Late in the afternoon, while tying grass bundles
at the edge of a low rolling plain, Locklear found
wood of the kind he'd hardly dared to hope for.
He simply had not expected it to grow horizon-
tally. With a thin bark that simulated its surroundings, it lay mostly below the surface with shallow
roots at intervals like bamboo. Kzinti probably
would've known to seek it from the first, damn
their hairy hides. The stuff—he dubbed it shamboo—grew parallel to the ground and arrow-
straight, and its foliage popped up at regular
intervals too. Some of its hard, hollow segments

stored water, and some specimens grew thick as his thighs and ten meters long, tapering to wicked growth spines on each end. Locklear had been walking over potential hiking staffs, construction shoring, and rafts for a week without noticing. He pulled up one the size of a javelin and clipped it smooth.

His grooming tool would do precision work, but Locklear abraded blisters on his palms fashioning an axehead from a chertlike stone common in seams where basalt crags soared from the prairie. He spent two days learning how to socket a handaxe in a shamboo handle, living mostly on tuberberries and grain from grassheads, and elevated his respect for the first tool-using creatures in the process.

By now, Locklear's right arm felt almost as good as new, and the process of rediscovering primitive technology became a compelling pastime. He was so intent on ways to weave split shamboo filaments into cordage for a firebow, while trudging just below the basalt heights, that he almost missed the most important moment of his life.

He stepped from savannah grass onto a gritty surface that looked like other dry washes, continued for three paces, stepped up onto grassy turf again, then stopped. He recalled walking across sand-sprinkled tiles as a youth, and something in that old memory made him look back. The dry wash held wavelike patterns of grit, pebbles, and sand, but here and there were bare patches.

And those bare patches were as black and as smooth as machine-polished obsidian.

Locklear crammed the half-braided cord into a pocket and began to follow that dry wash up a gentle slope, toward the cleft ahead, and toward his destiny.

*   *   *

His heart pounding with hope and fear, Locklear
stood five meters inside the perfect arc of obsidian
that formed the entrance to that cave. No runoff
had ever spilled grit across the smooth broad floor
inside, and he felt an irrational concern that his
footsteps were defiling something perfectly pris-
tine, clean and cold as an ice cavern. But a far, *far*
more rational concern was the portal before him,
its facing made of the same material as the floor,
the opening itself four meters wide and just as
high. A faint flickering luminescence, as of gossamer film stretched across the portal, gave barely
enough light to see. Locklear saw his reflection in
it, and wanted to laugh aloud at this ragged, skinny,
barrel-chested apparition with the stubble of beard
wearing stained flight togs. And the apparition
reminded him that he might not be alone.

He felt silly, but after clearing his throat twice
he managed to call out: "Anybody home?"

Echoes; several of them, more than this little
entrance space could possibly generate. He poked
his sturdy shamboo hiking staff into the gossamer
film and jumped when stronger light flickered in
the distance. "Maybe you just eat animal tissue,"
he said, with a wavering chuckle. "Well—" He
took his grooming pincers and cut away the dried
curl of skin around a broken blister on his palm,
clipped away sizeable crescents of fingernails, tossed
them at the film.

Nothing but the tiny clicks of cuticles on obsidian, inside; *that*'s how quiet it was. He held the
pointed end of the staff like a lance in his right
hand, extended the handaxe ahead in his left. He
was right-handed, after all, so he'd rather lose the
left one . . .

No sensation on his flesh, but a sudden flood of light as he moved through the portal, and Locklear dashed backward to the mouth of the cave. "Take it easy, fool," he chided himself. "What did you see?"

A long smooth passageway; walls without signs or features; light seeming to leap from obsidian walls, not too strong but damned disconcerting. He took several deep breaths and went in again, standing his ground this time when light flooded the artificial cave. His first thought, seeing the passageway's apparent end in another film-spanned portal two hundred meters distant, was, *Does it go all the way from Kzersatz to Newduvai?* He couldn't recall when he'd begun to think of this kzin compound as Kzersatz and the adjoining, Earthlike, compound as Newduvai.

Footfalls echoing down side corridors, Locklear hurried to the opposite portal, but frost glistened on its facing and his staff would not penetrate more than a half-meter through the luminous film. He could see his exhalations fogging the film. The resistance beyond it felt spongy but increasingly hard, probably an extension of that damned force wall. If his sense of direction was right, he should be just about beneath the rim of Kzersatz. No doubt someone or something knew how to penetrate that wall, because the portal was there. But Locklear knew enough about force walls and screens to despair of getting through it without better understanding. Besides, if he did get through he might punch a hole into vacuum. If his suspicions about the builders of Zoo were correct, that's exactly what lay beyond the portal.

Sighing, he turned back, counting nine secondary passages that yawned darkly on each side, choosing the first one to his right. Light flooded it instantly. Locklear gasped.

Row upon row of cubical, transparent containers stretched down the corridor for fifty meters, some of them tiny, some the size of a small room. And in each container floated a specimen of animal life, rotating slowly, evidently above its own gravity polarizer field. Locklear had seen a few of the creatures; had seen pictures of a few more; all, every last one that he could identify, native to the kzin homeworld. He knew that many museums maintained ranks of pickled specimens, and told himself he should not feel such a surge of anger about this one. *Well, you're an ethologist, you twit*, he told himself silently. *You're just pissed off because you can't study behaviors of dead animals.* Yet, even taking that into consideration, he felt a kind of righteous wrath toward builders who played at godhood without playing it perfectly. It was a responsibility he would never have chosen. He did not yet realize that he was surrounded with similar choices.

He stood before a floating *vatach*, in life a fast-moving burrower the size of an earless hare, reputedly tasty but too mild-mannered for kzinti sport. No symbols on any container, but obvious differences among the score of *vatach* in those containers.

How many sexes? He couldn't recall. "But I bet you guys would," he said aloud. He passed on, shuddering at the critters with fangs and leathery wings, marveling at the stump-legged creatures the height of a horse and the mass of a rhino, all in positions that were probably fetal though some were obviously adult.

Retracing his steps to the *vatach* again, Locklear

leaned a hand casually against the smooth metal base of one container. He heard nothing, but when he withdrew his hand the entire front face of the glasslike container levered up, the *vatach* settling gently to a cage floor that slid forward toward Locklear like an offering.

The *vatach* moved.

Locklear leaped back so fast he nearly fell, then darted forward again and shoved hard on the cage floor. Back it went, down came the transparent panel, up went the *vatach*, inert, into its permanent rotating waltz.

"Stasis fields! By God, they're alive," he said. The animals hadn't been pickled at all, only stored until someone was ready to stock Kzersatz. *Vatach* were edible herbivores—but if he released them without natural enemies, how long before they overran the whole damned compound? And did he really want to release their natural enemies, even if he could identify them?

"Sorry, fellas. Maybe I can find you an island," he told the little creatures, and moved on with an alertness that made him forget the time. He did not consider time because the glow of illumination did not dim when the sun of Kzersatz did, and only the growl of his empty belly sent him back to the cave entrance where he had left his jacket with his remaining food and water. Even then he chewed tuberberries from sheer necessity, his hands trembling as he looked out at the blackness of the Kzersatz night. Because he had passed down each of those eighteen side passages, and knew what they held, and knew that he had some godplaying of his own to ponder.

He said to the night and to himself, "Like for

instance, whether to take one of those goddamned kzinti out of stasis."

His wristcomp held a hundred megabytes, much of it concerning zoology and ethology. Some native kzin animals were marginally intelligent, but he found nothing whatever in memory storage that might help him communicate abstract ideas with them. "Except the tabbies themselves, eighty-one by actual count," he mused aloud the next morning, sitting in sunlight outside. "Damned if I do. Damned if I don't. Damn if I know which is the damnedest," he admitted. But the issue was never very much in doubt; if a kzin ship did return, they'd find the cave sooner or later because they were the best hunters in known space. He'd make it expensive in flying fur, maybe—but there seemed to be no rear entrance. Well, he didn't have to go it alone; Kdaptist kzinti made wondrous allies. Maybe he could convert one, or win his loyalty by setting him free.

If the kzin ship didn't return, he was stuck with a neolithic future or with playing God to populate Kzersatz, unless—"Aw shitshitshit," he said at last, getting up, striding into the cave. "I'll just wake the smallest one and hope he's reasonable."

But the smallest ones weren't male; the females, with their four small but prominent nipples and the bushier fur on their tails, were the runts of that exhibit. In their way they were almost beautiful, with longer hindquarters and shorter torsos than the great bulky males, all eighty-one of the species rotating nude in fetal curls before him. He studied his wristcomp and his own memory, uncomfortably aware that female kzin were, at best, morons. Bred for bearing kits, and for catering to their warrior males, female kzinti were little more than ferociously protected pets in their own culture.

"Maybe that's what I need anyhow," he muttered, and finally chose the female that bulked smallest of them all. When he pressed that baseplate, he did it with grim forebodings.

She settled to the cage bottom and slid out, and Locklear stood well away, axe in one hand, lance in the other, trying to look as if he had no intention of using either. His Adam's apple bobbed as the female began to uncoil from her fetal position.

Her eyes snapped open so fast, Locklear thought they should have clicked audibly. She made motions like someone waving cobwebs aside, mewing in a way that he found pathetic, and then she fully noticed the little man standing near, and she screamed and leaped. That leap carried her to the top of a nearby container, *away* from him, cowering, eyes wide, ear umbrellas folded flat.

He remembered not to grin as he asked, "Is this my thanks for bringing you back?"

She blinked. "You (something, something) a devil, then?"

He denied it, pointing to the scores of other kzin around her, admitting he had found them this way.

If curiosity killed cats, this one would have died then and there. She remained crouched and wary, her eyes flickering around as she formed more questions. Her speech was barely understandable. She used a form of verbal negation utterly new to him, and some familiar words were longer the way she pronounced them. The general linguistic rule was that abstract ideas first enter a lexicon as several words, later shortened by the impatient.

Probably her longer words were primitive forms;

God only knew how long she had been in stasis! He told her who he was, but that did not reduce her wary hostility much. She had never heard of men. Nor of any intelligent race other than kzinti. Nor, for that matter, of spaceflight. But she was remarkably quick to absorb new ideas, and from Locklear's demeanor she realized all too soon that *he*, in fact, was scared spitless of *her*. That was the point when she came down off that container like a leopard from a limb, snatched his handaxe while he hesitated, and poked him in the gut with its haft.

It appeared, after all, that Locklear had revived a very, *very* old-fashioned female.

"You (something or other) captive," she sizzled, unsheathing a set of shining claws from her fingers as if to remind him of their potency. She turned a bit away from him then, looking sideways at him. "Do you have sex?"

His Adam's apple bobbed again before he intuited her meaning. Her first move was to gain control, her second to establish sex roles. A bright female; yeah, that's about what an ethologist should expect . . . "Humans have two sexes just as kzinti do," he said, "and I am male, and I won't submit as your captive. You people eat captives. You're not all that much bigger than I am, and this lance is sharp. I'm your benefactor. Ask yourself why I didn't spear you for lunch before you awoke."

"If you could eat me, I could eat you," she said. "Why do you cut words short?"

Bewildering changes of pace but always practical, he thought. Oh yes, an exceedingly bright female. "I speak modern Kzinti," he explained. "One day we may learn how many thousands of years you have been asleep." He enjoyed the almost human widening of her yellow eyes, and went on doggedly. "Since I have honorably waked you from what might have been a permanent sleep, I ask this: what does your honor suggest?"

"That I (something) clothes," she said. "And owe you a favor, if nakedness is what you want."

"It's cold for me, too." He'd left his food outside but was wearing the jacket, and took it off. "I'll trade this for the axe."

She took it, studying it with distaste, and eventually tied its sleeves like an apron to hide her mammaries. It could not have warmed her much. His question was half disbelief: "That's it? Now you're clothed?"

"As (something) of the (something) always do," she said. "Do you have a special name?"

He told her, and she managed "Rockear." Her own name, she said, was (something fiendishly tough for humans to manage), and he smiled. "I'll call you 'Miss Kitty.'"

"If it pleases you," she said, and something in the way that phrase rolled out gave him pause.

He leaned the shamboo lance aside and tucked the axe into his belt. "We must try to understand each other better," he said. "We are not on your homeworld, but I think it is a very close approximation. A kind of incomplete zoo. Why don't we swap stories outside where it's warm?"

She agreed, still wary but no longer hostile, with a glance of something like satisfaction toward the massive kzin male rotating in the next container. And then they strolled outside into the wilderness of Kzersatz which, for same reason, forced thin mewling *miaows* from her. It had never occurred to Locklear that a kzin could weep.

*   *   *

As near as Locklear could understand, Miss Kitty's emotions were partly relief that she had lived to see her yellow fields and jungles again, and partly grief when she contemplated the loneliness she now faced. *I don't count*, he thought. *But if I expect to get her help, I'd best see that I do count.*

Everybody thinks his own dialect is superior, Locklear decided. Miss Kitty fumed at his brief forms of Kzinti, and he winced at her ancient elaborations, as they walked to the nearest stream. She had a temper, too, teaching him genteel curses as her bare feet encountered thorns. She seemed fascinated by this account of the kzin expansion, and that of humans, and others as well through the galaxy. She even accepted his description of the planet Zoo though she did not seem to understand it.

She accepted his story so readily, in fact, that he hit on an intuition. "Has it occurred to you that I might be lying?"

"Your talk is offensive," she flared. "My benefactor a criminal? No. Is it common among your kind?"

"More than among yours," he admitted, "but I have no reason to lie to you. Sorry," he added, seeing her react again. *Kzinti don't flare up at that word today; maybe all cusswords have to be replaced as they weaken from overuse.* Then he told her how man and kzin got along between wars, and ended by admitting it looked as if another war was brewing, which was why he had been abandoned here.

She looked around her. "Is Zoo your doing, or ours?"

"Neither. I think it must have been done by a

race we know very little about: Outsiders, we call them. No one knows how many years they have traveled space, but very, very long. They live without air, without much heat. Just beyond the wall that surrounds Kzersatz, I have seen airless corridors with the cold darkness of space and dapples of light. They would be quite comfortable there."

"I do not think I like them."

Then he laughed, and had to explain how the display of his teeth was the opposite of anger.

"Those teeth could not support much anger," she replied, her small pink ear umbrellas winking down and up. He learned that this was her version of a smile.

Finally, when they had taken their fill of water, they returned as Miss Kitty told her tale. She had been trained as a palace *prret*; a servant and casual concubine of the mighty during the reign of *Rrawlrit* Eight and Three. Locklear said that the 'Rrit' suffix meant high position among modern kzinti, and she made a sound very like a human sniff. *Rrawlrit* was the arrogant son of an arrogant son, and so on. He liked his females, lots of them, especially young ones. "I was (something) than most," she said, her four-digited hand slicing the air at her ear height.

"Petite, small?"

"Yes. Also smart. Also famous for my appearance," she added without the slightest show of modesty. She glanced at him as though judging which haunch might be tastiest. "Are you famous for yours?"

"Uh—not that I know of."

"But not unattractive?"

He slid a hand across his face, feeling its stubble. "I am considered petite, and by some as, uh, attractive." *Two or three are "Some." Not much, but some . . .*

"With a suit of fur you would be (something)," she said, with that ear-waggle, and he quickly asked about palace life because he damned well did not want to know what that final word of hers had meant. It made him nervous as hell. Yeah, but what *did* it mean? Mud-ugly? Handsome? Tasty? *Listen to the lady, idiot, and quit suspecting what you're suspecting.*

She had been raised in a culture in which females occasionally ran a regency, and in which males fought duels over the argument as to whether females were their intellectual equals. Most thought not. Miss Kitty thought so, and proved it, rising to palace prominence with her backside, as she put it.

"You mean you were no better than you should be," he commented.

"What does that mean?"

"I haven't the foggiest idea, just an old phrase." She was still waiting, and her aspect was not benign. "Uh, it means nobody could expect you to do any better."

She nodded slowly, delighting him as she adopted one of the human gestures he'd been using. "I did too well to suit the males jealous of my power, Rockear. They convinced the regent that I was conspiring with other palace *prrets* to gain equality for our sex."

"And were you?"

She arched her back with pride. "Yes. Does that offend you?"

"No. Would you care if it did?"

"It would make things difficult, Rockear. You

must understand that I loathe, admire, hate, desire kzintosh—male kzin. I fought for equality because it was common knowledge that some were planning to breed *kzinrret*, females, to be no better than pets."

"I hate to tell you this, Miss Kitty, but they've done it."

"Already?"

"I don't know how long it took, but—." He paused, and then told her the worst. Long before man and kzin first met, their females had been bred into brainless docility. Even if Miss Kitty found modern sisters, they would be of no help to her.

She fought the urge to weep again, strangling her miaows with soft snarls of rage.

Locklear turned away, aware that she did not want to seem vulnerable, and consulted his wristcomp's encyclopedia. The earliest kzin history made reference to the downfall of a *Rrawlrit* the fifty-seventh—Seven Eights and One, and he gasped at what that told him. "Don't feel too bad, Miss Kitty," he said at last. "That was at least forty thousand years ago; do you understand eight to the fifth power?"

"It is very, very many," she said in a choked voice.

"It's been more years than that since you were brought here. How did you get here, anyhow?"

"They executed several of us. My last memory was of grappling with the lord high executioner, carrying him over the precipice into the sacred lagoon with me. I could not swim with those heavy chains around my ankles, but I remember trying. I hope he drowned," she said, eyes slitted. "Sex with him had always been my most hated chore."

A small flag began to wave in Locklear's head; he furled it for further reference. "So you were trying to swim. Then?"

"Then suddenly I was lying naked with a very strange creature staring at me," she said with that ear-wink, and a sharp talon pointed almost playfully at him. "Do not think ill of me because I reacted in fright."

He shook his head, and had to explain what *that* meant, and it became a short course in subtle nuances for each of them. Miss Kitty, it seemed, proved an old dictum about downtrodden groups: they became highly expert at reading body language, and at developing secret signals among themselves. It was not Locklear's fault that he was constantly, and completely unaware, sending messages that she misread.

But already, she was adapting to his gestures as he had to her language. "Of all the kzinti I could have taken from stasis, I got you," he chuckled finally, and because her glance was quizzical, he told a gallant half-lie; "I went for the prettiest, and got the smartest."

"And the hungriest," she said. "Perhaps I should hunt something for us."

He reminded her that there was nothing to hunt. "You can help me choose animals to release here. Meanwhile, you can have this," he added, offering her the kzinti rations.

The sun faded on schedule, and he dined on tuberberries while she devoured an entire brick of meat. She amazed him by popping a few tuberberries for dessert. When he asked her about it, she replied that certainly kzinti ate vegetables in her time; why should they not?

"Males want only meat," he shrugged.

"They would," she snarled. "In my day, some select warriors did the same. They claimed it made them ferocious and that eaters of vegetation were mere *kshauvat*, dumb herbivores; we *prret* claimed their diet just made them hopelessly aggressive."

"The word's been shortened to *kshat* now," he mused. "It's a favorite cussword of theirs. At least you don't have to start eating the animals in stasis to stay alive. That's the good news; the bad news is that the warriors who left me here may return at any time. What will you do then?"

"That depends on how accurate your words have been," she said cagily.

"And if I'm telling the plain truth?"

Her ears smiled for her: "Take up my war where I left it," she said.

Locklear felt his control slipping when Miss Kitty refused to wait before releasing most of the *vatach*. They were nocturnal with easily-spotted burrows, she insisted, and yes, they bred fast— but she pointed to specimens of a winged critter in stasis and said they would control the *vatach* very nicely if the need arose. By now he realized that this kzin female wasn't above trying to vamp him; and when that failed, a show of fang and talon would succeed.

He showed her how to open the cages only after she threatened him, and watched as she grasped waking *vatach* by their legs, quickly releasing them to the darkness outside. No need to release the (something) yet, she said; Locklear called the winged beasts "batowls." "I hope you know what you're doing," he grumbled. "I'd stop you if I could do it without a fight."

"You would wait forever," she retorted. "I know

the animals of my world better than you do, and soon we may need a lot of them for food."

"Not so many; there's just the two of us."

The cat-eyes regarded him shrewdly. "Not for long," she said, and dropped her bombshell. "I recognized a friend of mine in one of those cages."

Locklear felt an icy needle down his spine. "A male?"

"Certainly not. Five of us were executed for the same offense, and at least one of them is here with us. Perhaps those Outsiders of yours collected us all as we sank in that stinking water."

"Not *my* Outsiders," he objected. "Listen, for all we know they're monitoring us, so be careful how you fiddle with their setup here."

She marched him to the kzin cages and purred her pleasure on recognizing two females, both *prret* like herself, both imposingly large for Locklear's taste. She placed a furry hand on one cage, enjoying the moment. "I could release you now, my sister in struggle," she said softly. "But I think I shall wait. Yes, I think it is best," she said to Locklear, turning away. "These two have been here a long time, and they will keep until——."

"Until you have everything under your control?"

"True," she said. "But you need not fear, Rockear. You are an ally, and you know too many things we must know. And besides," she added, rubbing against him sensuously, "you are (something)."

There was that same word again, *t'rralap* or some such, and now he was sure, with sinking heart, that it meant "cute". He didn't feel cute; he was beginning to feel like a Pomeranian on a short leash.

More by touch than anything else, they gath-

ered bundles of grass for a bower at the cave
entrance, and Miss Kitty showed no reluctance in
falling asleep next to him, curled becomingly into
a buzzing ball of fur. But when he moved away,
she moved too, until they were touching again.
He knew beyond doubt that if he moved too far in
the direction of his lance and axe, she would be
fully awake and suspicious as hell.

*And she'd call my bluff, and I don't want to kill
her,* he thought, settling his head against her furry
shoulder. *Even if I could, which is doubtful. I'm
no longer master of all I survey. In fact, now I
have a mistress of sorts, and I'm not too sure what
kind of mistress she has in mind. They used to
have a word for what I'm thinking. Maybe Miss
Kitty doesn't care who or what she diddles; hell,
she was a palace courtesan, doing it with males
she hated. She thinks I'm t'rralap. Yeah, that's
me, Locklear, Miss Kitty's trollop; and what the
hell can I do about it? I wish there were some way
I could get her back in that stasis cage . . .* And
then he fell asleep.

To Locklear's intense relief, Miss Kitty seemed
uninterested in the remaining cages on the following morning. They foraged for breakfast and he
hid his astonishment as she taught him a dozen
tricks in an hour. The root bulb of one spiny shrub
tasted like an apple; the seed pods of some weeds
were delicious; and she produced a tiny blaze by
rapidly pounding an innocent-looking nutmeat between two stones. It occurred to him that nuts
contained great amounts of energy. A pile of these
firenuts, he reflected, might be turned into a
weapon . . .

Feeding hunks of dry brush to the fire, she

announced that those root bulbs baked nicely in
coals. "If we can find clay, I can fire a few pottery
dishes and cups, Rockear. It was part of my training, and I intend to have everything in domestic
order before we wake those two."

"And what if a kzin ship returns and spots that
smoke?"

That was a risk they must take, she said. Some
woods burned more cleanly than others. He argued that they should at least build their fires far
from the cave, and while they were at it, the cave
entrance might be better disguised. She agreed,
impressed with his strategy, and then went down
on all-fours to inspect the dirt near a dry-wash. As he
admired her lithe movements, she shook her head
in an almost human gesture. "No good for clay."

"It's not important."

"It is vitally important!" Now she wheeled upright, impressive and fearsome. "Rockear, if any
kzintosh return here, we must be ready. For that,
we must have the help of others—the two *prret*.
And believe me, they will be helpful only if they
see us as their (something)."

She explained that the word meant, roughly,
"paired household leaders." The basic requirements
of a household, to a kzin female, included sleeping
bowers—easily come by—and enough pottery for
that household. A male kzin needed one more
thing, she said, her eyes slitting: a *wtsai*.

"You mean one of those knives they all wear?"

"Yes. And you must have one in your belt."
From the waggle of her ears, he decided she was
amused by her next statement: "It is a—badge, of
sorts. The edge is usually sharp but I cannot allow
that, and the tip must be dull. I will show you
why later."

"Dammit, these things could take weeks!"

"Not if we find the clay, and if you can make a *wtsai* somehow. Trust me, Rockear; these are the basics. Other kzinrret will not obey us otherwise. They must see from the first that we are proper providers, proper leaders with the pottery of a settled tribe, not the wooden implements of wanderers. And they must take it for granted that you and I," she added, "are (something)." With that, she rubbed lightly against him.

He caught himself moving aside and swallowed hard. "Miss Kitty, I don't want to offend you, but, uh, humans and kzinti do not mate."

"Why do they not?"

"Uhm. Well, they never have."

Her eyes slitted, yet with a flicker of her ears: "But they could?"

"Some might. Not me."

"Then they might be able to," she said as if to herself. "I thought I felt something familiar when we were sleeping." She studied his face carefully. "Why does your skin change color?"

"Because, goddammit, I'm upset!" He mastered his breathing after a moment and continued, speaking as if to a small child, "I don't know about kzinti, but a man can *not*, uh, mate unless he is, uh,—"

"Unless he is intent on the idea?"

"Right!"

"Then we will simply have to pretend that we do mate, Rockear. Otherwise, those two kzinrret will spend most of their time trying to become your mate and will be useless for work."

"Of all the," he began, and then dropped his chin and began to laugh helplessly. Human tribal customs had been just as complicated, once, and she was probably the only functioning expert in known space on the customs of ancient kzinrret. "We'll pretend, then, up to a point. Try and make that point, ah, not too pointed."

"Like your *wtsai*," she retorted. "I will try not to make your face change color."

"Please," he said fervently, and suggested that he might find the material for a *wtsai* inside the cave while she sought a deposit of clay. She bounded away on all-fours with the lope of a hunting leopard, his jacket a somehow poignant touch as it flapped against her lean belly.

When he looked back from the cave entrance, she was a tiny dot two kilometers distant, coursing along a shallow creekbed. "Maybe you won't lie, and I've got no other ally," he said to the swift saffron dot. "But you're not above misdirection with your own kind. I'll remember that."

Locklear cursed as he failed to locate any kind of tool chest or lab implements in those inner corridors. But he blessed his grooming tool when the tip of its pincer handle fitted screwheads in the cage that had held Miss Kitty prisoner for so long. He puzzled for minutes before he learned to turn screwheads a quarter-turn, release pressure to let the screwheads emerge, then another quarter-turn, and so on, nine times each. He felt quickening excitement as the cage cover detached, felt it stronger when he disassembled the base and realized its metal sheeting was probably one of a myriad stainless steel alloys. The diamond coating on his nail file proved the sheet was no indestructible substance. It was thin enough to flex, even to be dented by a whack against an adjoining cage. It might take awhile, but he would soon have his *wtsai* blade.

And two other devices now lay before him, ludicrously far advanced beyond an ornamental knife. The gravity polarizer's main bulk was a doughnut of ceramic and metal. Its switch, and that of the stasis field, both were energized by the sliding cage floor he had disassembled. The switches worked just as well with fingertip pressure. They boasted separate energy sources which Locklear dared not assault; anything that worked for forty thousand years without harming the creatures near it would be more sophisticated than any fumble-fingered mechanic.

Using the glasslike cage as a test load, he learned which of the two switches flung the load into the air. The other, then, had to operate the stasis field—and both devices had simple internal levers for adjustments. When he learned how to stop the cage from spinning, and then how to make it hover only a hand's breadth above the device or to force it against the ceiling until it creaked, he was ecstatic. Then he energized the stasis switch with a chill of gooseflesh. Any prying paws into those devices would not pry for long, unless someone knew about that inconspicuous switch. Locklear could see no interconnects between the stasis generator and the polarizer, but both were detachable. If he could get that polarizer outside—Locklear strode out of the cave laughing. It would be the damnedest vehicle ever, but its technologies would be wholly appropriate. He hid the device in nearby grass; the less his ally knew about such things, the more freedom he would have to pursue them.

Miss Kitty returned in late afternoon with a sopping mass of clay wrapped in greenish-yellow palm leaves. The clay was poor quality, she said, but it would have to serve—and why was he battering that piece of metal with his stone axe?

If she knew a better way to cut off a *wtsai*-sized strip of steel than bending it back and forth, he replied, he'd love to hear it. Bickering like an old married couple, they sat near the cave mouth until dark and pursued their separate Stone-Age tasks. Locklear, whose hand calluses were still forming, had to admit that she had been wonderfully trained for domestic chores; under those quick four-digited hands of hers, rolled coils of clay soon became shallow bowls with thin sides, so nearly perfect they might have been turned on a potter's wheel. By now he was calling her "Kit," and she seemed genuinely pleased when he praised her work. Ah, she said, but wait until the pieces were sun-dried to leather hardness; then she would make the bowls lovely with talon-etched decoration. He objected that decoration took time. She replied curtly that kzinrret did not live for utility alone.

He helped pull flat fibers from the stalks of palm leaves, which she began to weave into a mat. "For bedding," he asked? "Certainly not," she said imperiously: "for the clothing which modesty required of kzinrret." He pursued it: "Would they really care all that much with only a human to see them?" "A human *male*," she reminded him; if she considered him worthy of mating, the others would see him as a male first, and a non-kzin second. He was half-amused but more than a little uneasy as they bedded down, she curled slightly facing away, he crowded close at her insistence, "—For companionship," as she put it.

Their last exchange that night implied a difference between the rigorously truthful male kzin and their females. "Kit, you can't tell the others we're mated unless we are."

"I can ignore their questions and let them draw their own conclusions," she said sleepily.

"Aren't you blurring that fine line between half-truths and, uh, non-truths?"

"I do not intend to discuss it further," she said, and soon was purring in sleep with the faint growl of a predator.

He needed two more days, and a repair of the handaxe, before he got that jagged slice of steel pounded and, with abrasive stones, ground into something resembling a blade. Meanwhile, Kit built her open-fired kiln of stones in a ravine some distance from the cave, ranging widely with that leopard lope of hers to gather firewood. Locklear was glad of her absence; it gave him time to finish a laminated shamboo handle for his blade, bound with thread, and to collect the thickest poles of shamboo he could find. The blade was sharp enough to trim the poles quickly, and tough enough to hold an edge.

He was tying crosspieces with plaited fiber to bind thick shamboo poles into a slender raft when, on the third day of those labors, he felt a presence behind him. Whirling, he brandished his blade. "Oh," he said, and lowered the *wtsai*. "Sorry, Kit. I keep worrying about the return of those kzintosh."

She was not amused. "Give it to me," she said, thrusting her hand out.

"The hell I will. I need this thing."

"I can see that it is too sharp."

"I need it sharp."

"I am sure you do. I need it dull." Her gesture for the blade was more than impatient.

Half straightening into a crouch, he brought the blade up again, eyes narrowed. "Well, by God,

I've had about all your whims I can take. You want it? Come and get it."

She made a sound that was deeper than a purr, putting his hackles up, and went to all-fours, her furry tailtip flicking as she began to pace around him. She was a lovely sight. She scared Locklear silly. "When I take it, I will hurt you," she warned.

"If you take it," he said, turning to face her, moving the *wtsai* in what he hoped was an unpredictable pattern. *Dammit, I can't back down now. A puncture wound might be fatal to her, so I've got to slash lightly.* Or maybe he wouldn't have to, when she saw he meant business.

But he did have to. She screamed and leaped toward his left, her own left hand sweeping out at his arm. He skipped aside and then felt her tail lash against his shins like a curled rope. He stumbled and whirled as she was twisting to repeat the charge, and by sheer chance his blade nicked her tail as she whisked it away from his vicinity.

She stood erect, holding her tail in her hands, eyes wide and accusing. "You—you insulted my tail," she snarled.

"Damn tootin'," he said between his teeth.

With arms folded, she turned her back on him, her tail curled protectively at her backside. "You have no respect," she said, and because it seemed she was going to leave, he dropped the blade and stood up, and realized too late just how much peripheral vision a kzin boasted. She spun and was on him in an instant, her hands gripping his wrists, and hurled them both to the grass, bringing those terrible ripping foot talons up to his stomach. They lay that way for perhaps three seconds. "Drop the *wtsai*," she growled, her mouth near his throat. Locklear had not been sure until now whether a very small female kzin had more muscular strength than he. The answer was not just awfully encouraging.

He could feel sharp needles piercing the skin at his stomach, kneading, releasing, piercing; a reminder that with one move she could disembowel him. The blade whispered into the grass. She bit him lightly at the juncture of his neck and shoulder, and then faced him with their noses almost touching. "A love bite," she said, and released his wrists, pushing away with her feet.

He rolled, hugging his stomach, fighting for breath, grateful that she had not used those fearsome talons with her push. She found the blade, stood over him, and now no sign of her anger remained. *Right; she's in complete control*, he thought.

"Nicely made, Rockear. I shall return it to you when it is presentable," she said.

"Get the hell away from me," he husked softly.

She did, with a bound, moving toward a distant wisp of smoke that skirled faintly across the sky. If a kzin ship returned now, they would follow that wisp immediately.

Locklear trotted without hesitation to the cave, cursing, wiping trickles of blood from his stomach and neck, wiping a tear of rage from his cheek. There were other ways to prove to this damned tabby that he could be trusted with a knife. One, at least, if he didn't get himself wasted in the process.

She returned quite late, with half of a cooked *vatach* and tuberberries as a peace offering, to find him weaving a huge triangular mat. It was a sail, he explained, for a boat. She had taken the little animal on impulse, she said, partly because it was a male, and ate her half on the spot for old times' sake. He'd told her his distaste for raw meat and evidently she never forgot anything.

He sulked awhile, complaining at the lack of salt, brightening a bit when she produced the *wtsai* from his jacket which she still wore. "You've ruined it," he said, seeing the colors along the dull blade as he held it. "Heated it up, didn't you?"

"And ground its edge off on the stones of my hot kiln," she agreed. "Would you like to try its point?" She placed a hand on her flank, where a man's kidney would be, moving nearer.

"Not much of a point now," he said. It was rounded like a formal dinner knife at its tip.

"Try it here," she said, and guided his hand so that the blunt knifetip pointed against her flank. He hesitated. "Don't you want to?"

He dug it in, knowing it wouldn't hurt her much, and heard her soft miaow. Then she suggested the other side, and he did, feeling a suspicious unease. That, she said, was the way a *wtsai* was best used.

He frowned. "You mean, as a symbol of control?"

"More or less," she replied, her ears flicking, and then asked how he expected to float a boat down a dry wash, and he told her because he needed her help with it. "A skyboat? Some trick of man, or kzin?"

"Of man," he shrugged. It was, so far as he knew, uniquely his trick—and it might not work at all. He could not be sure about his other trick either, until he tried it. Either one might get him killed.

When they curled up to sleep again, she turned

her head and whispered, "Would you like to bite my neck?"

"I'd like to bite it off."

"Just do not break the skin. I did not mean to make yours bleed, Rockear. Men are tender creatures."

Feeling like an ass, he forced his nose into the fur at the curve of her shoulder and bit hard. Her miaow was familiar. And somehow he was sure that it was not exactly a cry of pain. She thrust her rump nearer, sighed, and went to sleep.

After an eternity of minutes, he shifted position, putting his knees in her back, flinging one of his hands to the edge of their grassy bower. She moved slightly. He felt in the grass for a familiar object; found it. Then he pulled his legs away and pressed with his fingers. She started to turn, then drew herself into a ball as he scrambled further aside, legs tingling.

He had not been certain the stasis field would operate properly when its flat field grid was positioned beneath sheaves of grass, but obviously it was working. Indeed, his lower legs were numb for several minutes, lying in the edge of the field as they were when he threw that switch. He stamped the pins and needles from his feet, barely able to see her inert form in the faint luminosity of the cave portal. Once, while fumbling for the *wtsai*, he stumbled near her and dropped to his knees.

He trembled for half a minute before rising. "Fall over her now and you could lie here for all eternity," he said aloud. Then he fetched the heavy coil of fiber he'd woven, with those super-strength threads braided into it. He had no way of lighting the place enough to make sure of his work, so he lay down on the sail mat inside the cave. One thing was sure: she'd be right there the next morning.

He awoke disoriented at first, then darted to the cave mouth. She lay inert as a carven image. The Outsiders probably had good reason to rotate their specimens, so he couldn't leave her there for the days—or weeks!—that temptation suggested. He decided that a day wouldn't hurt, and hurriedly set about finishing his airboat. The polarizer was lashed to the underside of his raft, with a slot through the shamboo so that he could reach down and adjust the switch and levers. The crosspieces, beneath, held the polarizer off the turf.

Finally, with a mixture of fear and excitement, he sat down in the middle of the raft-bottomed craft and snugged fiber straps across his lap. He reached down with his left hand, making sure the levers were pulled back, and flipped the switch. Nothing. Yet. When he had moved the second lever halfway, the raft began to rise very slowly. He vented a whoop—and suddenly the whole rig was tipping before he could snap the switch. The raft hit on one side and crashed flat like a barn door with a tooth-loosening impact.

Okay, the damn thing was tippy. He'd need a keel—a heavy rock on a short rope. Or a little rock on a long rope! He erected two short lengths of shamboo upright with a crosspiece like goalposts, over the seat of his raft, enlarging the hole under his thighs. Good; now he'd have a better view straight down, too. He used the cord he'd intended to bind Kit, tying it to a twenty-kilo stone, then feeding the cord through the hole and wrapping most of its fifteen-meter length around and around that thick crosspiece. Then he sighed, looked at the westering sun, and tried again.

The raft was still a bit tippy, but by paying the cordage out slowly he found himself ten meters up. By shifting his weight, he could make the little platform slant in any direction, yet he could move only in the direction the breeze took him. By adjusting the controls he rose until the heavy stone swung lazily, free of the ground, and then he was drifting with the breeze. He reduced power and hauled in on his keel weight until the raft settled, and then worked out the needed improvements. Higher skids off the ground, so he could work beneath the raft; a better method for winding that weight up and down; and a sturdy shamboo mast for his single sail—better still, a two-piece mast bound in a narrow A-frame to those goalposts. It didn't need to be high; a short catboat sail for tacking was all he could handle anyhow. And come to think of it, a pair of shamboo poles pivoted off the sides with small weights at their free ends just might make automatic keels.

He worked on that until a half-hour before dark, then carried his keel cordage inside the cave. First he made a slip noose, then flipped it toward her hands, which were folded close to her chin. He finally got the noose looped properly, pulled it tight, then moved around her at a safe distance, tugging the cord so that it passed under her neck and, with sharp tugs, down to her back. Then another pass. Then up to her neck, then around her flexed legs. He managed a pair of half-hitches before he ran short of cordage, then fetched his shamboo lance. With the lance against her throat, he snapped off the stasis field with his toe.

She began her purring rumble immediately. He

pressed lightly with the lance, and then she waked, and needed a moment to realize that she was bound. Her ears flattened. Her grin was nothing even faintly like enjoyment. "You drugged me, you little *vatach*."

"No. Worse than that. Watch," he said, and with his free hand he pointed at her face, staring hard. He toed the switch again and watched her curl into an inert ball. The half-hitches came loosed with a tug, and with some difficulty he managed to pull the cordage away until only the loop around her hand remained. He toed the switch again; watched her come awake, and pointed dramatically at her as she faced him. "I loosened your bonds," he said. "I can always tie you up again. Or put you back in stasis," he added with a tight smile, hoping this paltry piece of flummery would be taken as magic.

"May I rise?"

"Depends. Do you see that I can defeat you instantly, anytime I like?" She moved her hands, snarling at the loop, starting to bite it asunder. "Stop that! Answer my question," he said again, stern and unyielding, the finger pointing, his toe ready on the switch.

"It seems that you can," she said grudgingly.

"I could have killed you as you slept. Or brought one of the other *prret* out of stasis and made her my consort. Any number of things, Kit." Her nod was slow, and almost human, "Do you swear to obey me hereafter, and not to attack me again?"

She hated it, but she said it: "Yes. I—misjudged you, Rockear. If all men can do what you did, no wonder you win wars."

He saw that this little charade might get him in a mess later. "It is a special trick of mine; proba-

bly won't work for male kzin. In any case, I have
your word. If you forget it, I will make you sorry.
We need each other, Kit; just like I need a sharp
edge on my knife." He lowered his arm then,
offering her his hand. "Here, come outside and
help me. It's nearly dark again."

She was astonished to find, from the sun's position, that she had 'slept' almost a full day. But
there was no doubting he had spent many hours
on that airboat of his. She helped him for a few
moments, then remembered that her kiln would
now be cool, the bowls and water jug waiting in
its primitive chimney. "May I retrieve my pottery, Rockear?"

He smiled at her obedient tone. "If I say no?"

"I do it tomorrow."

"Go ahead, Kit. It'll be dark soon." He watched
her bounding away through high grass, then hurried into the cave. He had to put that stasis gadget
back where he'd got it or, sure as hell, she'd
figure it out and one fine day *he* would wake up
hogtied. Or worse.

Locklear's praise of the pottery was not forced;
Kit had a gift for handcrafts, and they ate from
decorated bowls that night. He sensed her new
deference when she asked, "Have you chosen a
site for the manor?"

"Not until I've explored further. We'll want a
hidden site we can defend and retreat from, with
reliable sources of water, firewood, food—not like
this cave. And I'll need your help in that decision,
Kit."

"It must be done before we wake the others,"
she said, adding as if to echo his own warnings,
"And soon, if we are to be ready for the kzintosh."

"Don't nag," he replied. He blew on blistered palms and lay full-length on their grassy bower. "We have to get that airboat working right away," he said, and patted the grass beside him. She curled up in her usual way. After a few moments he placed a hand on her shoulder.

"Thank you, Rockear," she murmured, and fell asleep. He lay awake for another hour, gnawing the ribs of two sciences. The engineering of the airboat would be largely trial and error. So would the ethology of a relationship between a man and a kzin female, with all those nuances he was beginning to sense. How, for example, did a kzin make love? Not that he intended to—*unless*, a vagrant thought nudged him, *I'm doing some of it already* . . .

Two more days and a near-disastrous capsizing later, Locklear found the right combination of ballast and sail. He found that Kit could sprint for short distances faster than he could urge the airboat, but over long distances he had a clear edge. Alone, tacking higher, he found stronger winds that bore him far across the sky of Kzersatz, and once he found himself drifting in cross-currents high above that frost line that curved visibly, now, tracing the edge of the force cylinder that was their cage.

He returned after a two-hour absence to find Kit weaving more mats, more cordage, for furnishings. She approached the airboat warily, mistrusting its magical properties but relieved to see him. "You'll be using this thing yourself, pretty soon, Kit," he confided. "Can you make us some decent ink and paper?"

In a day, yes, she said, if she found a scroll-leaf palm, to soak, pound, and dry its fronds. Ink was no problem. Then hop aboard, he said, and they'd go cruising for the palm. *That* was a problem; she was plainly terrified of flight in any form. Kzinti were fearless, he reminded her. Females were not, she said, adding that the sight of him dwindling in the sky to a scudding dot had "drawn up her tail"—a fear reaction, he learned.

He ordered her, at last, to mount the raft, sitting in tandem behind him. She found the position somehow obscene, but she did it. Evidently it was highly acceptable for a male to crowd close behind a female, but not the reverse. Then Locklear recalled how cats mated, and he understood. "Nobody will see us, Kit. Hang on to these cords and pull only when I tell you." With that, he levitated the airboat a meter, and stayed low for a time— until he felt the flexure of her foot talons relax at his thighs.

In another hour they were quartering the sky above the jungles and savannahs of Kzersatz, Kit enjoying the ride too much to retain her fears. They landed in a clearing near the unexplored end of the lake, Kit scrambling up a thick palm to return with young rolled fronds. "The sap stings when fresh," she said, indicating a familiar white substance. "But when dried and reheated it makes excellent glue." She also gathered fruit like purple leather melons, with flesh that smelled faintly of seafood, and stowed them for dinner.

The return trip was longer. He taught her how to tack upwind and later, watching her soak fronds that night inside the cave, exulted because soon they would have maps of this curious country. In only one particular was he evasive.

"Rockear, what is that thing I felt on your back under your clothing," she asked.

"It's, uh, just a thing your warriors do to captives. I have to keep it there," he said, and quickly changed the subject.

In another few days, they had crude air maps and several candidate sites for the manor. Locklear agreed to Kit's choice as they hovered above it, a gentle slope beneath a cliff overhang where a kzinrret could sun herself half the day. Fast-growing hardwoods nearby would provide timber and firewood, and the stream burbling in the throat of the ravine was the same stream where he had found that first waterfall down near the lake, and had conjectured on the age of Kzersatz. She rubbed her cheek against his neck when he accepted her decision.

He steered toward the hardwood grove, feeling a faint dampness on his neck. "What does that mean?"

"Why,—marking you, of course. It is a display of affection." He pursued it. The ritual transferred a pheromone from her furry cheeks to his flesh. He could not smell it, but she maintained that any kzin would recognize her marker until the scent evaporated in a few hours.

It was like a lipstick mark, he decided—"Or a hickey with your initials," he told her, and then had to explain himself. She admitted he had not guessed far off the mark. "But hold on, Kit. Could a kzin warrior track me by my scent?"

"Certainly. How else does one follow a spoor?"

He thought about that awhile. "If we come to the manor and leave it always by air, would that make it harder to find?"

Of course, she said. Trackers needed a scent trail; that's why she intended them to walk in the nearby stream, even if splashing in water was unpleasant. "But if they are determined to find you, Rockear, they will."

He sighed, letting the airboat settle near a stand of pole-straight trees, and as he hacked with the dulled *wtsai*, told her of the new weaponry: projectiles, beamers, energy fields, bombs. "When they do find us, we've got to trap them somehow; get their weapons. Could you kill your own kind?"

"They executed me," she reminded him and added after a moment, "Kzinrret weapons might be best. Leave it to me." She did not elaborate. Well, women's weapons had their uses.

He slung several logs under the airboat and left Kit stone-sharpening the long blade as he slowly tacked his way back to their ravine. Releasing the hitches was the work of a moment, thick poles thudding onto yellow-green grass, and soon he was back with Kit. By the time the sun faded, the *wtsai* was biting like a handaxe and Kit had prepared them a thick grassy pallet between the cliff face and their big foundation logs. It was the coldest night Locklear had spent on Kzersatz, but Kit's fur made it endurable.

Days later, she ate the last of the kzin rations as he chewed a fishnut and sketched in the dirt with a stick. "We'll run the shamboo plumbing out here from the kitchen," he said, "and dig our escape tunnel out from our sleep room parallel with the cliff. We'll need help, Kit. It's time."

She vented a long purring sigh. "I know. Things will be different, Rockear. Not as simple as our life has been."

He laughed at that, reminding her of the complications they had already faced, and then they resumed notching logs, raising the walls beyond window height. Their own work packed the earthen

floors, but the roofing would require more hands
than their own. That night, Kit kindled their first
fire in the central room's hearth, and they fell
asleep while she tutored him on the ways of ancient kzin females.

Leaning against the airboat alone near the cave,
Locklear felt new misgivings. Kit had argued that
his presence at the awakenings would be a Bad
Idea. Let them grow used to him slowly, she'd
said. Stand tall, give orders gently, and above all
don't smile until they understand his show of teeth.
No fear of that, he thought, shifting nervously a
half-hour after Kit disappeared inside. *I don't feel
like smiling*.

He heard a shuffling just out of sight; realized
he was being viewed covertly; threw out his chest
and flexed his pectorals. Not much by kzin standards, but he'd developed a lot of sinew during
the past weeks. He felt silly as hell, and those
other kzinrret had not made him any promises.
The *wtsai* felt good at his belt.

Then Kit was striding into the open, with an
expression of strained patience. Standing beside
him, she muttered, "Mark me." Then, seeing his
frown: "Your cheek against my neck, Rockear.
Quickly."

He did so. She bowed before him, offering the
tip of her tail in both hands, and he stroked it
when she told him to. Then he saw a lithe movement of orange at the cave and raised both hands
in a universal weaponless gesture as the second
kzinrret emerged, watching him closely. She was
much larger than Kit, with transverse stripes of
darker orange and a banded tail. Close on her
heels came a third, more reluctantly but staying

close behind as if for protection, with facial markings that reminded Locklear of an ocelot and very dark fur at hands and feet. They were admirable creatures, but their ear umbrellas lay flat and they were not yet his friends.

Kit moved to the first, urging her forward to Locklear. After a few tentative sniffs the big kzinrret said, in that curious ancient dialect, "I am (something truly unpronounceable), prret in service of Rockear." She bent toward him, her stance defensive, and he marked her as Kit had said he must, then stroked her tabby-banded tail. She moved away and the third kzinrret approached, and Locklear's eyes widened as he performed the greeting ritual. She was either potbellied, or carrying a litter!

Both of their names being beyond him, he dubbed the larger one Puss; the pregnant one, Boots. They accepted their new names as proof that they were members of a very different kind of household than any they had known. Both wore aprons of woven mat, Kit's deft work, and she offered them water from bowls.

As they stood eyeing one another speculatively, Kit surprised them all. "It is time to release the animals," she said. "My lord Rockear-the-magician, we are excellent herders, and from your flying boat you can observe our work. The larger beasts might also distract the kzintosh, and we will soon need meat. Is it not so?"

She *knew* he couldn't afford an argument now— and besides, she was right. He had no desire to try herding some of those big critters outside anyhow, and kzinti had been doing it from time immemorial. *Damned clever tactic, Kit; Puss and Boots will get a chance to work off their nerves, and so will I*. He swept a permissive arm outward and sat down in the airboat as the three kzin females moved into the cave.

The next two hours were a crash course in zoology for Locklear, safe at fifty-meter height as he watched herds, coveys, throngs and volleys of creatures as they crawled, flapped, hopped and galumphed off across the yellow prairie. A batowl found a perch atop his mast, trading foolish blinks with him until it whispered away after another of its kind. One huge ruminant with the bulk of a rhino and murderous spikes on its thick tail sat down to watch him, raising its bull's muzzle to issue a call like a wolf. An answering howl sent it lumbering off again, and Locklear wondered whether they were to be butchered, ridden, or simply avoided. He liked the last option best.

When at last Kit came loping out with shrill screams of false fury at the heels of a collie-sized, furry tyrannosaur, the operation was complete. He'd half-expected to see a troop of more kzinti bounding outside, but Kit was as good as her word. None of them recognized any of the other stasized kzinti, and all seemed content to let the strangers stay as they were.

The airboat did not have room for them all, but by now Kit could operate the polarizer levers. She sat ahead of Locklear for decorum's sake, making a show of her pairing with him, and let Puss and Boots follow beneath as the airboat slid ahead of a good breeze toward their tacky, unfinished little manor. "They will be nicely exhausted," she said to him, "by the time we reach home."

Home. My God, it may be my home for the rest of my life, he thought, watching the muscular Puss bound along behind them with Boots in arrears. *Three kzin courtesans for company; a sure 'nough cathouse! Is that much better than having those effing warriors return? And if they don't, is there any way I could get across to my own turf, to Newduvai?* The gravity polarizer could get him to orbit, but he would need propulsion, and a woven sail wasn't exactly de rigueur for travel in vacuum, and how the hell could he build an airtight cockpit anyhow? Too many questions, too few answers, and two more kzin females who might be more hindrance than help, hurtling along in the yellowsward behind him. One of them pregnant.

And kzin litters were almost all twins, one male. Like it or not, he was doomed to deal with at least one kzintosh. The notion of killing the tiny male forced itself forward. He quashed the idea instantly, and hoped it would stay quashed. *Yeah, and one of these days it'll weigh three times as much as I do, and two of these randy females will be vying for mating privileges.* The return of the kzin ship, he decided, might be the least of his troubles.

That being so, the least of his troubles could kill him.

Puss and Boots proved far more help than hindrance. Locklear admitted it to Kit one night, lying in their small room off the "great hall," itself no larger than five meters by ten and already pungent with cooking smokes. "Those two hardly talk to me, but they thatch a roof like crazy. How well can they tunnel?"

This amused her. "Every pregnant kzinrret is an expert at tunneling, as you will soon see. Except that you will not see. When birthing time nears, a mother digs her secret birthing place. The father sometimes helps, but oftener not."

"Too lazy?"

She regarded him with eyes that reflected a dim flicker from the fire dying in the next room's hearth, and sent a shiver through him. "Too likely to eat the newborn male," she said simply.

"Good God. Not among modern kzinti, I hope."

"Perhaps. Females become good workers; males become aggressive hunters likely to challenge for household mastery. Which would *you* value more?"

"My choice is a matter of record," he joked, adding that they were certainly shaping the manor up fast. That, she said, was because they knew their places and their leaders. Soon they would be butchering and curing meat, making (something) from the milk of ruminants, cheese perhaps, and making ready for the kittens. Some of the released animals seemed already domesticated. A few *vatach*, she said, might be trapped and released nearby for convenience.

He asked if the others would really fight the returning kzin warriors, and she insisted that they would, especially Puss. "She was a highly valued *prret*, but she hates males," Kit warned. "In some ways I think she wishes to be one."

"Then why did she ask if I'd like to scratch her flanks with my *wtsai*," he asked.

"I will claw her eyes out if you do," she growled. "She is only negotiating for status. Keep your blade in your belt," she said angrily, with a metaphor he could not miss.

That blade reminded him (as he idly scratched her flanks with its dull tip to calm her) that the cave was now a treasury of materials. He must study the planting of the fast-growing vines which, according to Kit, would soon hide the roof thatching; those vines could also hide the cave entrance. He could scavenge enough steel for lances, more of the polarizers to build a whopping big airsloop, maybe even— He sat up, startling her. "Meat storage!"

Kit did not understand. He wasn't sure he wanted her to. He would need wire for remote switches, which might be recovered from polarizer toroids if he had the nerve to try it. "I may have a way to keep meat fresh, Kit, but you must help me see that no one else touches my magics. They could be dangerous." She said he was the boss, and he almost believed it.

Once the females began their escape tunnel, Locklear rigged a larger sail and completed his mapping chores, amassing several scrolls which seemed gibberish to the others. And each day he spent two hours at the cave. When vines died, he planted others to hide the entrance. He learned that polarizers and stasis units came in three sizes, and brought trapped *vatach* back in large cages he had separated from their gravity and stasis devices. Those clear cage tops made admirable windows, and the cage metal was then reworked by firelight in the main hall.

Despite Kit's surly glances, he bade Puss sit beside him to learn metalwork, while Boots patiently wove mats and formed trays of clay to his specifications for papermaking. One day he might begin a journal. Meanwhile he needed awls, screwdrivers, pliers—and a longbow with arrows. He was all thumbs while shaping them.

Boots became more shy as her pregnancy advanced. Locklear's new social problem became the casual nuances from Puss that, by now, he knew were sexual. She rarely spoke unless spoken to, but one day while resting in the sun with the big kzinrret he noticed her tailtip flicking near his leg. He had noticed previously that a moving rope or vine seemed to mesmerize a kzin; they probably thought it fascinated him as well.

"Puss, I—uh—sleep only with Kit. Sorry, but that's the way of it."

"Pfaugh. I am more skilled at *ch'rowl* than she, and I could make you a pillow of her fur if I liked." Her gaze was calm, challenging; to a male kzin, probably very sexy.

"We must all work together, Puss. As head of the household, I forbid you to make trouble."

"My Lord," she said with a small nod, but her ear-flick was amused. "In that case, am I permitted to help in the birthing?"

"Of course," he said, touched. "Where is Boots, anyway?"

"Preparing her birthing chamber. It cannot be long now," Puss added, setting off down the ravine.

Locklear found Kit dragging a mat of dirt from the tunnel and asked her about the problems of birthing. The hardest part, she said, was the bower—and when males were near, the hiding. He asked why Puss would be needed at the birthing.

"Ah," said Kit. "It is symbolic, Rockear. You have agreed to let her play the mate role. It is not unheard-of, and the newborn male will be safe."

"You mean, symbolic like our pairing?"

"Not quite that symbolic," she replied with sarcasm as they distributed stone and earth outside. "Prret are flexible."

Then he asked her what *ch'rowl* meant.

Kit vented a tiny miaow of pleasure, then realized suddenly that he did not know what he had said. Furiously: "She used that word to you? I will break her tail!"

"I forbid it," he said. "She was angry because I told her I slept only with you." Pleased with this, Kit subsided as they moved into the tunnel again. Some kzin words, he learned, were triggers. At least one seemed to be blatantly lascivious. He was deflected from this line of thought only when Kit, digging upward now, broke through to the surface.

They replanted shrubs at the exit before dark, and lounged before the hearthfire afterward. At last Locklear yawned; checked his wristcomp. "They are very late," he said.

"Kittens are born at night," she replied, unworried.

"But—I assumed she'd tell us when it was time."

"She has not said eight-cubed of words to you. Why should she confide that to a male?"

He shrugged at the fire. Perhaps they would always treat him like a kzintosh. He wondered for the hundredth time whether, when push came to shove, they would fight with him or against him.

In his mapping sorties, Locklear had skirted near enough to the force walls to see that Kzersatz was adjacent to four other compounds. One, of course, was the tantalizing Newduvai. Another was hidden in swirling mists; he dubbed it Limbo. The others held no charm for him; he named them Who Needs It, and No Thanks. He wondered what collections of life forms roamed those mysterious lands, or slept there in stasis. The planet might have scores of such zoo compounds.

Meanwhile, he unwound a hundred meters of

wire from a polarizer, and stole switches from others. One of his jury-rigs, outside the cave, was a catapult using a polarizer on a sturdy frame. He could stand fifty meters away and, with his remote switch, lob a heavy stone several hundred meters. Perhaps a series of the gravity polarizers would make a kind of mass driver—a true space drive! There was yet hope, he thought, of someday visiting Newduvai.

And then he transported some materials to the manor where he installed a stasis device to keep meat fresh indefinitely; and late that same day, Puss returned. Even Kit, ignoring their rivalry, welcomed the big kzinrret.

"They are all well," Puss reported smugly, paternally. To Locklear's delighted question she replied in severe tones, "You cannot see them until their eyes open, Rockear."

"It is tradition," Kit injected. "The mother will suckle them until then, and will hunt as she must."

"I am the hunter," Puss said. "When we build our own manor, will your household help?"

Kit looked quickly toward Locklear, who realized the implications. *By God, they're really pairing off for another household*, he thought. After a moment he said, "Yes, but you must locate it nearby." He saw Kit relax and decided he'd made the right decision. To celebrate the new developments, Puss shooed Locklear and Kit outside to catch the late sun while she made them an early supper. They sat on their rough-hewn bench above the ravine to eat, Puss claiming she could return to the birthing bower in full darkness, and Locklear allowed himself to bask in a sense of well-being. It was not until Puss had headed back down the ravine with food for Boots, that Locklear realized she had stolen several small items from his storage shelves.

He could accept the loss of tools and a knife; Puss had, after all, helped him make them. What caused his cold sweat was the fact that the tiny *zzrou* transmitter was missing. The *zzrou* prongs in his shoulder began to itch as he thought about it. Puss could not possibly know the importance of the transmitter to him; maybe she thought it was some magical tool—and maybe she would destroy it while studying it. "Kit," he said, trying to keep the tremor from his voice, "I've got a problem and I need your help."

She seemed incensed, but not very surprised, to learn the function of the device that clung to his back. One thing was certain, he insisted: the birthing bower could not be more than a klick away. Because if Puss took the transmitter farther than that, he would die in agony. Could Kit lead him to the bower in darkness?

"I might find it, Rockear, but your presence there would provoke violence," she said. "I must go alone." She caressed his flank gently, then set off slowly down the ravine on all-fours, her nose close to the turf until she disappeared in darkness.

Locklear stood for a time at the manor entrance, wondering what this night would bring, and then saw a long scrawl of light as it slowed to a stop and winked out, many miles above the plains of Kzersatz. Now he knew what the morning would bring, and knew that he had not one deadly problem, but two. He began to check his pathetic little armory by the glow of his memocomp, because that was better than giving way entirely to despair.

*   *   *

When he awoke, it was to the warmth of Kit's fur nestled against his backside. *There was a time when she called this obscene,* he thought with a smile—and then he remembered everything, and lit the display of his memocomp. Two hours until dawn. How long until death, he wondered, and woke her.

She did not have the *zzrou* transmitter. "Puss heard my calls," she said, "and warned me away. She will return this morning to barter tools for things she wants."

"I'll tell you who else will return," he began. "No, don't rebuild the fire, Kit. I saw what looked like a ship stationing itself many miles away overhead, while you were gone. Smoke will only give us away. It might possibly be a Manship, but—expect the worst. You haven't told me how you plan to fight."

His hopes fell as she stammered out her ideas, and he countered each one, reflecting that she was no planner. They would hide and ambush the searchers—but he reminded her of their projectile and beam weapons. Very well, they would claim absolute homestead rights accepted by all ancient Kzinti clans—but modern Kzinti, he insisted, had probably forgotten those ancient immunities.

"You may as well invite them in for breakfast," he grumbled. "Back on earth, women's weapons included poison. I thought you had some kzinrret weapons."

"Poisons would take time, Rockear. It takes little time, and not much talent, to set warriors fighting to the death over a female. Surely they would still respond with foolish bravado?"

"I don't know; they've never seen a smart kzinrret. And ship's officers are very disciplined. I don't think they'd get into a free-for-all. Maybe lure them in here and hit 'em while they sleep . . ."

"As you did to me?"

"Uh no, I—yes!" He was suddenly galvanized by the idea, tantalized by the treasures he had left in the cave. "Kit, the machine I set up to preserve food is exactly the same as the one I placed under you, to make you sleep when I hit a foot switch." He saw her flash of anger at his earlier duplicity. "An ancient sage once said anything that's advanced enough beyond your understanding is indistinguishable from magic, Kit. But magic can turn on you. Could you get a warrior to sit or lie down by himself?"

"If I cannot, I am no *prret*," she purred. "Certainly I can *leave* one lying by himself. Or two. Or . . ."

"Okay, don't get graphic on me," he snapped. "We've got only one stasis unit here. If only I could get more— but I can't leave in the airboat without that damned little transmitter! Kit, you'll have to go and get Puss now. I'll promise her anything within reason."

"She will know we are at a disadvantage. Her demands will be outrageous."

"We're *all* at a disadvantage! Tell her about the kzin warship that's hanging over us."

"Hanging magically over us," she corrected him. "It is true enough for me."

Then she was gone, loping away in darkness, leaving him to fumble his way to the meat storage unit he had so recently installed. The memocomp's faint light helped a little, and he was too busy to notice the passage of time until, with its usual sudden blaze, the sunlet of Kzersatz began to shine.

He was hiding the wires from Puss's bed to the foot switch near the little room's single doorway when he heard a distant roll of thunder. No, not thunder: it grew to a crackling howl in the sky, and from the nearest window he saw what he most feared to see. The kzin lifeboat left a thin contrail in its pass, circling just inside the force cylinder of Kzersatz, and its wingtips slid out as it slowed. No doubt of the newcomer now, and it disappeared in the direction of that first landing, so long ago. If only he'd thought to booby-trap that landing zone with stasis units! Well, he might've, given time.

He finished his work in fevered haste, knowing that time was now his enemy, and so were the kzinti in that ship, and so, for all practical purposes, was the traitor Puss. *And Kit? How easy it will be for her to switch sides! Those females will make out like bandits wherever they are, and I may learn Kit's decision when these goddamned prongs take a lethal bite in my back. Could be any time now.* And then he heard movements in the high grass nearby, and leaped for his longbow.

Kit flashed to the doorway, breathless. "She is coming, Rockear. Have you set your sleeptrap?"

He showed her the rig. "Toe it once for sleep, again for waking, again for sleep," he said. "Whatever you do, don't get near enough to touch the sleeper, or stand over him, or you'll be in the same fix. I've set it for maximum power."

"Why did you put it here, instead of our own bed?"

He coughed and shrugged. "Uh,—I don't know. Just seemed like—well, hell, it's *our* bed, Kit! I, um, didn't like the idea of your using it, ah, the way you'll have to use it."

"You are an endearing beast," she said, pinching him lightly at the neck, "to bind me with tenderness."

They both whirled at Puss's voice from the main doorway: "Bind who with tenderness?"

"I will explain," said Kit, her face bland. "If you brought those trade goods, display them on your bed."

"I think not," said Puss, striding into the room she'd shared with Boots. "But I will show them to you." With that, she sat on her bed and reached into her apron pocket, drawing out a *wtsai* for inspection.

An instant later she was unconscious. Kit, with Locklear kibitzing, used a grass broom to whisk the knife safely away. "I should use it on her throat," she snarled, but she let Locklear take the weapon.

"She came of her own accord," he said, "and she's a fighter. We need her, Kit. Hit the switch again."

A moment later, Puss was blinking, leaping up, then suddenly backing away in fear. "Treachery," she spat.

In reply, Locklear tossed the knife onto her bed despite Kit's frown. "Just a display, Puss. You need the knife, and I'm your ally. But I've got to have that little gadget that looks like my wristcomp." He held out his hand.

"I left it at the birthing bower. I knew it was important," she said with a surly glance as she retrieved the knife. "For its return, I demand our total release from this household. I demand your help to build a manor as large as this, wherever I like. I demand teaching in your magical arts." She trembled, but stood defiant; a dangerous combination.

"Done, done, and done," he said. "You want equality, and I'm willing. But we may all be equally dead if that kzin ship finds us. We need a leader. Do you have a good plan?"

Puss swallowed hard. "Yes. Hunt at night, hide until they leave."

Sighing, Locklear told her that was no plan at all. He wasted long minutes arguing his case: Puss to steal near the landing site and report on the intruders; the return of his *zzrou* transmitter so he could try sneaking back to the cave; Kit to remain at the manor preparing food for a siege—and to defend the manor through what he termed guile, if necessary.

Puss refused. "My place," she insisted, "is defending the birthing bower."

"And you will not have a male as a leader," Kit said. "Is that not the way of it?"

"Exactly," Puss growled.

"I have agreed to your demands, Puss," Locklear reminded her. "But it won't happen if the kzin warriors get me. We've proved we won't abuse you. At least give me back that transmitter. Please," he added gently.

Too late, he saw Puss's disdain for pleading. "So that is the source of your magic," she said, her ears lifting in a kzinrret smile. "I shall discover its secrets, Rockear."

"He will die if you damage it," Kit said quickly, "or take it far from him. You have done a stupid thing; without this manbeast who knows our enemy well, we will be slaves again. To males," she added.

Puss sidled along the wall, now holding the knife at ready, menacing Kit until a single bound put her through the doorway into the big room.

Pausing at the outer doorway she stuck the *wtsai* into her apron. "I will consider what you say," she growled.

"Wait," Locklear said in his most commanding tone, the only one that Puss seemed to value. "The kzintosh will be searching for me. They have magics that let them see great distances even at night, and a big metal airboat that flies with the sound of thunder."

"I heard thunder this morning," Puss admitted.

"You heard their airboat. If they see you, they will probably capture you. You and Boots must be very careful, Puss."

"And do not hesitate to tempt males into (something) if you can," Kit put in.

"Now you would teach me my business," Puss spat at Kit, and set off down the ravine.

Locklear moved to the outer doorway, watching the sky, listening hard. Presently he asked, "Do you think we can lay siege to the birthing bower to get that transmitter back?"

"Boots is a suckling mother, which saps her strength," Kit replied matter-of-factly. "So Puss would fight like a crazed warrior. The truth is, she is stronger than both of us."

With a morose shake of his head, Locklear began to fashion more arrows while Kit sharpened his *wtsai* into a dagger, arguing tactics, drawing rough conclusions. They must build no fires at the manor, and hope that the searchers spread out for single, arrogant sorties. The lifeboat would hold eight warriors, and others might be waiting in orbit. Live captives might be better for negotiations than dead heroes—"But even as captives, the bastards would eat every scrap of meat in sight," Locklear admitted.

Kit argued persuasively that any warrior worth his *wtsai* would be more likely to negotiate with a potent enemy. "We must give them casualties," she insisted, "to gain their respect. Can these modern males be that different from those I knew?"

Probably not, he admitted. And knowing the modern breed, he knew they would be infuriated by his escape, dishonored by his shrewdness. He could expect no quarter when at last they did locate him. "And they won't go until they do," he said. On that, they agreed; some things never changed.

Locklear, dog-tired after hanging thatch over the gleaming windows, heard the lifeboat pass twice before dark but fell asleep as the sun faded.

Much later, Kit was shaking him. "Come to the door," she urged. "She refuses to come in."

He stumbled outside, found the bench by rote, and spoke to the darkness. "Puss? You have nothing to fear from us. Had a change of heart?"

Not far distant: "I hunted those slopes where you said the males left you, Rockear."

It was an obvious way to avoid saying she had reconnoitered as he'd asked, and he maintained the ruse. "Did you have good hunting?"

"Fair. A huge metal thing came and went and came again. I found four warriors, in strange costume and barbaric speech like yours, with strange weapons. They are making a camp there, and spoke with surprise of seeing animals to hunt." She spoke slowly, pausing often. He asked her to describe the males. She had no trouble with that, having lain in her natural camouflage in the jungle's verge within thirty paces of the ship until dark. *Must've taken her hours to get here in the dark over rough country*, he thought. *This is one tough bimbo.*

He waited, his hackles rising, until she finished. "You're sure the leader had that band across his face?" She was. She'd heard him addressed as "Grraf-Commander." One with a light-banded belly was called "Apprentice Something." And the other two tallied, as well. "I can't believe it," he said to the darkness. "The same foursome that left me here! If they're all down here, they're deadly serious. Damn their good luck."

"Better than you think," said Puss. "You told me they had magic weapons. Now I believe it."

Kit, leaning near, whispered into Locklear's ear. "If she were injured, she would refuse to show her weakness to us."

He tried again. "Puss, how do you know of their weapons?"

With dry amusement and courage, the disembodied voice said, "The usual way: the huge sentry used one. Tiny sunbeams that struck as I reached thick cover. They truly can see in full darkness."

"So they've seen you," he said, dismayed.

"From their shouts, I think they were not sure what they saw. But I will kill them for this, sentry or no sentry."

Her voice was more distant now. Locklear raised his voice slightly: "Puss, can we help you?"

"I have been burned before," was the reply.

Kit, moving into the darkness quietly: "You are certain there are only four?"

"Positive," was the faint reply, and then they heard only the night wind.

Presently Kit said, "It would take both of us, and when wounded she will certainly fight to the death. But we might overpower her now, if we can find the bower."

"No. She did more than she promised. And now she knows she can kill me by smashing the transmitter. Let's get same sleep, Kit," he said. Then, when he had nestled behind her, he added with a chuckle, "I begin to see why the kzinti decided to breed females as mere pets. Sheer self-defense."

"I would break your tail for that, if you had one," she replied in mock ferocity. Then he laid his hand on her flank, heard her soft miaow, and then they slept.

Locklear had patrolled nearly as far as he dared down the ravine at midmorning, armed with his *wtsai*, longbow, and an arrow-filled quiver rubbing against the *zzrou* when he heard the first scream. He knew that Kit, with her short lance, had gone in the opposite direction on her patrol, but the repeated kzin screams sent gooseflesh up his spine. Perhaps the tabbies had surrounded Boots, or Puss. He notched an arrow, half climbing to the lip of the ravine, and peered over low brush. He stifled the exclamation in his throat.

They'd found Puss, all right—or she'd found them. She stood on all-fours on a level spot below, her tail erect, its tip curled over, watching two hated familiar figures in a tableau that must have been as old as kzin history. Almost naked for this primitive duel, ebony talons out and their musky scent heavy on the breeze, they bulked stupefyingly huge and ferocious. The massive gunner, Goon, and engineer Yellowbelly circled each other with drawn stilettoes. What boggled Locklear was that their modern weapons lay ignored in neat groups. Were they going through some ritual?

They were like hell, he decided. From time to time, Puss would utter a single word, accompanied by a tremor and a tail-twitch; and each time, Yellowbelly and Goon would stiffen, then scream at each other in frustration.

The word she repeated was *ch'rowl*. No telling how long they'd been there, but Goon's right forearm dripped blood, and Yellowbelly's thigh was a sodden red mess. Swaying drunkenly, Puss edged nearer to the weapons. As Yellowbelly screamed and leaped, Goon screamed and parried, bearing his smaller opponent to the turf. What followed then was fast enough to be virtually a blur in a roil of Kzersatz dust as two huge tigerlike bodies thrashed and rolled, knives flashing, talons ripping, fangs sinking into flesh.

Locklear scrambled downward through the grass, his progress unheard in the earsplitting caterwauls nearby. He saw Puss reach a beam rifle, grasp it, swing it experimentally by the barrel. That's when he forgot all caution and shouted, "No, Puss! Put the stock to your shoulder and pull the trigger!"

He might as well have told her to bazzfazz the shimstock; and in any case, poor valiant Puss collapsed while trying to figure the rifle out. He saw the long ugly trough in her side then, caked with dried blood. A wonder she was conscious, with such a wound. Then he saw something more fearful still, the quieter thrashing as Goon found the throat of Yellowbelly, whose stiletto handle protruded from Goon's upper arm.

Ducking below the brush, Locklear moved to one side, nearer to Puss, whose breathing was as labored as that of the males. Or rather, of one male, as Goon stood erect and uttered a victory roar that must have carried to Newduvai. Yellowbelly's torn throat pumped the last of his blood onto alien dust.

"I claim my right," Goon screamed, and added a Word that Locklear was beginning to loathe. Only then did the huge gunner notice that Puss was in no condition to present him with what he had just killed to get. He nudged her roughly, and did not see Locklear approach with one arrow notched and another held between his teeth.

But his ear umbrellas pivoted as a twig snapped under Locklear's foot, and Goon spun furiously, the big legs flexed, and for one instant man and kzin stood twenty paces apart, unmoving. Goon leaped for the nearest weapon, the beam rifle Puss had dropped, and saw Locklear release the short arrow. It missed by a full armspan and now, his bloodlust rekindled and with no fear of such a marksman, Goon dropped the rifle and pulled Yellowbelly's stiletto from his own arm. He turned toward Locklear, who was unaccountably running *toward* him instead of fleeing as a monkey should flee a leopard, and threw his head back in a battle scream.

Locklear's second arrow, fired from a distance of five paces, pierced the roof of Goon's mouth, its stainless steel barb severing nerve bundles at the brain stem. Goon fell like a jointed tree, knees buckling first, arms hanging, and the ground's impact drove the arrow tip out the back of his head, slippery with gore. Goon's head lay two paces from Locklear's feet. He neither breathed nor twitched.

Locklear hurried to the side of poor, courageous, ill-starred Puss and saw her gazing calmly at him. "One for you, one for me, Puss. Only two more to go."

"I wish—I could live to celebrate that," she said, more softly than he had ever heard her speak.

"You're too tough to let a little burn," he began.

"They shot tiny things, too," she said, a finger migrating to a bluish perforation at the side of her rib cage. "Coughing blood. Hard to breathe," she managed.

He knew then that she was dying. A spray of slugs, roughly aimed at night from a perimeter-control smoothbore, had done to Puss what a beam rifle could not. Her lungs filling slowly with blood, she had still managed to report her patrol and then return to guard the birthing bower. He asked through the lump in his throat, "Is Boots all right?"

"They followed my spoor. When I—came out, twitching my best *prret* routine—they did not look into the bower."

"Smart, Puss."

She grasped his wrist, hard. "Swear to protect it—with your life." Now she was coughing blood, fighting to breathe.

"Done," he said. "Where is it, Puss?"

But her eyes were already glazing. Locklear stood up slowly and strode to the beam rifle, hefting it, thinking idly that these weapons were too heavy for him to carry in one trip. And then he saw Puss again, and quit thinking, and lifted the rifle over his head with both hands in a manscream of fury, and of vengeance unappeased.

The battle scene was in sight of the lake, fully in the open within fifty paces of the creek, and he found it impossible to lift Puss. Locklear cut bundles of grass and spread them to hide the bodies, trembling in delayed reaction, and carried three armloads of weapons to a hiding place far up the ravine just under its lip. He left the dead kzinti without stripping them; perhaps a mistake, but he had no time now to puzzle out tightband comm sets or medkits. Later, if there was a later . . .

He cursed his watery joints, knowing he could not carry a kzin beam rifle with its heavy accumulator up to the manor. He moved more cautiously now, remembering those kzin screams, wondering how far they'd carried on the breeze which was toward the lake. He read the safety legends on Goon's sidearm, found he could handle the massive piece with both hands, and stuck it and its twin from Yellowbelly's arsenal into his belt, leaving his bow and quiver with the other weapons.

He had stumbled within sight of the manor, planning how he could unmast the airboat and adjust its buoyancy so that it could be towed by a man afoot to retrieve those weapons, when a crackling hum sent a blast of hot air across his cheeks. Face down, crawling for the lip of the ravine, he heard a shout from near the manor.

"Grraf-Commander, the monkey approaches!" The reply, deep-voiced and muffled, seemed to come from inside the manor. So they'd known where the manor was. Heat or motion sensors, perhaps, during a pass in the lifeboat—not that it mattered now. A classic pincers from down and up the ravine, but one of those pincers now lay under shields of grass. They could not know that he was still tethered invisibly to that *zzrou* transmitter. But where was Kit?

Another hail from Brickshitter, whose tremors of impatience with a beam rifle had become Locklear's ally: "The others do not answer my calls, but I shall drive the monkey down to them."

Well, maybe he'd intended merely to wing his quarry, or follow him.

You do that, Locklear thought to himself in cold rage as he scurried back in the ravine toward his weapons cache; *you just do that, Brickshitter.* He had covered two hundred meters when another crackle announced the pencil-thin beam, brighter than the sun, that struck a ridge of stone above him.

White-hot bees stung his face, back and arms; tiny smoke trails followed fragments of superheated stone into the ravine as Locklear tumbled to the creek, splashing out again, stumbling on slick stones. He turned, intending to fire a sidearm, but saw no target and realized that firing from him would tell volumes to that big sonofabitchkitty behind and above him. Well, they wouldn't have returned unless they wanted him alive, so Brickshitter was just playing with him, driving him as a man drives cattle with a prod. Beam weapons were limited in rate of fire and accumulator charge; maybe Brickshitter would empty this one with his trembling.

Then, horrifyingly near, above the ravine lip, the familiar voice: "I offer you honor, monkey."

Whatthehell: the navigator knew where his quarry was anyhow. Mopping a runnel of blood from his face, Locklear called upward as he continued his scramble. "What, a prisoner exchange?" He did not want to be more explicit than that.

"We already have the beauteous kzinrret," was the reply that chilled Locklear to his marrows. "Is that who you would have sacrificed for your worthless hide?"

That tears it; no hope now, Locklear thought. "Maybe I'll give myself up if you'll let her go," he called. *Would I? Probably not. Dear God, please don't give me that choice because I know there would be no honor in mine . . .*

"We have you caged, monkey," in tones of scorn. "But Grraf-Commander warned that you may have some primitive hunting weapon, so we accord you some little honor. It occurs to me that you would retain more honor if captured by an officer than by a pair of rankings."

Locklear was now only a hundred meters from the precious cache. *He's too close; he'll see the weapons cache when I get near it and that'll be all she wrote. I've got to make the bastard careless and use what I've got.* He thought carefully how to translate a nickname into Kzin and began to ease up the far side of the ravine. "Not if the officer has no honor, you trembling shitter of bricks," he shouted, slipping the safety from a sidearm.

Instantly a scream of raw rage and astonishment from above at this unbelievably mortal insult, followed by the head and shoulders of an infuriated navigator. Locklear aimed fast, squeezed the firing stud, and saw a series of dirt clods spit from the verge of the ravine. The damned thing shot low!

But Brickshitter had popped from sight as though propelled by levers, and now Locklear was climbing, stuffing the sidearm into his belt again to keep both hands free for the ravine, and when he vaulted over the lip into low brush, he could hear Brickshitter babbling into his comm unit.

He wanted to hear the exchange more than he wanted to move. He heard: ". . . has two kzin handguns—of course I saw them, and heard them; had I been slower he would have an officer's ears on his belt now!—Nossir, no reply from the others. How else would he have hero's weapons? What do you think?—I think so, too."

Locklear began to move out again, below brushtops, as the furious Brickshitter was promising a mansack to his commander as a trophy. *And they won't get that while I live*, he vowed to himself. In fact, with his promise, Brickshitter was admitting they no longer wanted him alive. He did not hear the next hum, but saw brush spatter ahead of him, some of it bursting into flame, and then he was firing at the exposed Brickshitter who now stood with brave stance, seven and a half feet tall and weaving from side to side, firing once a second, as fast as the beam rifle's accumulator would permit.

Locklear stood and delivered, moving back and forth. At his second burst, the weapon's receiver locked open. He ducked below, discarded the thing, and drew its twin, estimating he had emptied the first one with thirty rounds. When next he lifted his head, he saw that Brickshitter had outpaced him across the ravine and was firing at the brush again. Even as the stuff ahead of him was kindling, Locklear noticed that the brush behind him flamed higher than a man, now a wildfire moving in the same direction as he, though the steady breeze swept it away from the ravine. His only path now was along the ravine lip, or in it.

He guessed that this weapon would shoot low as well, and opened up at a distance of sixty paces. Good guess; Brickshitter turned toward him and at the same instant was slapped by an invisible fist that flung the heavy rifle from his grasp. Locklear dodged to the lip of the ravine to spot the weapons, saw them twenty paces away, and dropped the sidearm so that he could hang onto brush as he vaulted over, now in full view of Brickshitter.

Whose stuttering fire with his good arm reminded Locklear, nearly too late, that Brickshitter had other weapons beside that beam rifle. Spurts of dirt flew into Locklear's eyes as he flung himself back to safety. He crawled back for the sidearm, watching the navigator fumble for his rifle, and opened up again just as Brickshitter dropped from sight. More wasted ammo.

Behind him, the fire was raging downslope toward their mutual dead. Across the ravine, Brickshitter's enraged voice: "Small caliber flesh wound in the right shoulder but I have started brush fires to flush him. I can see beam rifles, close-combat weapons and other things almost below him in the ravine.—Yessir, he is almost out of ammunition and wants that cache.— Yessir, a few more bolts. An easy shot."

Locklear had once seen an expedition bundle burn with a beam rifle in it. He began to run hard, skirting still-smouldering brush and grass, and had already passed the inert bodies of their unprotesting dead when the ground bucked beneath him. He fell to one knee, seeing a cloud of debris fan above the ravine, echoes of the explosion shouldering each other down the slopes, and he knew that Brickshitter's left-armed aim had been as good as necessary. Good enough, maybe, to get himself killed in that cloud of turf and stone and metal fragments, yes, and good wooden arrows that had made a warrior of Locklear. Yet any sensible warrior knows how to retreat.

The ravine widened now, the creek dropping in a series of lower falls, and Locklear knew that further headlong flight would send him far into

the open, so far that the *zzrou* would kill him if
Brickshitter didn't. And Brickshitter could track
his spoor—but not in water. Locklear raced to the
creek, heedless of the misstep that could smash a
knee or ankle, and began to negotiate the little
falls.

The last one faced the lake. He turned, recognizing that he had cached his pathetic store of
provisions behind that waterfall soon after his ar-
rival. It was flanked by thick fronds and ferns, and
Locklear ducked into the hideyhole behind that
sheet of water streaming wet, gasping for breath.

A soft inquiry from somewhere behind him. He
whirled in sudden recognition. *It's REALLY a
small world,* he thought idiotically. "Boots?" No
answer. Well, of course not, to his voice, but he
could see the dim outline of a deep horizontal
tunnel, turning left inside its entrance, with dry
grasses lining the floor. "Boots, don't be afraid of
me. Did you know the kzin males have returned?"

Guarded, grudging it: "Yes. They have wounded
my mate."

"Worse, Boots. But she killed one,"—*it was her
doing as surely as if her fangs had torn out Yellowbelly's throat*—and I killed another. She told
me to—to retrieve the things she took from me."
It seemed his heart must burst with this cowardly
lie. He was cold, exhausted, and on the run, and
with the transmitter he could escape to win another day, and, and—. And he wanted to slash his
wrists with his *wtsai.*

"I will bring them. Do not come nearer," said
the soft voice, made deeper by echoes. He squatted under the overhang, the plash of water now
dwindling, and he realized that the blast up the
ravine had made a momentary check-dam. He

distinctly heard the mewing of tiny kzin twins as Boots removed the security of her warm, soft fur. A moment later, he saw her head and arms. Both hands, even the one bearing a screwdriver and the transmitter, had their claws fully extended and her ears lay so flat on her skull that they might have been caps of skin. Still, she shoved the articles forward.

Pocketing the transmitter with a thrill of undeserved success, he bade her keep the other items. He showed her the sidearm. "Boots, one of these killed Puss. Do you see that it could kill you just as easily?"

The growl in her throat was an illustrated manual of counterthreat.

"But I began as your protector. I would never harm you or your kittens. Do you see that now?"

"My head sees it. My heart says to fight you. Go."

He nodded, turned away, and eased himself into the deep pool that was now fed by a mere trickle of water. Ahead was the lake, smoke floating toward it, and he knew that he could run safely in the shallows hidden by smoke without leaving prints. And fight another day. And, he realized, staring back at the once-talkative little falls, leave Boots with her kittens where the cautious Brickshitter would almost certainly find them because now the mouth of her birthing bower was clearly visible.

No, I'm damned if you will!

"So check into it, Brickshitter," he muttered softly, backing deep into the cool cover of yellow ferns. "I've still got a few rounds here, if you're still alive."

He was alive, all right. Locklear knew it in his

guts when a stone trickled its way down near the pool. He knew it for certain when he felt soft footfalls, the almost silent track of a big hunting cat, vibrate the damp grassy embankment against his back. He eased forward in water that was no deeper than his armpits, still hidden, but when the towering kzin warrior sprang to the verge of the water he made no sound at all. He carried only his sidearm and knife, and Locklear fired at a distance of only ten paces, actually a trifling space.

But a tremendous trifle, for Brickshitter was well-trained and did not pause after his leap before hopping aside in a squat. He was looking straight at Locklear and the horizontal spray of slugs ceased before it reached him. Brickshitter's arm was a blur. Foliage shredded where Locklear had hidden as the little man dropped below the surface, feeling two hot slugs trickle down his back after their velocity was spent underwater.

Locklear could not see clearly, but propelled himself forward as he broke the surface in a desperate attempt to reach the other side. He knew his sidearm was empty. He did not know that his opponent's was, until the kzin navigator threw the weapon at him, screamed, and leaped.

Locklear pulled himself to the bank with fronds as the big kzin strode toward him in water up to his belly. Too late to run, and Brickshitter had a look of cool confidence about him. *I like him better when he's not so cool.* "Come on, you *kshat*, you *vatach*'s ass," he chanted, backing toward the only place where he might have safety at his back— the stone shelf before Boots's bower, where great height was a disadvantage. "Come on, you fur-licking, brickshitting hairball, do it! Leaping and screaming, screaming and leaping; you stupid no-name," he finished, wondering if the last was an insult.

Evidently it was. With a howling scream of savagery, the big kzin tried to leap clear of the water, falling headlong as Locklear reached the stone shelf. Dagger now in hand, Brickshitter floundered to the bank spitting, emitting a string of words that doubled Locklear's command of kzinti curses. Then, almost as if reading Locklear's mind, the navigator paused a few paces away and held up his knife. And his voice, though quivering, was exceedingly mild. "Do you know what I am going to do with this, monkey?"

To break through this facade, Locklear made it offhanded. "Cut your *ch'rowl*ing throat by accident, most likely," he said.

The effect was startling. Stiffening, then baring his fangs in a howl of frustration, the warrior sprang for the shelf, seeing in midleap that Locklear was waiting for exactly that with his *wtsai* thrust forward, its tip made needle-sharp by the same female who had once dulled it. But a kzin warrior's training went deep. Pivoting as he landed, rolling to one side, the navigator avoided Locklear's thrust, his long tail lashing to catch the little man's legs.

Locklear had seen that one before. His blade cut deeply into the kzin's tail and Brickshitter vented a yelp, whirling to spring. He feinted as if to hurl the knife and Locklear threw both arms before his face, seeing too late the beginning of the kzin's squatting leap in close quarters, like a swordsman's balestra. Locklear slammed his back painfully against the side of the cave, his own blade slashing blindly, and felt a horrendous fiery trail of pain down the length of his knife arm before the graceful kzin moved out of range. He switched hands with the *wtsai*.

"I am going to carve off your maleness while you watch, monkey," said Brickshitter, seeing the blood begin to course from the open gash on Locklear's arm.

"One word before you do," Locklear said, and pulled out all the stops. "*Ch'rowl* your grandmother. *Ch'rowl* your patriarch, and *ch'rowl* yourself."

With each repetition, Brickshitter seemed to coil into himself a bit farther, his eyes not slitted but saucer-round, and with his last phrase Locklear saw something from the edge of his vision that the big kzin saw clearly. Ropelike, temptingly bushy, it was the flick of Boots's tail at the mouth of her bower.

Like most feline hunters from the creche onward, the kzin warrior reacted to this stimulus with rapt fascination, at least for an instant, already goaded to insane heights of frustration by the sexual triggerword. His eyes rolled upward for a flicker of time, and in that flicker Locklear acted. His headlong rush carried him in a full body slam against the navigator's injured shoulder, the *wtsai* going in just below the rib cage, torn from Locklear's grasp as his opponent flipped backward in agony to the water. Locklear cartwheeled into the pool, weaponless, choosing to swim because it was the fastest way out of reach.

He flailed up the embankment searching wildly for a loose stone, then tossed a glance over his shoulder. The navigator lay on his side, half out of the water, blood pumping from his belly, and in his good arm he held Locklear's *wtsai* by its handle. As if his arm were the only part of him still alive, he flipped the knife, caught it by the tip, forced himself erect.

Locklear did the first thing he could remember from dealing with vicious animals: reached down, grasped a handful of thin air, and mimicked hurling a stone. It did not deter the navigator's convulsive move in the slightest, the *wtsai* a silvery whirr before it thunked into a tree one pace from Locklear's breast. The kzin's motion carried him forward into water, face down. He did not entirely submerge, but slid forward inert, arms at his sides. Locklear wrestled his blade from the tree and waited, his chest heaving. The navigator did not move again.

Locklear held the knife aloft, eyes shut, for long moments, tears of exultation and vengeance coursing down his cheeks, mixing with dirty water from his hair and clean blood from his cheek. His eyes snapped open at the voice.

"May I name my son after you, Rockear?" Boots, just inside the overhang, held two tiny spotted kittens protectively where they could suckle. It was, he felt, meant to be an honor merely for him to see them.

"I would be honored, Boots. But the modern kzin custom is to make sons earn their names, I think."

"What do I care what they do? We are starting over here."

Locklear stuffed the blade into his belt, wiping wet stuff from his face again. "Not unless I can put away that scarfaced commander. He's got Kit at the manor— unless she has him. I'm going to try and bias the results," he said grimly, and scanned the heights above the ravine.

To his back, Boots said, "It is not traditional,

but—if you come for us, we would return to the manor's protection."

He turned, glancing up the ravine. "An honor. But right now, you'd better come out and wait for the waterfall to resume. When it does, it might flood your bower for a few minutes." He waved, and she waved back. When next he glanced downslope, from the upper lip of the ravine, he could see the brushfire dwindling at the jungle's edge, and water just beginning to carve its way through a jumble of debris in the throat of the ravine, and a small lithe orange-yellow figure holding two tiny spotted dots, patiently waiting in the sunlight for everything he said to come true.

"Lady," he said softly to the waiting Boots, "I sure hope you picked a winner."

He could have disappeared into the wilds of Kzersatz for months but Scarface, with vast advantages, might call for more searchers. Besides, running would be reactive, the act of mindless prey. Locklear opted to be *pro*active—a hunter's mindset. Recalling the violence of that exploding rifle, he almost ignored the area because nothing useful could remain in the crater. But curiosity made him pause, squinting down from the heights, and excellent vision gave him an edge when he saw the dull gleam of Brickshitter's beam rifle across the ravine. It was probably fully discharged, else the navigator would not have abandoned it. But Scarface wouldn't know that.

Locklear doubled back and retrieved the heavy weapon, chuckling at the sharp stones that lay atop the turf. Brickshitter must have expended a few curses as those stones rained down. The faint orange light near the scope was next to a legend in

Kzinti that translated as "insufficient charge." He thought about that a moment, then smeared his own blood over the light until its gleam was hidden. Shouldering the rifle, he set off again, circling high above the ravine so that he could come in from its upper end. Somehow the weapon seemed lighter now, or perhaps it was just his second wind. Locklear did not pause to reflect that his decision for immediate action brought optimism, and that optimism is another word for accumulated energy.

The sun was at his back when he stretched prone behind low cover and paused for breath. The zoom scope of the rifle showed that someone had ripped the thatches from the manor's window bulges, no doubt to give Scarface a better view. *Works both ways, hotshot,* he mused; but though he could see through the windows, he saw nothing move. Presently he began to crawl forward and down, holding the heavy rifle in the crooks of his arms, abrading his elbows as he went from brush to outcrop to declivity. His shadow stretched before him. Good; the sun would be in a watcher's eyes and he was dry-mouthed with awareness that Scarface must carry his own arsenal.

The vines they had planted already hid the shaft of their escape tunnel but Locklear paused for long moments at its mouth, listening, waiting until his breath was quiet and regular. What if Scarface were waiting in the tunnel? He ducked into the rifle sling, put his *wtsai* in his teeth, and eased down feet-first using remembered hand and footholds, his heart hammering his ribs. Then he scuffed earth with his knee and knew that his entry would no longer be a surprise if Scarface was waiting. He dropped the final two meters to soft dirt, squatting, hopping aside as he'd seen Brickshitter do.

Nothing but darkness. He waited for his panting to subside and then moved forward with great caution. It took him five minutes to stalk twenty meters of curving tunnel, feeling his way until he saw faint light filtering from above. By then, he could hear the fitz-rowr of kzin voices. He eased himself up to the opening and peered through long slits of shamboo matting that Boots had woven to cover the rough walls.

". . . Am learning, milady, that even the most potent Word loses its strength when used too often," a male voice was saying. Scarface, in tones Locklear had never expected to hear. "As soon as this operation is complete, rest assured I shall be the most gallant of suitors."

Locklear's view showed only their legs as modern warrior and ancient courtesan faced each other, seated on benches at the rough-hewn dining table. Kit, with a sulk in her voice, said, "I begin to wonder if your truthfulness extends to my attractions, milord."

Scarface, fervently: "The truth is that you are a warrior's wildest fantasies in fur. I cannot say how often I have wished for a mate I could actually talk to! Yet I am first Grraf-Commander, and second a kzintosh. Excuse me," he added, stood up, and strode to the main doorway, now in full view of Locklear. His belt held ceremonial *wtsai*, a sidearm and God knew what else in those pockets. His beam rifle lay propped beside the doorway. Taking a brick-sized device from his broad belt, he muttered, "I wonder if this rude hut is interfering with our signals."

A click and then, in gruff tones of frustrated

command, he said, "Hunt leader to all units: report! If you cannot report, use a signal bomb from your beltpacs, dammit! If you cannot do that, return to the hut at triple time or I will hang your hides from a pennant pole."

Locklear grinned as Scarface moved back to the table with an almost human sigh. *Too bad I didn't know about those signal bombs. Warm this place up a little. Maybe I should go back for those beltpacs.* But he abandoned the notion as Scarface resumed his courtship.

"I have hinted, and you have evaded, milady. I must ask you now, bluntly: will you return with me when this operation is over?"

"I shall do as the commander wishes," she said demurely, and Locklear grinned again. She hadn't said "Grraf-Commander"; and even if Locklear didn't survive, *she* might very well wind up in command. Oh sure, she'd do whatever the commander liked.

"Another point on which you have been evasive," Scarface went on; "your assessment of the monkey, and what relationship he had to either of you." Locklear did not miss this nuance; Scarface knew of two kzinrret, presumably an initial report from one of the pair who'd found Puss. He did not know of Boots, then.

"The manbeast ruled us with strange magic forces, milord. He made us fearful at times. At any time he might be anywhere. Even now." *Enough of that crap*, Locklear thought at her, even though he felt she was only trying to put the wind up Scarface's backside. *Fat chance! Lull the bastard, put him to sleep.*

Scarface went to the heart of his question. "Did he act honorably toward you both?"

After a long pause: "I suppose he did, as a manbeast saw honor. He did not *ch'rowl* me, if that is—"

"Milady! You will rob the Word of its meaning, or drive me mad."

"I have an idea. Let me dance for you while you lie at your ease. I will avoid the term and drive you only a little crazy."

"For the eighth-squared time, I do not need to lie down. I need to complete this hunt; duty first, pleasure after. I—what?"

Locklear's nose had brushed the matting. The noise was faint, but Scarface was on his feet and at the doorway, rifle in hand, in two seconds. Locklear's nose itched, and he pinched his nostrils painfully. It seemed that the damned tabby was never completely off-guard, made edgy as a *wtsai* by his failure to contact his crew. Locklear felt a sneeze coming, sank down on his heels, rubbed furiously at his nose. When he stood up again, Scarface stood a pace outside, demanding a response with his comm set while Kit stood at the doorway. Locklear scratched carefully at the mat, willing Kit alone to hear it. No such luck.

Scarface began to pace back and forth outside, and Locklear scratched louder. Kit's ear-umbrellas flicked, lifted. Another scratch. She turned, and saw him move the matting. Her mouth opened slightly. *She's going to warn him,* Locklear thought wildly.

"Perhaps we could stroll down the ravine, milord," she said easily, taking a few steps outside.

Locklear saw the big kzin commander pass the doorway once, twice, muttering furiously about indecision. He caught the words, ". . . Return to the lifeboat with you now if I have not heard from them very soon," and knew that he could never regain an advantage if that happened. He paced his advance past the matting to coincide with Scarface's movements, easing the beam rifle into plain sight on the floor, now with his head and shoulders out above the dusty floor, now his waist, now his—his—his sneeze came without warning.

Scarface leaped for the entrance, snatching his sidearm as he came into view, and Locklear gave himself up then even though he was aiming the heavy beam rifle from a prone position, an empty threat. But a bushy tail flashed between the warrior's ankles, and his next bound sent him skidding forward on his face, the sidearm still in his hand but pointed away from Locklear.

And the muzzle of Locklear's beam rifle poked so near the commander's nose that he could only focus on it cross-eyed. Locklear said it almost pleasantly: "Could even a monkey miss such a target?"

"Perhaps," Scarface said, and swallowed hard. "But I think that rifle is exhausted."

"The one your nervous brickshitting navigator used? It probably was," said Locklear, brazening it out, adding the necessary lie with, "I broiled him with this one, which doesn't have that cute little light glowing, does it? Now then: skate that little shooter of yours across the floor. Your crew is all bugbait, Scarface, and the only thing between you and kitty heaven is my good humor."

Much louder than need be, unless he was counting on Kit's help: "Have you no end of insults? Have you no sense of honor? Let us settle this as equals." Kit stood at the doorway now.

"The sidearm, Grraf-Commander. Or meet your

ancestors. Your crew tried to kill me—and monkey see, monkey do."

The sidearm clattered across the rough floor mat. Locklear chose to avoid further insult; the last thing he needed was a loss of self-control from the big kzin. "Hands behind your back. Kit, get the strongest cord we have and bind him; the feet, then the hands. And stay to one side. If I have to pull this trigger, you don't want to get splattered."

Minutes later, holding the sidearm and sitting at the table, Locklear studied the prisoner who sat, legs before him, back against the doorway, and explained the facts of Kzersatz life while Kit cleaned his wounds. She murmured that his cheek scar would someday be *t'rralap* as he explained the options. "So you see, you have nothing to lose by giving your honorable parole, because I trust your honor. You have everything to lose by refusing, because you'll wind up as barbecue."

"Men do not eat captives," Scarface said. "You speak of honor and yet you lie."

"Oh, I wouldn't eat you. But *they* would. There are two kzinrret here who, if you'll recall, hate everything you stand for."

Scarface looked glumly at Kit. "Can this be true?"

She replied, "Can it be true that modern kzinrret have been bred into cattle?"

"Both can be true," he conceded. "But monk—men are devious, false, conniving little brutes. How can a kzinrret of your intelligence approve of them?"

"Rockear has defeated your entire force—with a little help," she said. "I am content to pledge my honor to a male of his resourcefulness, especially when he does not abuse his leadership. I only wish he were of our race," she added wistfully.

Scarface: "My parole would depend on your absolute truthfulness, Rockear."

A pause from Locklear, and a nod. "You've got it as of now, but no backing out if you get some surprises later."

"One question, then, before I give my word: *are all my crew truly casualties?*"

"Deader than this beam rifle," Locklear said, grinning, holding its muzzle upward, squeezing its trigger.

Later, after pledging his parole, Scarface observed reasonably that there was a world of difference between an insufficient charge and *no* charge. The roof thatching burned slowly at first; slowly enough that they managed to remove everything worth keeping. But at last the whole place burned merrily enough. To Locklear's surprise, it was Scarface who mentioned safe removal of the *zzrou*, and pulled it loose easily after a few deft manipulations of the transmitter.

Kit seemed amused as they ate al fresco, a hundred meters from the embers of their manor. "It is a tradition in the ancient culture that a major change of household leadership requires burning of the old manor," she explained with a smile of her ears.

Locklear, still uneasy with the big kzin warrior so near and now without his bonds, surreptitiously felt of the sidearm in his belt and asked, "Am I not still the leader?"

"Yes," she said. "But what kind of leader would deny happiness to his followers?" Her lowered glance toward Scarface could hardly be misunderstood.

The ear umbrellas of the big male turned a deeper hue. "I do not wish to dishonor another warrior, Locklear, but—if I am to remain your captive here as you say, um, such females may be impossibly overstimulating."

"Not to me," Locklear said. "No offense, Kit; I'm half in love with you myself. In fact, I think the best thing for my own sanity would be to seek, uh, females of my own kind."

"You intended to take us back to the manworlds, I take it," said Scarface with some smugness.

"After a bit more research here, yes. The hell with wars anyhow. There's a lot about this planet you don't know about yet. Fascinating!"

"You will never get back in a lifeboat," said Scarface, "and the cruiser is now only a memory."

"You didn't!"

"I assuredly did, Locklear. My first act when you released my bonds was to send the self-destruct signal."

Locklear put his head between his hands. "Why didn't we hear the lifeboat go up?"

"Because I did not think to set it for destruct. It is not exactly a major asset."

"For me it damned well is," Locklear growled, then went on. "Look here: I won't release Kit from any pair-bonding to me unless you promise not to sabotage me in any way. And I further promise not to try turning you over to some military bunch, because I'm the, uh, mayor of this frigging planet and I can declare peace on it if I want to. Honor bound, honest injun, whatever the hell that means, and all the rigamarole that goes with it. Goddammit, I could have blown your head off."

"But you did not know that."

"With the sidearm, then! Don't *ch'r*—don't fiddle me around. Put your honor on the line, mister, and put your big paw against mine if you mean it."

After a long look at Kit, the big kzin commander reached out a hand, palm vertical, and Locklear met it with his own. "You are not the man we left here," said the vanquished kzin, eyeing Locklear without malice. "Brown and tough as dried meat—and older, I would say."

"Getting hunted by armed kzinti tends to age a feller," Locklear chuckled. "I'm glad we found peace with honor."

"Was any commander," the commander asked no one in particular, "ever faced with so many conflicts of honor?"

"You'll resolve them," Locklear predicted. "Think about it: I'm about to make you the head captive of a brand new region that has two newborn babes in it, two intelligent kzinrret at least, and over an eight-squared other kzinti who have been in stasis for longer than you can believe. Wake 'em, or don't, it's up to you, just don't interfere with me because I expect to be here part of the time, and somewhere else at other times. Kit, show him how to use the airboat. If you two can't figure out how to use the stuff in this Outsider zoo, I miss my—"

"Outsiders?" Scarface did not seem to like the sound of that.

"That's just my guess," Locklear shrugged. "Maybe they have hidden sensors that tell 'em what happens on the planet Zoo. Maybe they don't care. What I care about, is exploring the other compounds on Zoo, one especially. I may not find any of my kind on Newduvai, and if I do they might have foreheads a half-inch high, but it bears looking into. For that I need the lifeboat. Any reason why it wouldn't take me to another compound on Zoo?"

"No reason." After a moment of rumination, Scarface put on his best negotiation face again. "If I teach you to be an expert pilot, would you let me disable the hyperwave comm set?"

Locklear thought hard for a similar time. "Yes, if you swear to leave its local functions intact. Look, fella, we may want to talk to one another with it."

"Agreed, then," said the kzin commander.

That night, Locklear slept poorly. He lay awake for a time, wondering if Newduvai had its own specimen cave, and whether he could find it if one existed. The fact was that Kzersatz simply lacked the kind of company he had in mind. *Not even the right kind of cathouse*, he groused silently. He was not enormously heartened by the prospect of wooing a Neanderthal nymphet, either. Well, that was what field research was for. *Please, God, at least a few Cro-Magnons! Patience, Locklear, and earplugs*, because he could not find sleep for long.

It was not merely that he was alone, for the embers near his pallet kept him as toasty as kzinrret fur. No, it was the infernal yowling of those cats somewhere below in the ravine.

BRIAR PATCH

If Locklear had been thinking straight, he never would have stayed in the god business. But when a man has been thrust into the Fourth Man–Kzin War, won peace with honor from the tigerlike kzinti on a synthetic zoo planet, and released long-stored specimens so that his vast prison compound resembles the kzin homeworld, it's hard for that man to keep his sense of mortality.

It's hard, that is, until someone decides to kill him. His first mistake was lust, impure and simple. A week after he paroled Scarface, the one surviving kzin warrior, Locklear admitted his problem during supper. "All that caterwauling in the ravine," he said, refilling his bowl from the hearth stewpot, "is driving me nuts. Good thing you haven't let the rest of those kzinti out of stasis; the racket would be unbelievable!"

Scarface wiped his muzzle with a brawny forearm and handed his own bowl to Kit, his new mate. The darkness of the huge Kzersatz region was tempered only by coals, but Locklear saw those coals flicker in Scarface's cat eyes. "A condition of my surrender was that you release Kit to me," the big kzin growled. "And besides: do humans mate so quietly?"

Because they were speaking Kzin, the word

Scarface had used was actually "ch'rowl"—itself a sexual goad. Kit, who was refilling the bowl, let slip a tiny mew of surprise and pleasure. "Please, milord," she said, offering the bowl to Scarface. "Poor Rockear is already overstimulated. Is it not so?" Her huge eyes flicked to Locklear, whom she had grown to know quite well after Locklear waked her from age-long sleep.

"Dead right," Locklear agreed with a morose glance. "Not by the word; by the goddamn deed!"

"She is mine," Scarface grinned; a kzin grin, the kind with big fangs and no amusement.

"Calm down. I may have been an animal psychologist, but I only have letches for human females," Locklear gloomed toward his kzin companions. "And every night when I hear you two flattening the grass out there," he nodded past the half-built walls of the hut, "I get, uh, . . ." He did not know how to translate "horny" into Kzin.

"You get the urge to travel," Scarface finished, making it not quite a suggestion. The massive kzin stared into darkness as if peering across the force walls surrounding Kzersatz. Those towering invisible walls separated the air, and lifeforms, of Kzersatz from other synthetic compounds of this incredible planet, Zoo. "I can see the treetops in the next compound as easily as you, Locklear. But I see no monkeys in them."

Before his defeat, Scarface had been "Tzak–Commander." The same strict kzin honor that bound him to his surrender, forbade him to curse his captor as a monkey. But he could still sharpen the barb of his wit. Kit, with real affection for Locklear, did not approve. "Be nice," she hissed to her mate.

"Forget it," Locklear told her, stabbing with his

Kzin *wtsai* blade for a hunk of meat in his stew. "Kit, he's stuck with his military code, and it won't let him insist that his captor get the hell out of here. But he's right. I still don't know if that next compound I call Newduvai is really Earthlike." He smiled at Scarface, remembering not to show his teeth, and added, "Or whether it has my kind of monkey."

"And we must not try to find out until your war wounds have completely healed," Kit replied.

The eyes of man and kzin warrior met. "Whoa," Locklear said quickly, sparing Scarface the trouble. "*We* won't be scouting over there; I will, but you won't. I'm an ethologist," he went on, holding up a hand to bar Kit's interruption. "If Newduvai is as completely stocked as Kzersatz, somebody—maybe the Outsiders, maybe not, but damn certain a long time ago—*some*body intended all these compounds to be kept separate. Now, I won't say I haven't played god here a little, . . ."

"And intend to play it over there a lot," said Kit, who had never yet surrendered to anyone.

"Hear me out. I'm not going to start mixing species from Kzersatz and Newduvai any more than I already have, and that's final." He pried experimentally at the scab running down his knife arm. "But I'm pretty much healed, thanks to your medkit, Scarface. And I meant it when I said you'd have free run of this place. It's intended for kzinti, not humans. High time I took your lifeboat over those force walls to Newduvai."

"Boots will miss you," said Kit.

Locklear smiled, recalling the other kzin female he'd released from stasis in a very pregnant condition. According to Kit, a kzin mother would not emerge from her birthing creche until the eyes of her twins had opened—another week, at least. "Give her my love," he said, and swilled the last of his stew.

"A pity you will not do that yourself," Kit sighed.

"Milady." Scarface became, for the moment, every inch a Tzak-Commander. "Would you ask me to ch'rowl a human female?" He waited for Kit to control her mixed expression. "Then please be silent on the subject. Locklear is a warrior who knows what he fights for."

Locklear yawned. "There's an old song that says, 'Ain't gonna study war no more,' and a slogan that goes, 'Make love, not war.' "

Kit stood up with a fetching twitch of her tail. "I believe our leader has spoken, milord," she purred.

Locklear watched them swaying together into the night, and his parting call was plaintive. "Just try and keep it down, okay? A fellow needs his sleep."

The kzin lifeboat was over ten meters long, well-armed and furnished with emergency rations. In accord with their handshake armistice, Scarface had given flight instructions to his human pupil after disabling the hyperwave portion of its comm set. He had given no instructions on armament because Locklear, a peaceable man, saw no further use for anything larger than a sidearm. Neither of them could do much to make the lifeboat seating comfortable for Locklear, who was small even by human standards in an acceleration couch meant for a two-hundred-kilo kzin.

Locklear paused in the air lock in midmorning and raised one arm in a universal peace sign. Scarface returned it. "I'll call you now and then, if those force walls don't stop the signal," Locklear called. "If you let your other kzinti out of stasis, call and tell me how it works out."

"Keep your tail dry, Rockear," Kit called, perhaps forgetting he lacked that appendage—a compliment, of sorts.

"Will do," he called back as the air lock swung shut. Moments later, he brought the little craft to life and, cursing the cradle-rock motion that branded him a novice, urged the lifeboat into the yellow sky of Kzersatz.

Locklear made one pass, a "goodbye sweep," high above the region with its yellow and orange vegetation, taking care to stay well inside the frostline that defined those invisible force walls. He spotted the cave from the still-flattened grass where Kit had herded the awakened animals from the crypt and their sleep of forty thousand years, then steepened his climb and used aero boost to begin his trajectory. No telling whether the force walls stopped suddenly, but he did not want to find out by plowing into the damned things. It was enough to know they stopped below orbital height, and that he could toss the lifeboat from Kzersatz to Newduvai in a low-energy ballistic arc.

And he knew enough to conserve energy in the craft's main accumulators because one day, when the damned stupid Man–Kzin War was over, he'd need that energy to jump from Zoo to some part of known space. Unless, he amended silently, somebody found Zoo first. The war might already be over, and certainly the warlike kzinti must have the coordinates of Zoo . . .

Then he was at the top of his trajectory, seeing the planetary curvature of Zoo, noting the tiny satellite sunlets that bathed hundred-mile-diameter regions in light, realizing that a warship could condemn any one of those circular regions to death with one well-placed shot against its synthetic, automated little sun. He was already past the circular force walls now, and felt an enormous temptation to slow the ship by main accumulator energy. A good pilot could lower that lifeboat down between the walls of those force cylinders, in the hard vacuum between compounds. Outsiders might be lurking there, idly studying the specimens through invisible walls.

But Locklear was no expert with a kzin lifeboat, not yet, and he had to use his wristcomp to translate the warning on the console screen. He set the wing extensions just in time to avoid heavy buffeting, thankful that he had not needed orbital speed to manage his brief trajectory. He bobbled a maneuver once, twice, then felt the drag of Newduvai's atmosphere on the lifeboat and gave the lifting surfaces full extension. He put the craft into a shallow bank to starboard, keeping the vast circular frostline far to portside, and punched in an autopilot instruction. Only then did he dare to turn his gaze down on Newduvai.

Like Kzersatz it boasted a big lake, but this one glinted in a sun heartbreakingly like Earth's. A rugged jumble of cliffs soared into cloud at one side of the region, and green hills mounded above plains of mottled hues: tan, brown, green, Oh, God, all that green! He'd forgotten, in the saffron of Kzersatz, how much he missed the emerald of grass, the blue of sky, the darker dusty green of Earth forests. For it was, in every respect, perfectly Earthlike. He wiped his misting eyes, grinned at himself for such foolishness, and eased the lifeboat down to a lazy circular course that kept him two thousand meters above the terrain. If the builders of Zoo were consistent, one of those shallow creekbeds would begin not in a marshy meadow but in a horizontal shaft. And there he would find—he dared not think it through any further.

After his first complete circuit of Newduvai, he knew it had no herds of animals. No birds dotted the lakeshore; no bugs whacked his viewport. A dozen streams meandered and leapt down from the frostline where clouds dumped their moisture against cold encircling force walls. One stream ended in a second small lake with no obvious outlet, but none of the creeks or dry washes began with a cave.

Mindful of his clumsiness in this alien craft, Locklear set it down in soft sand where a dry wash delta met the kidney-shaped lake. After further consulting between his wristcomp and the ship's computer, he punched in his most important queries and listened to the ship cool while its sensors analyzed Newduvai.

Gravity: Earth normal. Atmosphere, solar flux, and temperature: all Earth normal. "And not a critter in sight," he told the cabin walls. In a burst of insight, he asked the computer to list anything that might be a health hazard to a kzin. If man and kzin could make steaks of each other, they probably should fear the same pathogens. The computer took its time, but its most fearsome finding was of tetanus in the dust.

He waited no longer, thrusting at the air lock in his hurry, filling his lungs with a rich soup of odors, and found his eyes brimming again as he stepped onto a little piece of Earth. Smells, he reflected, really got you back to basics. Scents of cedar, of dust, of grasses and yes, of wildflowers.

Just like home—yet, in some skinprickling way, not quite.

Locklear sat down on the sand then, with an earthlike sunlet baking his back from a turquoise sky, and he wept. Outsiders or not, any bunch that could engineer a piece of home on the rim of known space couldn't be all bad.

He was tasting the lake water's very faint brackishness when, in a process that took less than a minute, the sunlight dimmed and was gone. "But it's only noontime," he protested, and then laughed at himself and made a notation on his wristcomp, using its faint light to guide him back to the air lock.

As with Kzersatz, he saw no stars; and then he realized that the position of Newduvai's sun had been halfway to the horizon when—almost as it happened on Kzersatz—the daily ration of sunlight was quenched. Why should Newduvai's sun keep the same time as that of Kzersatz? It didn't; nor did it wink off as suddenly as that of Kzersatz.

He activated the still-functioning local mode of the lifeboat's comm set, intending to pass his findings on to Scarface. No response. Scarface's handset was an allband unit; perhaps some wavelength could bounce off of debris from the kzin cruiser scuttled in orbit—but Locklear knew that was a slender hope, and soon it seemed no hope at all. He spent the longest few hours of his life then, turning floodlights on the lake in the forlorn hope of seeing a fish leap, and with the vague fear that a tyrannosaur might pay him a social call. But no matter where he turned the lights he saw no gleam of eyes, and the sand was innocent of any tracks. Sleep would not come until he began to address the problem of the stasis crypt in logical ways.

Locklear came up from his seat with a bound, facing a sun that brightened as he watched. His wristcomp said not quite twelve hours had passed since the sunlet dimmed. His belly said it was late. His memory said yes, by God, there was one likely plan for locating that horizontal shaft: fly very near the frostline and scan every dark cranny that was two hundred meters or so inside the force walls. On Kzersatz, the stasis crypt had ended exactly beneath the frostline, perhaps a portal for those who'd built Zoo. And the front entrance had been two hundred meters inside the force walls.

He lifted the lifeboat slowly, ignoring hunger pangs, beginning to plot a rough map of Newduvai on the computer screen because he did not know how to make the computer do it for him. Soon, he passed a dry plateau with date palms growing in its declivities and followed the ship's shadow to more fertile soil. Near frostline, he set the aeroturbine reactor just above idle and, moving briskly a hundred meters above the ground, began a careful scan of the terrain because he was not expert enough with kzin computers to automate the search.

After three hours he had covered more than half of his sweep around Newduvai, past semidesert and grassy fields to pine-dotted mountain slopes, and the lifeboat's reactor coolant was overheating from the slow pace. Locklear set the craft down nicely near that smaller mountain lake, chopped all power systems, and headed for scrubby trees in the near distance. Scattered among the pines were cedar and small oak. Nearer stood tall poplar and chestnut, invaded by wild grape with immature fruit. But nearest of all, the reason for his landing here, were gnarled little pear trees and, amid wild shoots of rank growth, trees laden with small ripe plums. He wolfed them down until juice dripped from his chin, washed in the lake, and then found the pears unripe. No matter: he'd seen dates, grapes, and chestnut, which suggested a model of some Mediterranean region. After identifying juniper, oleander and honeysuckle, he sent his wristcomp scurrying through its megabytes and narrowed his opinion of the area: a surrogate slice of Asia Minor.

He might have sat on sunwarmed stones until dark, lulled by this sensation of being, somehow, back home without a care. But then he glanced far across the lower hills and saw, proceeding slowly across a parched desert plateau many miles distant, a whirlwind with its whiplike curve and bloom of dust where it touched the soil.

"Uh-huh! That's how you reseed plants without insect vectors," he said aloud to the builders of Zoo. "But whirlwinds don't make honey, and they'll sting anyway. Hell, even *I* can play god better than that," he said, and bore a pocketful of plums into the lifeboat, filled once more with the itch to find the cave that might not even exist on Newduvai.

But it was there, all right. Locklear saw it only because of the perfect arc of obsidian, gleaming through a tangle of brush that had grown around the cave mouth.

He made a botch of the landing because he was trembling with anticipation. A corner of his mind kept warning him not to assume everything here was the same as on Kzersatz, so Locklear stopped just outside that brush-choked entrance. His wtsai blade made short work of the brush, revealing a polished floor. He strode forward, wtsai in one hand, his big kzin sidearm in the other, to the now-familiar luminous film that flickered, several meters inside the cave mouth, across an obsidian portal. He thrust his blade through the film and saw, as he had expected to see, stronger light flash behind the portal. Then he stepped through and stopped, listening.

He might have been back in the Kzersatz crypt: a quiet so deep his own breathing made echoes; the long obsidian central passage, with nine branches on each side, ending in a frost-covered force wall that filled the passageway. And the clear plastic containers ranked in the side passages were of three sizes on smooth metal bases, as expected. But Locklear took one look at the nearest specimen, spinning slowly in its stasis cage, and knew that here the resemblance to Kzersatz ended forever.

The monster lay in something like a fetal crouch, tumbling slowly in response to the grav polarizer as it had been doing for many thousands of years. It was black, with great forward-curving horns and heavy shoulders, and when released—*if* anyone dared, he amended—it would stand six feet at the shoulder. Locklear figured its weight at a ton. Some European zoologists had once tried to breed cattle back to this brute, but with scant success, and Locklear had not seen so much as a sketch of it since his undergrad work. It was a bull aurochs, a beast which had survived on Earth into historic times; and counting the cows, Locklear realized there were over forty of them.

No point in kidding himself about his priorities.

Locklear walked past the stasized camels and gerbils, hurried faster beyond small horses and chee-
tahs and bats, began to trot as he ran to the next
passage past lions and hares and grouse, and was
sprinting as he passed whole schools of fish (without water? Why the hell not? They were in stasis,
he reminded himself—) in their respective containers. He was out of breath by the time he
dashed between specimens of reindeer and saw
the monkeys.

NO! A mistake any kzin might have made, but:
"How could I play such a shameful joke on myself?" They were in fetal curls, and some of them
boasted a lot of body hair. And each of them,
Locklear realized, was human.

In a kind of reverence he studied them all,
careful to avoid touching the metal bases which,
on Kzersatz, opened the cages and released the
specimens. Narrowheaded and swarthy they were,
no taller than he, with heavy brow ridges and high
cheekbones. Noses like prizefighters; forearms like
blacksmiths; and some had pendulous mammaries
and a few had—had—"Tits," he breathed. "There's
a difference! Thank you, God."

Men and women like these had first been studied in a river valley near old Dusseldorf, hardy
folk who had preceded modern humans on Earth
and, in all probability, had intermarried with them
until forty or fifty thousand years before. Locklear,
rubbing at the gooseflesh on his arms, began to
study each of the stasized nudes with great care.
He would need every possible advantage because
they would be disoriented, perhaps even furious,
when they waked. And the last thing Locklear
needed was to start off on the wrong foot with a
frenzied Neanderthaler.

Only an idiot would release a mob of Neanderthal hunters into a tiny world without taking steps to protect endangered game animals. The killing of a dozen deer might doom the rest of that species to slow extinction here. On the other hand, Locklear might have released all the animals and waited for a season or more. But certain of the young women in stasis were not exactly repellant, and he did not intend to wait a year before making their acquaintance. Besides, his notes on a Neanderthal community could make him famous on a dozen worlds, and Locklear was anxious to get on with it.

His second option was to wake the people and guide them, by force if necessary, outside to fruits and grains. But each of them would see those stasized animals, probably as meat on the hoof, and might not respond to his demands. It was beyond belief that any of them would speak a language he knew. Then it struck him that he already knew how to disassemble a stasis cage, and that he had as much time as he needed. With a longing glance backward, Locklear retraced his steps to the lifeboat and started looking for something with wheels.

But kzin lifeboats do not carry cargo dollies, and the sun of Newduvai had dimmed before he found a way to remove the wheeled carriage below the reactor's heat exchanger unit. Evidently the unit needed replacement often enough that kzin engineers installed a carriage with it. That being so, Locklear decided not to use the lifeboat's reactor any more than he had to.

He worked until hunger and aching muscles drove him to the cabin where he cut slices of bricklike kzin rations and ate plums for dessert.

But before he fell asleep, Locklear made some decisions that might save his hide. The lifeboat must be hidden away from inquisitive savage fingers; he would even camouflage the stasis crypt so that those savages would not know what lay inside; and it was absolutely crucial that he present himself as a shaman of great power. Without a few tawdry magics, he might not be able to distance himself as an observer; might even be challenged to combat by some strong male. And Locklear remembered those hornlike fingernails and bulging muscles all too well. He saw no sense in shooting a man, even a Neanderthal, merely to prove a point that could be made in peaceable ways.

He spent over a week preparing his hardware. His trials on Kzersatz had taught him how, when all you've got is a hammer, the whole world is a nail; and that you must hammer out a few other tools as soon as possible. He soon found the lifeboat's military toolbox complete with wire, pistol-grip arc welder, and motorized drill.

He took time off to gather fruit and to let his frustrations drain away. It was hard not to throw rocks at the sky when he commanded a state-of-the-art kzin craft, yet could not cannibalize much of it for the things he needed. "Maybe I should release a dog from stasis so I could kick it," he told himself aloud, while attaching an oak branch as a wagon tongue for the wheeled carriage. But lacking any other game, he figured, the dog would probably attack before he did.

Then he used oak staves to lever a cage base up, with flat stones as blocks, and eased his makeshift wagon beneath. The doe inside was heavy with young. Most likely, she would retreat far

from him before bearing her fawns, and he knew
what to do with the tuneable gray polarizer below
that cage. Soon the clear plastic container sat gleaming in the sun, and Locklear poked hard at the
base before retreating to the cave mouth.

As on Kzersatz, the container levered up, the
red doe sank to the cage base, and the base slid
forward. A moment later the creature moved, stood
with lovely slender limbs shaking, and then saw
him waving an oak stave. She reached grassy turf
in one graceful bound and sped off with leaps he
watched in admiration. Then, feeling somehow
more lonely as the doe vanished, he sighed and
disconnected the plastic container, then set about
taking the entire cage to pieces. Already experi-
enced with these gadgets, he would need at least
two of the grav polarizer units before he could
move stasized specimens outside with ease.

Disconnected from the stasis unit, a polarizer
toroid with its power source and wiring could be
tuned to lift varied loads; for example, a container
housing a school of fish. The main thing was to
avoid tipping it, which Locklear managed by wiring the polarizer securely to the underside of his
wheeled carriage. Another hour saw him tugging
his burden to the air lock, where he wrestled that
entire, still-functioning cageful of fish inside. The
fish, he saw, had sucking mouths meant for bottom-
feeding on vegetable trash. They looked rather
like carp or tilapia. Raising the lifeboat with great
care, he eased toward the big lake some miles
distant. It was no great trick to dump the squirm-
ing mass of life from the air lock port into the lake
from a height of two meters, and then he cele-
brated by landing near the first laden fig tree he
saw. Munching and lazing in the sun, he decided

that his fortunes were looking up. But then, Locklear had been wrong before . . .

He knew that his next steps must be planned carefully. Before hiding the kzin craft away he must duplicate the airboat he had built on Kzersatz. After an exhaustive search—meanwhile mapping Newduvai's major features—he felled and stripped slender pines, hauling them in the lifeboat to his favorite spot near the small mountain lake. By now he had found a temporary spot in a barren cleft near frostline to hide the lifeboat itself, and began by stripping off its medium-caliber beam weapons from extension struts. The strut skins were attached by long screws, which Locklear saved. The weapon wiring came in handy, too, as he began fitting the raftlike platform of his airboat together. When he realized that the lifeboat's slings and emergency seats could be stripped for a fabric sail, he began to feel a familiar excitement.

This airboat was larger than his first, with its single sail and swiveling double-pole keel for balance. With wires for rigging, he could hunker down just behind the mast and operate the gravity control vernier through a slot in the flat deck. He could carry over two hundred kilos of ballast, the mass of a stasis cage with a human specimen inside, far from the crypt before setting that specimen free. "I'll have to carry the cage back, of course. Who knows what trouble a savage might create, fiddling with a stasis cage?" He snorted at himself; he'd almost said "monkeying," and it was dangerous to assume he was smarter than these ancient people. But wasn't he, really? If Neanderthalers had died out on Earth, they must have been inferior in some way. Well, he was sure as hell going to find out.

If his new airboat was larger than the first, it was also more unwieldy. He used it to ferry logs to his cabin site at the small lake, cursing his need to tack in the light breezes, wishing he had a better propulsion system, for over a week before the solution hit him.

At the time he was debating the release of more animals. The mammoths, he promised himself, would come last. No wonder the builders of Newduvai had left them nearest the crypt entrance! Their cage tops would each make a dandy greenhouse and their grav polarizers would lift tons. *Or push tons*.

"Some things don't change," he told himself, laughing aloud. "I was dumb on Kzersatz and I've been dumb here." So he released the hares, gerbils, grouse and some other species of bird with beaks meant for crunching seeds. He promptly installed their grav units around his airboat seat for propulsion, removing the mast and keel poles for reuse as cabin roof beams. That was the day Locklear nearly killed himself caroming off the lake's surface at sixty miles an hour, whooping like a fool. Now the homemade craft was no longer a boat; it was a scooter, and would scoot with an extra fifty kilos of cargo.

It might have been elation with the sporty performance of his scooter that made him so optimistic, failing to remember that you have to kill pessimists, but optimists do it themselves. The log cabin, five meters square with fireplace and frond-thatched shed roof, needed only a pallet of sling fabric and fragrant boughs beneath. A *big* pallet, he decided. It had been Kit who taught him that he should have food and shelter ready before waking strangers in strange lands. He had figs and apricot slices drying, kzin rations for the strong of tooth, and kzin-sized drinking vessels from the lifeboat. He moved a few more items, including a clever kzin memory pad with electronic stylus and screen, from lifeboat to cabin, then attached a ten-meter cable harness from the scooter to the lifeboat's overhead weapon pylon.

It was only necessary then to set the scooter's bottom grav unit to slight buoyancy, and to pilot the kzin lifeboat very slowly, towing the scooter.

The cleft where he landed had become a soggy meadow from icemelt near the frostline high on Newduvai's perimeter, protected on one side by the towering force wall and on the other by jagged basalt. The lifeboat could not be seen from below, and if his first aerial visitors were kzinti, they'd have to fly dangerously near that force wall before they saw it. He sealed the lifeboat and then hauled the scooter down hand over hand, puffing with exertion, letting the scooter bounce harmlessly off the lifeboat's hull as he clambered aboard. Then he cast off and twiddled with those grav unit verniers until the wind whistled in his ears en route to the stasis crypt. He was already expert at modifying stasis units, and he would have lots of them to play with. If he had to protect himself from a wild woman, he could hardly wish for anything better.

He trundled the crystal cage into sunlight still wondering if he'd chosen the right—specimen? Subject? "Woman, dammit; woman!" He was trying to wear too many hats, he knew, with the one labeled "lecher" perched on top. He landed the scooter near his cabin, placed bowls of fruit and water nearby, and pressed the cage baseplate, retreating beyond his offerings.

She sank to the cage floor but only shifted position, still asleep, the breeze moving strands of chestnut hair at her cheeks. She was small and muscular, her breasts firm and immature, pubic hair sparse, limbs slender and marked with scratches; and yes, he realized as he moved nearer, she had a forty-thousand-year-old zit on her little chin. Easily the best-looking choice in the crypt, not yet fully developed into the Neanderthal body shape, she seemed capable of sleep in any position and was snoring lightly to prove it.

A genuine teen-ager, he mused, grinning. Aloud he said, "Okay, Lolita, up and at 'em." She stirred; a hand reached up as if tugging at an invisible blanket. "You'll miss the school shuttle," he said louder. It had never failed back on Earth with his sister.

It didn't fail here, either. She waked slowly, blinking as she sat up in lithe, nude, heartbreaking innocence. But her yawn snapped in two as she focused on him, and her pantomime of snatching a stone and hurling it at Locklear was convincing enough to make him duck. She leaped away scrabbling for real stones, and between her screams and her clods, all in Locklear's direction, she seemed to be trying to cover herself.

He retreated, but not far enough, and grabbed a chunk of dirt only after taking one clod on his thigh. He threatened a toss of his own, whereupon she ducked behind the cage, watching him warily.

Well, it wouldn't matter what he said, so long as he said it calmly. His tone and gestures would have to serve. "You're a real little shit before breakfast, Lolita," he said, smiling, tossing his clod gently toward the bowls.

She saw the food then, frowning. His open hands and strained smile invited her to the food, and she moved toward it still holding clods ready. Wolfing plums, she paused to gape as he pulled a plum from a pocket and began to eat. "Never seen pockets, hm? Stick around, little girl, I'll show you lots of interesting things." The humor didn't work, even on himself; and at his first step toward her she ran like a deer.

Every time he pointed to himself and said his name, she screamed something brief. She moved around the area, checking out the cabin, draping a vine over her breasts, and after an hour Locklear gave up. He'd made a latchcord for the cabin door, so she couldn't do much harm. She watched from fifty meters distance with great wondering brown eyes as he waved, lifted the scooter, and sped away with her cage and a new idea.

An hour later he returned with a second cage, cursing as he saw Lolita trying to smash his cabin window with an oak stave. The clear plastic, of cage material, was tough stuff and he laughed as the scooter settled nearby, pretending he didn't itch to whack her rump. She began a litany of stone-age curses, then, as she saw the new cage and its occupant. Locklear actually had to mount the scooter and chase her off before she would quit pelting him with anything she could throw.

He made the same preparations as before, this time with shreds of smelly kzin rations as well, and stood leaning against the cage for long moments, facing Lolita who lurked fifty meters away, to make his point. The young woman revolving slowly inside the cage was at his mercy. Then he pressed the baseplate, turned his back as the plastic levered upward, and strode off a few paces with a sigh. This one was a Neanderthal and no mistake: curves a little too broad to be exciting, massive forearms and calves, pug nose, considerable body hair. *Nice tits, though. Stop it, fool!*

The young woman stirred, sat up, looked around, then let her big jaw drop comically as she stared at Locklear, whose smile was a very rickety construction. She cocked her head at him, impassive, an instant before he spoke.

"You're no beauty, lady, so maybe you won't throw rocks at *me*. Too late for breakfast," he continued in his sweetest tones and a pointing finger. "How about lunch?"

She saw the bowls. Slowly, with caution and surprising grace, she stepped from the scooter's deck still eyeing him without smile or frown. Then she squatted to inspect the food, knees apart, facing him, and Locklear grew faint at the sight. He looked away quickly, flushing, aware that she continued to stare at him while sampling human and kzin rations with big strong teeth and wrinklings of her nose that made her oddly attractive. *More attractive. Why the hell doesn't she cover up or something?*

He pulled another plum from a pocket, and this magic drew a smile from her as they ate. He realized she was through eating when she wiped sticky fingers in her straight black hair, and stepped back by reflex as she stepped toward him. She stopped, with a puzzled inclination of her head, and smiled at him. That was when he stood his ground and let her approach. He had hoped for something like this, so the watching Lolita could see that he meant no harm.

When the woman stood within arm's length of him she stopped. He put a hand on his breast. "Me Locklear, you Jane," he said.

"(Something,)" she said. Maybe *Kh-roofeh*.

He was going to try saying it himself when she startled him into a wave of actual physical weakness. With eyes half-closed, she cupped her full breasts in both hands and smiled. He looked at her erect nipples, feeling the rush of blood to his face, and showed her his hands in a broad helpless shrug. Whereupon, she took his hands and placed them on her breasts, and now her big black eyes were not those of a savage Neanderthal but a sultry smiling Levantine woman who knew how to make a point. Two points.

Three points, as he felt a rising response and knew her hands were seeking that rise, hands that had never known velcrolok closures yet seemed to have an intelligence of their own. His whole body was tingling now as he caressed her, and when her hands found that fabric closure, she shared a fresh smile with him, and tried to pull him down on the ground with her.

So he took her hands in his and walked her to the cabin. She "hmm"ed when he pulled the latchcord loop to open the door, and "ahh"ed when she saw the big pallet, and then offered those swarthy full breasts again and put her face against the hollow of his throat, and toyed inside his velcrolok closure until he astonished her by pulling his entire flight suit off, and offered her body in ways simple and sophisticated, and Locklear accepted all the offers he could, and made a few of his own, all of which she accepted expertly.

He had his first sensation of something eerie, something just below his awareness, as he lay inert on his back bathed in honest sweat, his partner lying facedown more or less across him like one stick abandoned across another stick after both had been rubbed to kindle a blaze. He saw a movement at his window and knew it was Lolita, peering silently in. He sighed.

His partner sighed too, and turned toward the window with a quick, vexed burst of some command. The face disappeared.

He chuckled, "Did you hear the little devil, or smell her?" Actually, his partner had more of the *eau de sweatsock* perfume than Lolita did; now more pronounced than ever. He didn't care. If the past half-hour had been any omen, he might never care again.

She stretched then, and sat up, dragging a heel that was rough as a rasp across his calf. Her heavy ragged nails had scratched him, and he was oily from God knew what mixture of greases in her long hair. He didn't give a damn about that either, reflecting that a man should allow a few squeaks in the hinges of the pearly gates.

She said something then, softly, with that tilt of her head that suggested inquiry. "Locklear," he replied, tapping his chest again.

Her look was somehow pitying then, as she repeated her phrase, placing one hand on her head, the other on his.

"Oh yeah, you're my girl and I'm your guy," he said, nodding, placing his hands on hers.

She sat quite still for a moment, her eyes sad on his. Then, delighting him, she placed one hand on his breast and managed a passable, "Loch-leah."

He grinned and nodded, then cocked his head and placed a hand between her (wonderful!) breasts.

No homecoming queen, but dynamite in deep shadows . . .

He paid more attention as she said, approximately, "Ch'roof'h," and when he repeated it she laughed, closing her eyes with downcast chin. *A big chin, a really whopping big one to be honest about it,* and then he caught her gaze, not angry but perhaps reproachful, and again he felt the passage of something like a cold breeze through his awareness.

She rubbed his gooseflesh down for him, responding to his "ahh"s, and presently she astonished him again by beginning to query him on the names of things. Locklear knew that he could thoroughly confuse her if he insisted on perfectly grammatical tenses, cases, and syntax. He tried to keep it simple, and soon learned that "head down, eyes shut" was the same as a negative headshake. "Chin elevated, smiling" was the same as a nod—and now he realized he'd seen her giving him yesses that way from the first moment she awoke. A smile or a frown was the same for her as for him—but that heads-up smile was a definite gesture.

She drew him outside again presently, studying the terrain with lively curiosity, miming actions and listening as he provided words, responding with words of her own.

The name he gave her was, in part, because it was faintly like the one she'd offered; and in part because she seemed willing to learn his ways while revealing ancient ways of her own. He named her "Ruth." Locklear felt crestfallen when, by midafternoon, he realized Ruth was learning his language much faster than he was learning hers. And then, as he glanced over her shoulder to see little

Lolita creeping nearer, he began to understand why.

Ruth turned quickly, with a shouted command and warning gestures, and Lolita dropped the sharpened stick she'd been carrying. Locklear knew beyond doubt that Lolita had made no sound in her approach. There was only one explanation that would fit all his data: Ruth unafraid of him from the first; offering herself as if she knew his desires; keeping track of Lolita without looking; and her uncanny speed in learning his language.

And that moment when she'd placed her hand on his head, with an inquiry that was somehow pitying. Now he copied her gesture with one hand on his own head, the other on hers, and lowered his head, eyes shut. "No," he said. "Locklear, no telepath. Ruth, yes?"

"Ruth, yes." She pointed to Lolita then. "No—telpat."

She needed another ten minutes of pantomime, attending to his words and obviously to his thoughts as he spoke them, to get her point across. Ruth was a "gentle," but like Locklear himself, Lolita was a "new."

When darkness came to Newduvai, Lolita got chummier in a hurry, complaining until Ruth let her into the cabin. Despite that, Ruth didn't seem to like the girl much and accepted Locklear's name for her, shortening it to "Loli." Ruth spoke to her in their common tongue, not so much gutteral as throaty, and Locklear had a strong impression that they were old acquaintances. Either of them could tend a fire expertly, and both were wary of the light from his kzin memory screen until they found that it would not singe a curious finger.

Locklear was bothered on two counts by Loli's insistence on taking pieces of kzin plastic film to make a bikini suit: first because Ruth plainly thought it silly, and second because the kid was more appealing with it than she was when stark naked. At least the job kept Loli silently occupied, listening and watching as Locklear got on with the business of talking with Ruth.

Their major breakthrough for the evening came when Locklear got the ideas of past and future, "before" and "soon," across to Ruth. Her telepathy was evidently the key to her quick grasp of his language; yet it seemed to work better with emotional states than with abstract ideas, and she grew upset when Loli became angry with her own first clumsy efforts at making her panties fit. Clearly, Ruth was a lady who liked her harmony.

For Ruth was, despite her rude looks, a lady—when she wasn't in the sack. Even so, when at last Ruth had seen to Loli's comfort with spare fabric and Locklear snapped off the light, he felt inviting hands on him again. "No thanks," he said, chuckling, patting her shoulder, even though he wanted her again. And Ruth *knew* he did, judging from her sly insistence.

"No. Loli here," he said finally, and felt Ruth shrug as if to say it didn't matter. Maybe it didn't matter to Neanderthals, but—"Soon," he promised, and shared a hug with Ruth before they fell asleep.

During the ensuing week, he learned much. For one thing, he learned that Loli was a chronic pain in the backside. She ate like a kzin warrior. She liked to see if things would break. She liked to spy. She interfered with Locklear's pace during his afternoon "naps" with Ruth by whacking on the door with sticks and stones, until he swore he would " . . . hit Loli soon."

But Ruth would not hear of that. "Hit Loli, same hit Ruth head. Locklear like hit Ruth head?"

But one afternoon, when she saw Locklear studying her with friendly intensity, Ruth spoke to Loli at some length. The girl picked up her short spear and, crooning her happiness, loped off into the forest. Ruth turned to Locklear smiling. "Loli find fruitwater, soon Ruth make fruitfood." A few minutes of miming showed that she had promised to make some kind of kind of dessert, if Loli could find a beehive for honey.

Locklear had seen beehives in stasis, but explained that there were very few animals loose on Newduvai, and no hurtbugs.

"No hurtbugs? Loli no find, long time. Good," Ruth replied firmly, and led him by the hand into their cabin, and "good" was the operative word.

On his next trip to the crypt, Locklear needed all day for his solitary work. He might put it off forever, but it was clear by now that he must populate Newduvai with game before he released their most fearsome predators. The little horses needed only to see daylight before galloping off. Camels were quicker still, and the deer bounded off like golf balls down a freeway. The predators would simply have to wait until the herds were larger, and the day was over before he could rig grav polarizers to trundle mammoths to the mouth of the crypt. His last job of the day was his most troublesome, releasing small cages of bees near groves of fruit trees and wildflowers.

Locklear and Ruth managed to convey a lot with only a few hundred words, though some of those words had to do multiple duty while Ruth expanded her vocabulary. When she said "new," for example, it often carried a stigma. Neanderthals, he decided, were very conservative folk, and they sensed a lie before you told it. If Ruth was any measure, they also had little aptitude for math. She understood one and two and many. She understood "none," but not as a number. If there wasn't any, she conveyed to him, why try to count it? She had him there.

Eventually, between food-gathering forays, he used pebbles and sketches to tell Ruth of the many, many other animals and people he could bring to the scene. She was no sketch artist; in fact, she insisted, women were not supposed to draw things—especially huntthings. Ah, he said, magics were only for men? Yes, she said, then mystified him with pantomimes of sleep and pain. That was for men, too, and food-gathering was for women.

He pursued the mystery, sketching with the kzin memo screen. At last, when she pretended to cut her throat with his wtsai knife, he understood, and added the word "kill" to her vocabulary. Men hunted and killed.

Dry-mouthed, he asked, "Man like kill Locklear?"

Now it was her turn to be mystified. "No kill. Why kill magic man?"

Because, he replied, "Locklear like Ruth, one-two other man like Ruth. Kill Locklear for Ruth?"

He had never seen her laugh aloud, but he saw it now, the big teeth gleaming, breasts shaking with merriment. "Locklear like Ruth, good. Many man like Ruth, good."

He was silent for a long time, fighting the temptation to tell her that many men liking Ruth was *not* good. Then: "Ruth like many man?"

She had learned to nod by now, and did it happily.

The next five minutes were troubled ones for Locklear. Ruth did not seem to understand monogamy in any form. Apparently, everybody took potluck in the sex department and was free to accept or reject. Some people were simply more popular than others. "Many man like Ruth," she said. "Many, many, many . . ."

"Okay, for Christ's sake, I get the idea," he exploded, and again he saw that look of sadness—or perhaps pain. "Locklear see, Ruth popular with man."

It seemed to be their first quarrel. Tentatively, she said, "Locklear popular with woman."

"No. Little popular with woman."

"Much popular with Ruth," she said, and began to rub his shoulders. That was the day she asked him about her appearance, and he responded the best way he could. She thought it silly to trim her strong, useful nails; sillier to wash her hair. Still, she did it, and he claimed she was pretty, and she knew he lied.

When it occured to him to ask how he could look nice for her, Ruth said, "Locklear pretty now." But he never thought to wonder if *she* might be lying.

Whatever Ruth said about women and hunting, it did not seem to apply to Loli. While aloft in the scooter one day to study distribution of the animals, Locklear saw the girl chasing a hare across a meadow. She was no slouch with a short spear and nailed the hare on her second toss, dispatching it with a stone after a brief struggle. He lowered the scooter very, very slowly, watching her tear at the

animal, disgusted when he realized she was eating
it raw.

She saw his shadow when the scooter was hovering very near, and sat there blushing, looking at
him with the innards of the hare across her lap.

She understood few of his words—or seemed
to, at the cabin—but his tone was clear enough.
"You couldn't share it, you little bastard. No, you
sneak out here and stuff yourself." She began to
suck her thumb, pouting. Then perhaps Loli realized the boss must be placated; she tried a smile
on her blood-streaked face and held her grisly
trophy out.

"No. Ruth. Give to Ruth," he scowled, pointing
toward the cabin. She elevated her chin and smiled,
and he flew off grumbling. He couldn't much blame
the kid; kzin rations and fruit were getting pretty
tiresome, and the gruel Ruth made from grain
wasn't all that exciting without bits of meat. It was
going to be rougher on the animals when he woke
the men.

*And why wake them at all? You've got it good
here,* he reminded himself in Sequence Umpteen
of his private dialogue. *You have your own little
world and a harem of one, and you know when
her period comes so you know when not to play.
And one of these days, Loli will be a knockout, I
suspect. A much niftier dish than poor Ruth, who
doesn't know what a skag she'd be in modern
society, thank God.*

Moments like this made him squirm. Setting
Ruth's looks aside, he had no complaint, not even
about the country itself. *Not much seasonal change,
no dangerous animals unless you want to release
them, certainly none of the most dangerous animal of all.* Except for kzinti, of course. One on

one, they were meaner predators than men—even Neanderthal savages.

"That's why I have to release 'em," he said to the wind. "If a fully-manned kzin ship comes, I'll need an army." He no longer kidded himself about scholarship and the sociology of *homo neanderthalensis*, which was strictly a secondary item. It was sobering to look yourself over and see self-interest riding you like a hunchback. So he flew directly to the crypt and spent the balance of the day releasing the whoppers: aurochs and bison, which didn't make him sweat much, and a half-dozen mammoths, which did.

A mammoth, he found, was a flighty beast not given to confrontations. He could set one shambling off with a shout, its trunk high like a periscope tasting the breeze. Every one of them turned into the wind and disappeared toward the frostline, and now the crypt held only its most dangerous creatures.

He returned to the cabin perilously late, the sun of Newduvai dying while he was still a hundred meters from the wisp of smoke rising from the cabin. He landed blind near the cabin, very slowly but with a jolt, and saw the faint gleam of the kzin light leap from the cabin window. Ruth might not have a head for figures, but she'd seen him snap that light on fifty times. *And she must've sensed my panic. I wonder how far off she can do that.* . . .

Ruth already had succulent broiled haunches of Loli's hare, keeping them warm over coals, and it wrenched his heart as he saw she was drooling as she waited for him. He wiped the corner of her mouth, kissed her anyhow, and sat at the rough pole table while she brought his supper. Loli had obviously eaten, and watched him as if fearful that he would order her outside.

Hauling mammoths, even with a grav polarizer, is exhausting work. After finishing off a leg of hare, and falling asleep at the table, Locklear was only half-aware when Ruth picked him up and carried him to their pallet as easily as she would have carried a child.

The next day, he had Ruth convey to Loli that she was not to hunt without permission. Then, with less difficulty than he'd expected, he sketched and quizzed her about the food of a Neanderthal tribe. Yes, they hunted everything: bugs to mammoths, it was all protein, but chiefly they gathered roots, grains, and fruits.

That made sense. Why risk getting killed hunting when tubers didn't fight back? He posed his big question then. If he brought a tribe to Newduvai (this brought a smile of anticipation to her broad face), and forbade them to hunt without his permission, would they obey?

Gentles might, she said. New people, such as Loli, were less obedient. She tried to explain why, conveying something about telepathy and hunting, until he waved the question aside. If he showed her sleeping gentles, would she tell him which ones were good? Oh yes, she said, adding a phrase she knew he liked: "No problem."

But it took him an hour to get Ruth on the scooter. That stuff was all very well for great magic men, she implied, but women's magics were more prosaic. After a few minutes idling just above the turf, he sped up, and she liked that fine. Then he slowed and lifted the scooter a bit. By noon, he was cruising fast as they surveyed groups of aurochs, solitary gazelles, and skittish horses from high above. It was she, sampling the wind with her nose, who directed him higher and then pointed out a mammoth, a huge specimen using its tusks to find roots.

He watched the huge animal briefly, estimating how many square miles a mammoth needed to feed, and then made a decision that saddened him. Earth had kept right on turning when the last mammoths disappeared. Newduvai could not afford many of them, ripping up foliage by the roots. Perhaps the Outsiders didn't care about that, but Locklear did. If you had to start sawing off links in your food chain, best if you started at the top. And he didn't want to pursue that thought by himself. At the very top was man. And kzin. It was the kind of thing he'd like to discuss with Scarface, but he'd made two trips to the lifeboat without a peep from its all-band comm set.

Finally, he flew to the crypt and set his little craft down nearby, reassuring Ruth as they walked inside. She paused for flight when she saw the rest of the mammoths, slowly tumbling inside their cages. "Much, much, much magic," she said, and patted him with great confidence.

But it was the sight of forty Neanderthals in stasis that really affected Ruth. Her face twisted with remorse, she turned from the nearest cage and faced Locklear with tears streaming down her cheeks. "Locklear kill?"

"No, no! Sleep," he insisted, miming it.

She was not convinced. "No sleeptalk," she protested, placing a hand on her head and pointing toward the rugged male nearby. And doubtless she was right; in stasis you didn't even dream.

"Before, Locklear take Ruth from little house," he said, tapping the cage, and then she remembered, and wanted to take the man out then and there. Instead, he got her help in moving the cage onto his improvised dolly and outside to the scooter.

They were halfway to the cabin and a thousand feet up on the heavily-laden scooter when Ruth somehow struck the cage base with her foot. Locklear saw the transparent plastic begin to rise, shouted, and nearly turned the scooter on its side as he leaped to slam the plastic down.

"Good God! You nearly let a wild man loose on a goddamn raft, a thousand feet in the air," he raged, and saw her cringe, holding her head in both hands. "Okay, Ruth. Okay, no problem," he continued more slowly, and pointed at the cage base. "Ruth no hit little house more. Locklear hit, soon."

They remained silent until they landed, and Locklear had time to review Newduvai's first in-flight airline emergency. Ruth had not feared a beating. No, it was his own panic that had punished her. That figured: a kzin telepath sometimes suffered when someone nearby was suffering.

He brought food and water from the cabin, placed it near the scooter, then paused before pressing the cage base. "Ruth: gentle man talk in head same Ruth talk in head?"

"Yes, all gentles talk in head." She saw what he was getting at. "Ruth talk to man, say Locklear much, much good magic man."

He pointed again at the man, a muscular young specimen who, without so much body hair, might have excited little comment at a collegiate wrestling match. "Ruth friend of man?"

She blushed as she replied: "Yes. Friend long time."

"That's what I was afraid of," he muttered with

a heavy sigh, pressed the baseplate, and then stepped back several paces, nearly bumping into the curious Loli.

The man's eyes flicked open. Locklear could see the heavy muscles tense, yet the man moved only his eyes, looking from him to Ruth, then to him again. When he did move, it was as though he'd been playing possum for forty thousand years, and his movements were as oddly graceful as Ruth's. He held up both hands, smiling, and it was obvious that some silent message had passed between them.

Locklear advanced with the same posture. A flat touch of hands, and then the man turned to Ruth with a burst of throaty speech. He was no taller than Locklear, but immensely more heavily-boned and muscled. He stood as erect as any man, unconcerned in his nakedness, and after a double handclasp with Ruth he made a smiling motion toward her breasts.

Again, Locklear saw the deeper color of flushing over her face and, after a head-down gesture of negation, she said something while staring at the young man's face. Puzzled, he glanced at Locklear with a comical half-smile, and Locklear tried to avoid looking at the man's budding erection. He told the man his name, and got a reply, but as usual Locklear gave him a name that seemed appropriate. He called him "Minuteman."

After a quick meal of fruit and water, Ruth did the translating. From the first, Minuteman accepted the fact that Locklear was one of the "new" people. After Locklear's demonstrations with the kzin memo screen and a levitation of the scooter, Minuteman gave him more physical space, perhaps a sign of deference. Or perhaps wariness; time would tell.

Though Loli showed no fear of Minuteman, she spoke little to him and kept her distance—with an egg-sized stone in her little fist at all times. Minuteman treated Loli as a guest might treat an unwelcome pet. *Oh yes*, thought Locklear, *he knows her, all righty. . . .*

The hunt, Locklear claimed, was a celebration to welcome Minuteman, but he had an ulterior motive. He made his point to Ruth, who chattered and gestured and, no doubt, silently communed with Minuteman for long moments. It would be necessary for Minuteman to accompany Locklear on the scooter, but without Ruth if they were to lug any sizeable game back to the cabin.

When Ruth stopped, Minuteman said something more. "Yes, no problem," Ruth said then.

Minuteman, his facial scars writhing as he grinned, managed, "Yef, no pobbem," and laughed when Locklear did. *Amazing how fast these people adapt*, Locklear thought. *He wakes up on a strange planet, and an hour later he's right at home. A wonderful trusting kind of innocence; even childlike*. Then Locklear decided to see just how far that trust went, and gestured for Minuteman to sit down on the scooter after he wrestled the empty stasis cage to the ground.

Soon they were scudding along just above the trees at a pace guaranteed to scare the hell out of any sensible Neanderthal, Minuteman desperately trying to make a show of confidence in the leadership of this suicidal shaman, and Locklear was satisfied on two counts, with one count yet to come. First, the scooter's pace near trees was enough to make Minuteman hold on for dear life.

Second, the young Neanderthal would view Locklear's easy mastery of the scooter as perhaps the very greatest of magics—and maybe Minuteman would pass that datum on, when the time came.

The third item was a shame, really, but it had to be done. A shaman without the power of ultimate punishment might be seen as expendable, and Locklear had to show that power. He showed it after passing over specimens of aurochs and horse, both noted with delight by Minuteman.

The goat had been grazing not far from three does until he saw the scooter swoop near. He was an old codger, probably driven off by the younger buck nearby, and Locklear recalled that the gestation period for goats was only five months—and besides, he told himself, the Outsiders could be pretty dumb in some matters. You didn't need twenty bucks for twenty does.

All of the animals bounded toward a rocky slope, and Minuteman watched them as Locklear maneuvered, forcing the old buck to turn back time and again. When at last the buck turned to face them, Locklear brought the scooter down, moving straight toward the hapless old fellow. Minuteman did not turn toward Locklear until he heard the report of the kzin sidearm which Locklear held in both hands, and by that time the scooter was only a man's height above the rocks.

At the report, the buck slammed backward, stumbling, shot in the breast. Minuteman ducked away from the sound of the shot, seeing Locklear with the sidearm, and then began to shout. Locklear let the scooter settle but Minuteman did not wait, leaping down, rushing at the old buck which still kicked in its death agony.

By the time Locklear had the scooter resting on

the slope, Minuteman was tearing at the buck's throat with his teeth, trying to dodge flinty hooves, the powerful arms locked around his prey. In thirty seconds the buck's eyes were glazing and its movements grew more feeble by the moment. Locklear put away the sidearm, feeling his stomach churn. Minuteman was drinking the animal's blood; sucking it, in fact, in a kind of frenzy.

When at last he sat up, Minuteman began to massage his temples with bloody fingers—perhaps a ritual, Locklear decided. The young Neanderthal's gaze at Lucklear was not pleasant, though he was suitably impressed by the invisible spear that had noisily smashed a man-sized goat off its feet leaving nothing more than a tiny hole in the animal's breast. Locklear went through a pantomime of shooting, and Minuteman gestured his "yes." Together, they placed the heavy carcass on the scooter and returned to the cabin. Minuteman seemed oddly subdued for a hunter who had just chewed a victim's throat open.

Locklear guffawed at what he saw at the cabin: in the cage so recently vacated by Minuteman was Loli, revolving in the slow dance of stasis. Ruth explained, "Loli like little house, like sleep. Ruth like for Loli sleep. Many like for Loli sleep long time," she added darkly.

It was Ruth who butchered the animal with the wtsai, while talking with Minuteman. Locklear watched smugly, noting the absence of flies. Damned if he was going to release those from their cages, nor the mosquitoes, locusts and other pests which lay with the predators in the crypt. Why would any god worth his salt pester a planet with flies, anyhow? The butterflies might be worth the trouble.

He was still ruminating on these matters when Ruth handed him the wtsai and entered the cabin silently. She seemed preoccupied, and Minuteman had wandered off toward the oaks so, just to be sociable, he said, "Minuteman see Locklear kill with magic. Minuteman like?"

She built a smoky fire, stretching skewers of stringy meat above the smoke, before answering. "No good, talk bad to magic man."

"It's okay, Ruth. Talk true to Locklear."

She propped the cabin door open to adjust the draft, then sat down beside him. "Minuteman feel bad. Locklear no kill meat fast, meat hurt long time. Meat feel much, much bad, so Minuteman feel much bad before kill meat. Locklear new person, no feel bad. Loli no feel bad. Minuteman no want hunt with Locklear."

As she attended to the barbecue and Locklear continued to ferret out more of this mystery, he grew more chastened. Neanderthal boys, learning to kill for food, began with animals that did not have a highly developed nervous system. Because when the animal felt pain, all the gentles nearby felt some of it too, especially women and girls. Neanderthal hunt teams were all-male affairs, and they learned every trick of stealth and quick kills because a clumsy kill meant a slow one. Minuteman had known that, lacking a club, he himself would feel the least pain if the goat bled to death quickly.

And large animals? You dug pit traps and visited them from a distance, or drove your prey off a distant cliff if you could. Neanderthal telepathy did not work much beyond twenty meters. The hunter who approached a wounded animal to pierce its throat with a spear was very brave, or very hungry. Or he was one of the new people, perfectly capable of irritating or even fighting a gentle without feeling the slightest psychic pain. The gentle Neanderthal, of course, was not protected against the new person's reflected pain. No wonder Ruth took care of Loli without liking her much!

He asked if Loli was the first "new" Ruth had seen. No, she said, but the only one they had allowed in the tribe. A hunt team had found her wandering alone, terrified and hungry, when she was only as high as a man's leg. Why hadn't the hunters run away? They had, Ruth said, but even then Loli had been quick on her feet. Rather than feel her gnawing fear and hunger on the perimeter of their camp, they had taken her in. And had regretted it ever since, " . . . long time. Long, long, long time!"

Locklear knew that he had gained a crucial insight; a Neanderthal behaved gently because it was in his own best interests. It was, at least, until modern Cro-Magnon man appeared without the blessing, and the curse, of telepathy.

Ruth's first telepathic greeting to the waking Minuteman had warned that he was in the presence of a great shaman, a "new" but nonetheless a good man. Minuteman had been so glad to see Ruth that he had proposed a brief roll in the grass, which involved great pleasure to participants—and it was expected that the audience could share their joy by telepathy. But Ruth knew better than that, reminding her friend that Locklear was not telepathic. Besides, she had the strongest kind of intuition that Locklear did not want to see her enjoying any other man. Peculiar, even bizarre; but new people were hard to figure. . . .

It was clear now, why Ruth's word "new" seemed

to have an unpleasant side. New people were savage people. *So much for labels*, Locklear told himself. *Modern man is the real savage!*

Ruth took Loli out of stasis for supper, perhaps to share in the girl's pleasure at such a feast. Through Ruth, Locklear explained to Minuteman that he regretted giving pain to his guest. He would be happy to let gentles do the hunting, but all animals belonged to Locklear. No animals must be hunted without prior permission. Minuteman was agreeable, especially with a mouthful of succulent goat rib in his big lantern jaws. Tonight, Minuteman could share the cabin. Tomorrow he must choose a site for a camp, for Locklear would soon bring many, many more gentles.

Locklear fell asleep slowly, no thanks to the ache in his jaws. The others had wolfed down that barbecued goat as if it had been well-aged porterhouse, but he had been able to choke only a little of it down after endless chewing because, savory taste or not, that old goat had been tough as a kzin's knuckles.

He wondered how Kit and Scarface were getting along, on the other side of those force walls. He really ought to fire up the lifeboat and visit them soon. Just as soon as he got things going here. With his mind-bending discovery of the truly gentle nature of Neanderthals, he was feeling very optimistic about the future. And modestly hungry. And very, very sleepy.

Minuteman spent two days quartering the vast circular expanse of Newduvai while Locklear piloted the scooter. In the process, he picked up a smatter of modern words though it was Ruth, in the evenings, who straightened out misunderstandings. Minuteman's clear choice for a major encampment was beside Newduvai's big lake, near the point where a stream joined the "big water." The site was a day's walk from the cabin, and Minuteman stressed that his choice might not be the choice of tribal elders. Besides, gentles tended to wander from season to season.

Though tempted by his power to command, Locklear decided against using it unless absolutely necessary. He would release them all and let them sort out their world, with the exception of excess hunting or tribal warfare. That didn't seem likely, but: "Ruth," he asked after the second day of recon, "see all people in little houses in cave?"

"Yes," she said firmly. "Many many in tribe of Minuteman and Ruth. Many many in other tribe."

But "many many" could mean a dozen or less. "Ruth see all in other tribe before?"

"Many times," she assured him. "Others give killstones, Ruth tribe give food."

"You trade with them," he said. After she had studied his face a moment, she agreed. He persisted: "Bad trades? Problem?"

"No problem," she said. "Trade one, two man or woman sometime, before big fire."

He asked about that, of course, and got an answer to a question he hadn't thought to ask. Ruth's last memory before waking on Newduvai— and Minuteman's too—was of the great fire that had driven several tribes to the base of a cliff. There, with trees bursting into flame nearby, the men had gathered around their women and children, beginning their song to welcome death. It was at that moment when the Outsiders must have put them in stasis and whisked them off to the rim of Known Space.

Almost an ethical decision, Locklear admitted. *Almost.* "No little gentles in cave," he reminded Ruth. "Locklear much sorry.."

"No good, think of little gentles," she said glumly. And with that, they passed to matters of tribal leadership. The old men generally led, though an old woman might have followers. It seemed a loose kind of democracy and, when some faction disagreed, they could simply move out—perhaps no farther than a short walk away.

Locklear soon learned why the gentles tended to stay close: "Big, bad animals eat gentles," Ruth said. "New people take food, kill gentles," she added. Lions, wolves, bears—and modern man—were their reasons for safety in numbers.

Ruth and Minuteman had both seen much of Newduvai from the air by now. To check his own conclusions, Locklear said, "Plenty food for many people. Plenty for many, many, many people?"

"Plenty," said Ruth, "for all people in little houses; no problem." Locklear ended the session on that note and Minuteman, perhaps with some silent urging from Ruth, chose to sleep outside.

Again, Locklear had a trouble getting to sleep, even after a half-hour of delightful tussle with the willing, homely, gentle Ruth. He could hardly wait for morning and his great social experiment.

His work would have gone much faster with Minuteman's muscular help, but Locklear wanted to share the crypt's secrets with as few as possible. The lake site was only fifteen minutes from the crypt by scooter, and there were no predators to attack a stasis cage, so Locklear transported the gentles by twos and left them in their cages, cursing his rotten time-management. It soon was obvious that the job would take two days and he'd set his heart on results now, now, now!

He was setting the scooter down near his cabin when Minuteman shot from the doorway, began to lope off, and then turned, approaching Locklear with the biggest, ugliest smile he could manage. He chattered away with all the innocence of a ferret in a birdhouse, his maleness in repose but rather large for that innocence. And wet.

Ruth waved from the cabin doorway.

"Right," Locklear snarled, too exhausted to let his anger kindle to white-hot fury. "Minuteman, I named you well. Your pants would be down, if you had any. Ahh, the hell with it."

Loli was asleep in her cage, and Minuteman found employment elsewhere as Locklear ate chopped goat, grapes, and gruel. He did not look at Ruth, even when she sat near him as he chewed.

Finally he walked to the pallet, looking from it to Ruth, shook his head and then lay down.

Ruth cocked her head in that way she had. "Like Ruth stay at fire?"

"I don't give a good shit. Yes, Ruth stay at fire. Good." Some perversity made him want her, but it was not as strong as his need for sleep. And rejecting her might be a kind of punishment, he thought sleepily. . . .

Late the next afternoon, Locklear completed his airlift and returned to the cabin. He could see Minuteman sitting disconsolate, chin in hands, at the edge of the clearing. Apparently, no one had seen fit to take Loli from stasis. He couldn't blame them much. Actually, he thought as he entered the cabin, he had no logical reason to blame them for anything. They enjoyed each other according to their own tradition, and he was out of step with it. *Damn right, and I don't know if I could ever get in step.*

He called Minuteman in. "Many, many gentles at big water," he said. "No big bad meat hurt gentles. Like see gentles now?" Minuteman wanted to very much. So did Ruth. He urged them onto the scooter and handed Ruth her woven basket full of dried apricots, giving both hindquarters of the goat to Minuteman without comment. Soon they were flitting above conifers and poplars, and then Ruth saw the dozens of cages glistening beside the lake.

"Gentles, gentles," she exclaimed, and began to weep. Locklear found himself angry at her pleasure, the anger of a wronged spouse, and set the scooter down abruptly some distance from the stasis cages.

Minuteman was off and running instantly. Ruth disembarked, turned, held a hand out. "Locklear like wake gentles? Ruth tell gentles, Locklear good, much good magics."

"Tell 'em anything you like," he barked, "after you screw 'em all!"

In the distance, Minuteman was capering around the cages, shouting in glee. After a moment, Ruth said, "Ruth like go back with Locklear."

"The hell you will! No, Ruth like push-push with many gentles. Locklear no like." And he twisted a vernier hard, the scooter lifting quickly.

Plaintively, growing faint on the breeze: "Ruth hurt in head. Like Locklear much . . ." And whatever else she said was lost.

He returned to the hidden kzin lifeboat, hating the idea of the silent cabin, and monitored the comm set for hours. It availed him nothing, but its boring repetitions eventually put him to sleep.

* * *

For the next week, Locklear worked like a man demented. He used a stasis cage, as he had on Kzersatz, to store his remaining few hunks of smoked goat. He flew surveillance over the new encampment, so high that no one would spot him, which meant that he could see little of interest, beyond the fact that they were building huts of bundled grass and some dark substance, perhaps mud. The stasis cages lay in disarray; he must retrieve them soon.

It was pure luck that he spotted a half-dozen deer one morning, a half-day's walk from the encampment, running as though from a predator. Presently, hovering beyond big chestnut trees, he saw them: men, patiently herding their prey toward an arroyo. He grinned to himself and waited until a rise of ground would cover his maneuver. Then he swooped low behind the deer, swerving from side to side to group them, yelping and growling until he was hoarse. By that time, the deer had put a mile between themselves and their real pursuers.

No better time than now to get a few things straight. Locklear swept the scooter toward the encampment at a stately pace, circling twice, hearing thin shouts as the Neanderthals noted his approach. He watched them carefully, one hand checking his kzin sidearm. They might be gentle but a few already carried spears and they were, after all, experts at the quick kill. He let the scooter hover at knee height, a constant reminder of his great magics, and noted the stir he made as the scooter glided silently to a stop at the edge of the camp.

He saw Ruth and Minuteman emerge from one

of the dozen beehive-shaped, grass-and-wattle huts. No, it wasn't Ruth; he admitted with chagrin that they all looked very much alike. The women paused first, and then he did spot Ruth, waving at him, a few steps nearer. The men moved nearer, falling silent now, laying their new spears and stone axes down as if by prearrangement. They stopped a few paces ahead of the women.

An older male, almost covered in curly gray hair, continued to advance using a spear—no, it was only a long walking staff—to aid him. He too stopped, with a glance over his shoulder, and then Locklear saw a bald old fellow with a withered leg hobbling past the younger men. Both of the old-sters advanced together then, full of years and dignity without a stitch of clothes. The gray man might have been sixty, with a little pot belly and knobby joints suggesting arthritis. The cripple was perhaps ten years younger but stringy and meatless, and his right thigh had been hideously smashed a long time before. His right leg was inches too short, and his left hip seemed disfigured from years of walking to compensate.

Locklear knew he needed Ruth now, but feared to risk violating some taboo so soon. "Locklear," he said, showing empty hands, then tapping his breast.

The two old men cocked their heads in a parody of Ruth's familiar gesture, then the curly one began to speak. Of course it was all gibberish, but the walking staff lay on the ground now and their hands were empty.

Wondering how much they would understand telepathically, Locklear spoke with enough volume for Ruth to hear. "Gentles hunt meat in hills," he said. "Locklear no like." He was not smiling.

The old men used brief phrases to each other, and then the crippled one turned toward the huts. Ruth began to walk forward, smiling wistfully at Locklear as she stopped next to the cripple.

She waited to hear a few words from each man, and then faced Locklear. "All one tribe now, two leaders," she said. "Skywater and Shortleg happy to see great shaman who save all from big fire. Ruth happy see Locklear too," she added softly.

He told her about the men hunting deer, and that it must stop; they must make do without meat for awhile. She translated. The old men conferred, and their gesture for "no" was the same as Ruth's. They replied through Ruth that young men had always hunted, and always would.

He told them that the animals were his, and they must not take what belonged to another. The old men said they could see that he felt in his head the animals were his, but no one owned the great mother land, and no one could own her children. They felt much bad for him. He was a very, very great shaman, but not so good at telling gentles how to live.

With great care, having chosen the names Cloud and Gimp for the old fellows, he explained that if many animals were killed, soon there would be no more. One day when many little animals were born, he would let them hunt the older ones.

The gist of their reply was this: Locklear obviously thought he was right, but they were older and therefore wiser. And because they had never run out of game no matter how much they killed, they *never could* run out of game. If it hadn't already happened, it wouldn't ever happen.

Abruptly, Locklear motioned to Cloud and had Ruth translate: he could prove the scarcity of game if Cloud would ride the scooter as Ruth and Minuteman had ridden it.

Much silent discussion and some out loud. Then old Cloud climbed aboard and in a moment, the scooter was above the trees.

From a mile up, they could identify most of the game animals, especially herd beasts in open plains. There weren't many to see. "No babies at all," Locklear said, trying to make gestures for "small." "Cloud, gentles *must* wait until babies are born." The old fellow seemed to understand Locklear's thoughts well enough, and spoke a bit of gibberish, but his head gesture was a Neanderthal "no."

Locklear, furious now, used the verniers with abandon. The scooter fled across parched arroyo and broken hill, closer to the ground and now so fast that Locklear himself began to feel nervous. Old Cloud sensed his unease, grasping handholds with gnarled knuckles and hunkering down, and Locklear knew a savage elation. *Serve the old bastard right if I splattered him all over Newduvai.* And then he saw the old man staring at his eyes, and knew that the thought had been received.

"No, I won't do it," he said. But a part of him had wanted to; *still* wanted to out of sheer frustration. Cloud's face was a rigid mask of fear, big teeth showing, and Locklear slowed the scooter as he approached the encampment again.

Cloud did not wait for the vehicle to settle, but debarked as fast as painful old joints would permit and stood facing his followers without a sound.

After a moment, with dozens of Neanderthals staring in stunned silence, they all turned their backs, a wave of moans rising from every throat.

Ruth hesitated, but she too faced away from Locklear.

"Ruth! No hurt Cloud. Locklear no like hurt gentles."

The moans continued as Cloud strode away. "Locklear need to talk to Ruth!" And then as the entire tribe began to walk away, he raised his voice: "No hurt gentles, Ruth!"

She stopped, but would not look at him as she replied. "Cloud say new people hurt gentles and not know. Locklear hurt Cloud before, want kill Cloud. Locklear go soon soon," she finished in a sob. Suddenly, then, she was running to catch the others.

Some of the men were groping for spears now. Locklear did not wait to see what they might do with them. A half-hour later he was using the dolly in the crypt, ranking cage upon cage just inside the obscuring film. With several lion cages stacked like bricks at the entrance, no sensible Neanderthal would go a step further. Later, he could use disassembled stasis units as booby traps as he had done on Kzersatz. But it was nearly dark when he finished, and Locklear was hurrying. Now, for the first time ever on Newduvai, he felt goose-flesh when he thought of camping in the open.

For days, he considered a return to Kzersatz in the lifeboat, meanwhile improving the cabin with Loli's help. He got that help very simply, by refusing to let her sleep in her stasis cage unless she did help. Loli was very bright, and learned his language quickly because she could not rely on telepathy. Operating on the sour-grape theory, he told himself that Ruth had been mud-fence ugly;

he hadn't felt any real affection for a Neanderthal bimbo. Not *really* . . .

He managed to ignore Loli's budding charms by reminding himself that she was no more than twelve or so, and gradually she began to trust him. He wondered how much that trust would suffer if she found he was taking her from stasis only on the days he needed help.

As the days faded into weeks, the cabin became a two-room affair with a connecting passage for firewood and storage. Loli, after endless scraping and soaking of the stiff goathide in acorn water, fashioned herself a one-piece garment. She taught Locklear how repeated boiling turned acorns into edible nuts, and wove mats of plaited grass for the cabin.

He let her roam in search of small game once a week until the day she returned empty-handed. He was cutting hinge material of stainless steel from a stasis cage with Kzin shears at the time, and smiled. "Don't feel bad, Loli. There's plenty of meat in storage." The more he used complete sentences, the more she seemed to be picking up the lingo.

She shrugged, picking at a scab on one of her hard little feet. "Loli not hunt. Gentles hunt Loli." She read his stare correctly. "Gentles not try to hurt Loli; this many follow and hide," she said, holding up four fingers and making a comical pantomime of a stealthy hunter.

He held up four fingers. "Four," he reminded her. "Did they follow you here?"

"Maybe want to follow Loli here," she said, grinning. "Loli think much. Loli go far far—"

"Very far," he corrected.

"Very far to dry place, gentles no follow feet

there. Loli hide, run very far where gentles not see. Come back to Locklear."

Yes, they'd have trouble tracking her through those desert patches, he realized, and she could've doubled back unseen in the arroyos. Or she might have been followed after all. "Loli is smart," he said, patting her shoulder, "but gentles are smart too. Gentles maybe want to hurt Locklear."

"Gentles cover big holes, spears in holes, come back, maybe find kill animal. Maybe kill Locklear."

Yeah, they'd do it that way. Or maybe set a fire to burn him out of the cabin. "Loli, would you feel bad if the gentles killed me?"

In her vast innocence, Loli thought about it before answering. "Little while, yes. Loli don't like to live alone. Gentles alltime like to play," she said, with a bump-and-grind routine so outrageous that he burst out laughing. "Locklear don't trade food for play," she added, making it obvious that Neanderthal men *did*.

"Not until Loli is older," he said with brutal honesty.

"Loli is a woman," she said, pouting as though he had slandered her.

To shift away from this dangerous topic he said, "Yes, and you can help me make this place safe from gentles." That was the day he began teaching the girl how to disassemble cages for their most potent parts, the grav polarizers and stasis units.

They burned off the surrounding ground cover bit by bit during the nights to avoid telltale smoke, and Loli assured him that Neanderthals never ventured from camp on nights as dark as Newduvai's. Sooner or later, he knew, they were bound to discover his little homestead and he intended to make it a place of terrifying magics.

As luck would have it, he had over two months to prepare before a far more potent new magic thundered across the sky of Newduvai.

Locklear swallowed hard the day he heard that long roll of synthetic thunder, recognizing it for what it was. He had told Loli about the kzinti, and now he warned her that they might be near, and saw her coltish legs flash into the forest as he sent the scooter scudding close to the ground toward the heights where his lifeboat was hidden. He would need only one close look to identify a kzin ship.

Dismounting near the lifeboat, peering past an outcrop and shivering because he was so near the cold force walls, he saw a foreshortened dot hovering near Newduvai's big lake. Winks of light streaked downward from it; he counted five shots before the ship ceased firing, and knew that its target had to be the big encampment of gentles.

"If only I had those beam cannons I took apart," he growled, unconsciously taking the side of the Neanderthals as tendrils of smoke fingered the sky. But he had removed the weapon pylon mounts long before. He released a long-held breath as the ship dwindled to a dot in the sky, hunching his shoulders, wondering how he could have been so naive as to forswear war altogether. Killing was a bitter draught, yet not half so bitter as dying.

The ship disappeared. Ten minutes later he saw it again, making the kind of circular sweep used for cartography, and this time it passed only a mile distant, and he gasped—for it was not a kzin ship. The little cruiser escort bore Interworld Commission markings.

"The goddamn tabbies must have taken one of

ours," he muttered to himself, and cursed as he saw the ship break off its sweep. No question about it: they were hovering very near his cabin.

Locklear could not fight from the lifeboat, but at least he had plenty of spare magazines for his kzin sidearm in the lifeboat's lockers. He crammed his pockets with spares, expecting to see smoke roiling from his homestead as he began to skulk his scooter low toward home. His little vehicle would not bulk large on radar. And the tabbies might not realize how soon it grew dark on Newduvai. Maybe he could even the odds a little by landing near enough to snipe by the light of his burning cabin. He sneaked the last two hundred meters afoot, already steeling himself for the sight of a burning cabin.

But the cabin was not burning. And the kzinti were not pillaging because, he saw with utter disbelief, the armed crew surrounding his cabin was human. He had already stood erect when it occurred to him that humans had been known to defect in previous wars—and he was carrying a kzin weapon. He placed the sidearm and spare magazines beneath a stone overhang. Then Locklear strode out of the forest rubber-legged, too weak with relief to be angry at the firing on the village.

The first man to see him was a rawboned, ruddy private with the height of a belter. He brought his assault rifle to bear on Locklear, then snapped it to "port arms." Three others spun as the big belter shouted, "Gomulka; We've got one!"

A big fireplug of a man, wearing sergeant's stripes, whirled and moved away from a cabin window, motioning a smaller man beneath the other window to stay put. Striding toward the belter, he used the heavy bellow of command.

"Parker; escort him in! Schmidt, watch the perimeter."

The belter trotted toward Locklear while an athletic specimen with a yellow crew cut moved out to watch the forest where Locklear had emerged. Locklear took the belter's free hand and shook it repeatedly. They walked to the cabin together, and the rest of the group relaxed visibly to see Locklear all but capering in his delight. Two other armed figures appeared from across the clearing, one with curves too lush to be male, and Locklear invited them all in with, "There are no kzinti on this piece of the planet; welcome to Newduvai."

Leaning, sitting, they all found their ease in Locklear's room, and their gazes were as curious as Locklear's own. He noted the varied shoulder patches: We Made It, Jinx, Wunderland. The woman, wearing the bars of a lieutenant, was evidently a Flatlander like himself. Commander Curt Stockton wore a Canyon patch, standing wiry and erect beside the woman, with pale gray eyes that missed nothing.

"I was captured by a kzin ship," Locklear explained, "and marooned. But I suppose that's all in the records; I call the planet 'Zoo' because I think the Outsiders designed it with that in mind."

"We had these co-ordinates, and something vague about prison compounds, from translations of kzin records," Stockton replied. "You must know a lot about this Zoo place by now."

"A fair amount. Listen, I saw you firing on a village near the big lake an hour ago. You mustn't do it again, Commander. Those people are real Earth Neanderthals, probably the only ones in the entire galaxy."

The blocky sergeant, David Gomulka, slid his

gaze to lock on Stockton's and shrugged big sloping shoulders. The woman, a close-cropped brunette whose cinched belt advertised her charms, gave Locklear a brilliant smile and sat down on his pallet. "I'm Grace Agostinho; Lieutenant, Manaus Intelligence Corps, Earth. Forgive our manners, Mr. Locklear, we've been in heavy fighting along the Rim and this isn't exactly what we expected to find."

"Me neither," Locklear smiled, then turned serious. "I hope you didn't destroy that village."

"Sorry about that," Stockton said. "We may have caused a few casualties when we opened fire on those huts. I ordered the firing stopped as soon as I saw they weren't kzinti. But don't look so glum, Locklear; it's not as if they were human."

"Damn right they are," Locklear insisted. "As you'll soon find out, if we can get their trust again. I've even taught a few of 'em some of our language. And that's not all. But hey, I'm dying of curiosity without any news from outside. Is the war over?"

Commander Stockton coughed lightly for attention and the others seemed as attentive as Locklear. "It looks good around the core worlds, but in the Rim sectors it's still anybody's war." He jerked a thumb toward the two-hundred-ton craft, twice the length of a kzin lifeboat, that rested on its repulsor jacks at the edge of the clearing with its own small pinnace clinging to its back. "The *Anthony Wayne* is the kind of cruiser escort they don't mind turning over to small combat teams like mine. The big brass gave us this mission after we captured some kzinti files from a tabby dreadnaught. Not as good as R & R back home, but we're glad of the break." Stockton's grin was infectious.

"I haven't had time to set up a distillery," Locklear said, "or I'd offer you drinks on the house."

"A man could get parched here," said a swarthy little private.

"Good idea, Gazho. You're detailed to get some medicinal brandy from the med stores," said Stockton.

As the private hurried out, Locklear said, "You could probably let the rest of the crew out to stretch their legs, you know. Not much to guard against on Newduvai."

"What you see is all there is," said a compact private with high cheekbones and a Crashlander medic patch. Locklear had not heard him speak before. Softly accented, laconic; almost a scholar's diction. But that's what you might expect of a military medic.

Stockton's quick gaze riveted the man as if to say, "that's enough." To Locklear he nodded. "Meet Soichiro Lee; an intern before the war. Has a tendency to act as if a combat team is a democratic outfit but," his glance toward Lee was amused now, "he's a good sawbones. Anyhow, the *Wayne* can take care of herself. We've set her auto defenses for voice recognition when the hatch is closed, so don't go wandering closer than ten meters without one of us. And if one of those hairy apes throws a rock at her, she might just burn him for his troubles."

Locklear nodded. "A crew of seven; that's pretty thin."

Stockton, carefully: "You want to expand on that?"

Locklear: "I mean, you've got your crew pretty thinly spread. The tabbies have the same problem, though. The bunch that marooned me here had only four members."

Sergeant Gomulka exhaled heavily, catching Stockton's glance. "Commander, with your permission: Locklear here might have some ideas about those tabby records."

"Umm. Yeah, I suppose," with some reluctance. "Locklear, apparently the kzinti felt there was some valuable secret, a weapon maybe, here on Zoo. They intended to return for it. Any idea what it was?"

Locklear laughed aloud. "Probably it was me. It ought to be the whole bleeding planet," he said. "If you stand near the force wall and look hard, you can see what looks like a piece of the Kzin homeworld close to this one. You can't imagine the secrets the other compounds might have. For starters, the life forms I found in stasis had been here forty thousand years, near as I can tell, before I released 'em."

"*You* released them?"

"Maybe I shouldn't have, but—" He glanced shyly toward Lieutenant Agostinho. "I got pretty lonesome."

"Anyone would," she said, and her smile was more than understanding.

Gomulka rumbled in evident disgust, "Why would a lot of walking fossils be important to the tabby war effort?"

"They probably wouldn't," Locklear admitted. "And anyhow, I didn't find the specimens until after the kzinti left." He could not say exactly why, but this did not seem the time to regale them with his adventures on Kzersatz. Something just beyond the tip of his awareness was flashing like a caution signal.

Now Gomulka looked at his commander. "So that's not what we're looking for," he said. "Maybe it's not on this Newduvai dump. Maybe next door?"

"Maybe. We'll take it one dump at a time," said Stockton, and turned as the swarthy private popped into the cabin. "Ah. I trust the Armagnac didn't insult your palate on the way, Nathan," he said.

Nathan Gazho looked at the bottle's broken seal, then began to distribute nested plastic cups, his breath already laced with his quick nip of the brandy. "You don't miss much," he grumbled.

But I'm missing something, Locklear thought as he touched his half-filled cup to that of the sloe-eyed, languorous lieutenant. *Slack discipline? But combat troups probably ignore the spit and polish. Except for this hotsy who keeps looking at me as if we shared a secret, they've all got the hand calluses and haircuts of shock troops. No, it's something else . . .*

He told himself it was reluctance to make himself a hero; and next he told himself they wouldn't believe him anyway. And then he admitted that he wasn't sure exactly why, but he would tell them nothing about his victory on Kzersatz unless they asked. *Maybe because I suspect they'd round up poor Scarface, maybe hunt him down and shoot him like a mad dog no matter what I said. Yeah, that's reason enough. But something else, too.*

Night fell, with its almost audible thump, while they emptied the Armagnac. Locklear explained his scholarly fear that the gentles were likely to kill off animals that no other ethologist had ever studied on the hoof; mentioned Ruth and Minute-

man as well; and decided to say nothing about
Loli to these hardbitten troops. Anse Parker, the
gangling belter, kept bringing the topic back to
the tantalizingly vague secret mentioned in kzin
files. Parker, Locklear decided, thought himself
subtle but managed only to be transparently
cunning.

Austin Schmidt, the wide-shouldered blond, had
little capacity for Armagnac and kept toasting the
day when ". . . all this crap is history and I'm a
man of means," singing that refrain from an old
barracks ballad in a surprisingly sweet tenor.
Locklear could not warm up to Nathan Gazho,
whose gaze took inventory of every item in the
cabin. The man's expensive wristcomp and pinky
ring mismatched him like earrings on a weasel.

David Gomulka was all noncom, though, with a
veteran's gift for controlling men and a sure hand
in measuring booze. If the two officers felt any
unease when he called them "Curt" and "Grace,"
they managed to avoid showing it. Gomulka spun
out the tale of his first hand-to-hand engagement
against a kzin penetration team with details that
proved he knew how the tabbies fought. Locklear
wanted to say, "That's right; that's how it is," but
only nodded.

It was late in the evening when the commander
cut short their speculations on Zoo, stood up,
snapped the belt flash from its ring and flicked it
experimentally. "We could all use some sleep," he
decided, with the smile of a young father at his
men, some of whom were older than he. "Mr.
Locklear, we have more than enough room. Please
be our guest in the *Anthony Wayne* tonight."

Locklear, thinking that Loli might steal back to
the cabin if she were somewhere nearby, said, "I

appreciate it, Commander, but I'm right at home here. Really."

A nod, and a reflective gnawing of Stockton's lower lip. "I'm responsible for you now, Locklear. God knows what those Neanderthals might do, now that we've set fire to their nests."

"But—" The men were stretching out their kinks, paying silent but close attention to the interchange.

"I must insist. I don't want to put it in terms of command, but I *am* the local sheriff here now, so to speak." The engaging grin again. "Come on, Locklear, think of it as repaying your hospitality. Nothing's certain in this place, and—" his last phrase bringing soft chuckles from Gomulka, "they'd throw me in the brig if I let anything happen to you now."

The taciturn Parker led the way, and Locklear smiled in the darkness thinking how Loli might wonder at the intensely bright, intensely magical beams that bobbed toward the ship. After Parker called out his name and a long number, the ship's hatch steps dropped at their feet and Locklear knew the reassurance of climbing into an Interworld ship with its familiar smells, whines and beeps.

Parker and Schmidt were loudly in favor of a nightcap, but Stockton's, "Not a good idea, David," to the sergeant was met with a nod and barked commands by Gomulka. Grace Agostinho made a similar offer to Locklear.

"Thanks anyway. You know what I'd really like?"

"Probably," she said, with a pursed-lipped smile.

He was blushing as he said, "Ham sandwiches. Beer. A slice of thrillcake," and nodded quickly when she hauled a frozen shrimp teriyaki from their food lockers. When it popped from the radioven, he sat near the ship's bridge to eat it, idly noting a few dark foodstains on the bridge linolamat and listening to Grace tell of small news from home. The Amazon dam, a new "mustsee" holo musical, a controversial cure for the common cold; the kind of tremendous trifles that cemented friendships.

She left him briefly while he chased scraps on his plate, and by the time she returned most of the crew had secured their pneumatic cubicle doors. "It's always satisfying to feed a man with an appetite," said Grace, smiling at his clean plate as she slid it into the galley scrubber. "I'll see you're fed well on the *Wayne*." With hands on her hips, she said, "Well: Private Schmidt has sentry duty. He'll show you to your quarters."

He took her hand, thanked her, and nodded to the slightly wavering Schmidt who led the way back toward the ship's engine room. He did not look back but, from the sound of it, Grace entered a cubicle where two men were arguing in subdued tones.

Schmidt showed him to the rearmost cubicle but not the rearmost dozen bunks. Those, he saw, were ranked inside a cage of duralloy with no privacy whatever. Dark crusted stains spotted the floor inside and outside the cage. A fax sheet lay in the passageway. When Locklear glanced toward it, the private saw it, tried to hide a startled response, and then essayed a drunken grin.

"Gotta have a tight ship," said Schmidt, banging his head on the duralloy as he retrieved the fax and balled it up with one hand. He tossed the wadded fax into a flush-mounted waste receptacle, slid the cubicle door open for Locklear, and managed a passable salute. "Have a good one, pal. You know how to adjust your rubberlady?"

Locklear saw that the mattresses of the two bunks were standard models with adjustable inflation and webbing. "No problem," he replied, and slid the door closed. He washed up at the tiny inset sink, used the urinal slot below it, and surveyed his clothes after removing them. They'd all seen better days. Maybe he could wangle some new ones. He was sleepier than he'd thought, and adjusted his rubberlady for a soft setting, and was asleep within moments.

He did not know how long it was before he found himself sitting bolt-upright in darkness. He knew what was wrong, now: *everything*. It might be possible for a little escort ship to plunder records from a derelict mile-long kzin battleship. It was barely possible that the same craft would be sent to check on some big kzin secret—*but not without at least a cruiser, if the kzinti might be heading for Zoo.*

He rubbed a trickle of sweat as it counted his ribs. He didn't have to be a military buff to know that ordinary privates do not have access to medical lockers, and the commander had told Gazho to get that brandy from med stores. Right; and all those motley shoulder patches didn't add up to a picked combat crew, either. And one more thing: even in his half-blotted condition, Schmidt had snatched that fax sheet up as though it was evidence against him. Maybe it was . . .

He waved the overhead lamp on, grabbed his ratty flight suit, and slid his cubicle door open. If anyone asked, he was looking for a cleaner unit for his togs.

A low thrum of the ship's sleeping hydraulics; a

slightly louder buzz of someone sleeping, most likely Schmidt while on sentry duty. *Not much discipline at all. I wonder just how much commanding Stockton really does.* Locklear stepped into the passageway, moved several paces, and eased his free hand into the waste receptacle slot. Then he thrust the fax wad into his dirty flight suit and padded silently back, cursing the sigh of his door. A moment later he was colder than before.

The fax was labeled, "PRISONER RIGHTS AND PRIVILEGES," and had been signed by some Provost Marshall—or a doctor, to judge from its illegibility. He'd bet anything that fax had fallen, or had been torn, from those duralloy bars. Rust-colored crusty stains on the floor; a similar stain near the ship's bridge; but no obvious damage to the ship from kzin weapons.

It took all his courage to go into the passageway again, flight suit in hand, and replace the wadded fax sheet where he'd found it. And the door seemed much louder this time, almost a sob instead of a sigh.

Locklear felt like sobbing too. He lay on his rubberlady in the dark, thinking about it. A hundred scenarios might explain some of the facts, but only one matched them all: the *Anthony Wayne* had been a prisoner ship, but now the prisoners were calling themselves "commander" and "sergeant," and the real crew of the *Anthony Wayne* had made those stains inside the ship with their blood.

He wanted to shout it, but demanded it silently: *So why would a handful of deserters fly to Zoo?* Before he fell at last into a troubled sleep, he had asked it again and again, and the answer was always the same: somehow, one of them had learned of the kzin records and hoped to find Zoo's secret before either side did.

These people would be deadly to anyone who knew their secret. And almost certainly, they'd never buy the truth, that Locklear himself was the secret because the kzinti had been so sure he was an Interworld agent.

Locklear awoke with a sensation of dread, then a brief upsurge of joy at sleeping in modern accomodations, and then he remembered his conclusions in the middle of the night, and his optimism fell off and broke.

To mend it, he decided to smile with the innocence of a Candide and plan his tactics. If he could get to the kzin lifeboat, he might steer it like a slow battering ram and disable the *Anthony Wayne*. Or they might blow him to flinders in midair—and what if his fears were wrong, and despite all evidence this combat team was genuine? In any case, disabling the ship meant marooning the whole lot of them together. It wasn't a plan calculated to lengthen his life expectancy; maybe he would think of another.

The crew was already bustling around with breakfasts when he emerged, and yes, he could use the ship's cleaning unit for his clothes. When he asked for spare clothing, Soichiro Lee was first to deny it to him. "Our spares are still—contaminated from a previous engagement," he explained, with a meaningful look toward Gomulka.

I bet they are, with blood, Locklear told himself as he scooped his synthesized eggs and bacon. Their uniforms all seemed to fit well. Probably their own, he decided. The stylized winged gun on Gomulka's patch said he could fly gunships.

Lee might be a medic, and the sensuous Grace might be a real intelligence officer—and all could be renegades.

Stockton watched him eat, friendly as ever, arms folded and relaxed. "Gomulka and Gazho did a recon in our pinnace at dawn," he said, sucking a tooth. "Seems your apemen are already rebuilding at another site; a terrace at this end of the lake. A lot closer to us."

"I wish you could think of them as people," Locklear said. "They're not terribly bright, but they don't swing on vines."

Chuckling: "Bright enough to be nuisances, perhaps try and burn us out if they find the ship here," Stockton said. "Maybe bright enough to know what it is the tabbies found here. You said they can talk a little. Well, you can help us interrogate 'em."

"They aren't too happy with me," Locklear admitted as Gomulka sat down with steaming coffee. "But I'll try on one condition."

Gomulka's voice carried a rumble of barely hidden threat. "Conditions? You're talking to your commander, Locklear."

"It's a very simple one," Locklear said softly. "No more killing or threatening these people. They call themselves 'gentles,' and they are. The New Smithson, or half the Interworld University branches, would give a year's budget to study them alive."

Grace Agostinho had been working at a map terminal, but evidently with an ear open to their negotiations. As Stockton and Gomulka gazed at each other in silent surmise, she took the few steps to sit beside Locklear, her hip warm against his. "You're an ethologist. Tell me, what could the kzinti do with these gentles?"

Locklear nodded, sipped coffee, and finally said, "I'm not sure. Study them hoping for insights into the underlying psychology of modern humans, maybe."

Stockton said, "But you said the tabbies don't know about them."

"True; at least I don't see how they could. But you asked. I can't believe the gentles would know what you're after, but if you have to ask them, of course I'll help."

Stockton said it was necessary, and appointed Lee acting corporal at the cabin as he filled most of the pinnace's jumpseats with himself, Locklear, Agostinho, Gomulka, and the lank Parker. The little craft sat on downsloping delta wings that ordinarily nested against the *Wayne*'s hull, and had intakes for gas-reactor jets. "Newest piece of hardware we have," Stockton said, patting the pilot's console. It was Gomulka, however, who took the controls.

Locklear suggested that they approach very slowly, with hands visibly up and empty, as they settled the pinnace near the beginnings of a new gentles campsite. The gentles, including their women, all rushed for primitive lances but did not flee, and Anse Parker was the only one carrying an obvious weapon as the pinnace's canopy swung back. Locklear stepped forward, talking and smiling, with Parker at their backs. He saw Ruth waiting for old Gimp, and said he was much happy to see her, which was an understatement. Minuteman, too, had survived the firing on their village.

Cloud had not. Ruth told him so immediately. "Locklear make many deaths to gentles," she accused. Behind her, some of the gentles stared with faces that were anything but gentle. "Gentles

not like talk to Locklear, he says. Go now. Please,"
she added, one of the last words he'd taught her,
and she said it with urgency. Her glance toward
Grace Agostinho was interested, not hostile but
perhaps pitying.

Locklear moved away from the others, farther
from the glaring Gimp. "More new people come,"
he called from a distance, pleading. "Think gentles big, bad animals. Stop when they see gentles;
much much sorry. Locklear say not hurt gentles
more."

With her head cocked sideways, Ruth seemed
to be testing his mind for lies. She spoke with
Gimp, whose face registered a deep sadness and,
perhaps, some confusion as well. Locklear could
hear a buzz of low conversation between Stockton
nearby and Gomulka, who still sat at the pinnace
controls.

"Locklear think good, but bad things happen,"
Ruth said at last. "Kill Cloud, many more. Gentles not like fight. Locklear know this," she said,
almost crying now. "Please go!"

Gomulka came out of the pinnace with his sidearm drawn, and Locklear turned toward him,
aghast. "No shooting! You promised," he reminded
Stockton.

But: "We'll have to bring the ape-woman with
the old man," Stockton said grimly, not liking it
but determined. Gomulka stood quietly, the big
sloping shoulders hunched.

Stockton said, "This is an explosive situation,
Locklear. We must take those two for interroga-
tion. Have the woman tell them we won't hurt
them unless their people try to hunt us."

Then, as Locklear froze in horrified anger,
Gomulka bellowed, *"Tell 'em!"*

Locklear did it and Ruth began to call in their language to the assembled throng. Then, at Gomulka's command, Parker ran forward to grasp the pathetic old Gimp by the arm, standing more than a head taller than the Neanderthal. That was the moment when Minuteman, who must have understood only a little of their parley, leaped weaponless at the big belter.

Parker swept a contemptuous arm at the little fellow's reach, but let out a howl as Minuteman, with those blacksmith arms of his, wrenched that arm as one would wave a stick.

The report was shattering, with echoes slapping off the lake, and Locklear whirled to see Gomulka's two-handed aim with the projectile sidearm. "No! Goddammit, these are human beings," he screamed, rushing toward the fallen Minuteman, falling on his knees, placing one hand over the little fellow's breast as if to stop the blood that was pumping from it. The gentles panicked at the thunder from Gomulka's weapon, and began to run.

Minuteman's throat pulse still throbbed, but he was in deep shock from the heavy projectile and his pulse died as Locklear watched helpless. Parker was already clubbing old Gimp with his riflebutt and Gomulka, his sidearm out of sight, grabbed Ruth as she tried to interfere. The big man might as well have walked into a train wreck while the train was still moving.

Grace Agostinho seemed to know she was no fighter, retreating into the pinnace. Stockton, whipping the ornamental braid from his epaulets, began to fashion nooses as he moved to help Parker, whose left arm was half-useless. Locklear came to his feet, saw Gomulka's big fist smash at Ruth's temple, and dived into the fray with one arm locked around Gomulka's bull neck, trying to haul him off-balance. Both of Ruth's hands grappled with Gomulka's now, and Locklear saw that she was slowly overpowering him while her big teeth sought his throat, only the whites of her eyes showing. It was the last thing Locklear would see for awhile, as someone raced up behind him.

He awoke to a gentle touch and the chill of antiseptic spray behind his right ear, and focused on the real concern mirrored on Stockton's face. He lay in the room he had built for Loli, Soichiro Lee kneeling beside him, while Ruth and Gimp huddled as far as they could get into a corner. Stockton held a standard issue parabellum, arms folded, not pointing the weapon but keeping it in evidence. "Only a mild concussion," Lee murmured to the commander.

"You with us again, Locklear?" Stockton got a nod in response, motioned for Lee to leave, and sighed. "I'm truly sorry about all this, but you were interfering with a military operation. Gomulka is—he has a lot of experience, and a good commander would be stupid to ignore his suggestions."

Locklear was barely wise enough to avoid saying that Gomulka did more commanding than Stockton did. Pushing himself up, blinking from the headache that split his skull like an axe, he said, "I need some air."

"You'll have to get it right here," Stockton said, "because I can't—won't let you out. Consider yourself under arrest. Behave yourself and that could change." With that, he shouldered the woven mat aside and his slow footsteps echoed down the connecting corridor to the other room.

Without a door directly to the outside, he would

have to run down that corridor where armed ya-
hoos waited. Digging out would make noise and
might take hours. Locklear slid down against the
cabin wall, head in hands. When he opened them
again he saw that poor old Gimp seemed coma-
tose, but Ruth was looking at him intently. "I
wanted to be friend of all gentles," he sighed.

"Yes. Gentles know," she replied softly. "New
people with gentles not good. Stok-Tun not want
hurt, but others not care about gentles. Ruth hear
in head," she added, with a palm against the top
of her head.

"Ruth must not tell," Locklear insisted. "New
people maybe kill if they know gentles hear that
way."

She gave him a very modern nod, and even in
that hopelessly homely face, her shy smile held a
certain beauty. "Locklear help Ruth fight. Ruth
like Locklear much, much; even if Locklear is
—new."

"Ruth, 'new' means 'ugly,' doesn't it? New, new,"
he repeated, screwing his face into a hideous cari-
cature, making claws of his hands, snarling in
exaggerated mimicry.

He heard voices raised in muffled excitement in
the other room, and Ruth's head was cocked again
momentarily. "Ugly?" She made faces, too. "Part
yes. New means not same as before but also ugly,
maybe bad."

"All the gentles considered me the ugly man. Yes?"

"Yes," she replied sadly. "Ruth not care. Like
ugly man if good man, too."

"And you knew I thought you were, uh . . ."

"Ugly? Yes. Ruth try and fix before."

"I know," he said, miserable. "Locklear like
Ruth for that and many, many more things."

Quickly, as boots stamped in the corridor, she said, "Big problem. New people not think Locklear tell truth. New woman—"

Schmidt's rifle barrel moved the mat aside and he let it do his gesturing to Locklear. "On your feet, buddy, you've got some explaining to do."

Locklear got up carefully so his head would not roll off his shoulders. Stumbling toward the doorway he said to Ruth: "What about new woman?"

"Much, much new in head. Ruth feel sorry," she called as Locklear moved toward the other room.

They were all crowded in, and seven pairs of eyes were intent on Locklear. Grace's gaze held a liquid warmth but he saw nothing warmer than icicles in any other face. Gomulka and Stockton sat on the benches facing him across his crude table like judges at a trial. Locklear did not have to be told to stand before them.

Gomulka reached down at his own feet and grunted with effort, and the toolbox crashed down on the table. His voice was not its usual command timbre, but menacingly soft. "Gazho noticed this was all tabby stuff," he said.

"Part of an honorable trade," Locklear said, dry-mouthed. "I could have killed a kzin and didn't."

"They trade you a fucking LIFEBOAT, too?"

Those goddamn pinnace sorties of his! The light of righteous fury snapped in the big man's face, but Locklear stared back. "Matter of fact, yes. The kzin is a cat of his word, sergeant."

"Enough of your bullshit, I want the truth!"

Now Locklear shifted his gaze to Stockton. "I'm telling it. Enough of your bullshit, too. How did your bunch of bozos get out of the brig, Stockton?"

Parker blurted, "How the hell did—" before Gomulka spun on his bench with a silent glare. Parker blushed and swallowed.

"We're asking the questions, Locklear. The tabbies must've left you a girlfriend, too," Stockton said quietly. "Lee and Schmidt both saw some little hotsy queen of the jungle out near the perimeter while we were gone. Make no mistake, they'll hunt her down and there's nothing I can say to stop them."

"Why not, if you're a commander?"

Stockton flushed angrily, with a glance at Gomulka that was not kind. "That's my problem, not yours. Look, you want some straight talk, and here it is: Agostinho has seen the goddamned translations from a tabby dreadnaught, and there *is* something on this godforsaken place they think is important, and we were in this Rim sector when—when we got into some problems, and she told me. I'm an officer, I really am, believe what you like. But we have to find whatever the hell there is on Zoo."

"So you can plea-bargain after your mutiny?"

"That's ENOUGH," Gomulka bellowed. "You're a little too cute for your own good, Locklear. But if you're ever gonna get off this ball of dirt, it'll be after you help us find what the tabbies are after."

"It's me," Locklear said simply. "I've already told you."

Silent consternation, followed by disbelief. "And what the fuck are you," Gomulka spat.

"Not much, I admit. But as I told you, they captured me and got the idea I knew more about the Rim sectors than I do."

"How much kzinshit do you think I'll swallow?" Gomulka was standing, now, advancing around

the table toward his captive. Curt Stockton shut
his eyes and sighed his helplessness.

Locklear was wondering if he could grab anything from the toolbox when a voice of sweet
reason stopped Gomulka. "Brutality hasn't solved
anything here yet," said Grace Agostinho. "I'd
like to talk to Locklear alone." Gomulka stopped,
glared at her, then back at Locklear. "I can't do
any worse than you have, David," she added to
the fuming sergeant.

Beckoning, she walked to the doorway and Gazho
made sure his rifle muzzle grated on Locklear's
ribs as the ethologist followed her outside. She
said, "Do I have your honorable parole? Bear in
mind that even if you try to run, they'll soon have
you and the girl who's running loose, too. They've
already destroyed some kind of flying raft; yours, I
take it," she smiled.

Damn, hell, shit, and blast! "Mine. I won't run,
Grace. Besides, you've got a parabellum."

"Remember that," she said, and began to stroll
toward the trees while the cabin erupted with
argument. Locklear vented more silent damns and
hells; she wasn't leading him anywhere near his
hidden kzin sidearm.

Grace Agostinho, surprisingly, first asked about
Loli. She seemed amused to learn he had waked
the girl first, and that he'd regretted it at his
leisure. Gradually, her questions segued to answers. "Discipline on a warship can be vicious,"
she mused as if to herself. "Curt Stockton was—is
a career officer, but it's his view that there must
be limits to discipline. His own commander was a
hard man, and—"

"Jesus Christ; you're saying he mutinied like
Fletcher Christian?"

"That's not entirely wrong," she said, now very feminine as they moved into a glade, out of sight of the cabin. "David Gomulka is a rougher sort, a man of some limited ideas but more of action. I'm afraid Curt filled David with ideas that, ah, . . ."

"Stockton started a boulder downhill and can't stop it," Locklear said. "Not the first time a man of ideas has started something he can't control. How'd you get into this mess?"

"An affair of the heart; I'd rather not talk about it. When I'm drawn to a man, . . . well, I tend to show it," she said, and preened her hair for him as she leaned against a fallen tree. "You must tell them what they want to know, my dear. These are desperate men, in desperate trouble."

Locklear saw the promise in those huge dark eyes and gazed into them. "I swear to you, the kzinti thought I was some kind of Interworld agent, but they dropped me on Zoo for safekeeping."

"And were you?" Softly, softly, catchee monkey . . .

"Good God, no! I'm an—"

"Ethologist. I heard it. But the kzin suspicion does seem reasonable, doesn't it?"

"I guess, if you're paranoid." *God, but this is one seductive lieutenant.*

"Which means that David and Curt could sell you to the kzinti for safe passage, if I let them," she said, moving toward him, her hands pulling apart the closures on his flight suit. "But I don't think that's the secret, and I don't think *you* think so. You're a fascinating man, and I don't know when I've been so attracted to anyone. Is this so awful of me?"

He knew damned well how powerfully persuasive a woman like Grace could be with that voluptuous willowy sexuality of hers. And he remembered Ruth's warning, and believed it. But he would rather drown in honey than in vinegar, and when she turned her face upward, he found her mouth with his, and willingly let her lust kindle his own.

Presently, lying on forest humus and watching Grace comb her hair clean with her fingers, Locklear's breathing slowed. He inventoried her charms as she shrugged into her flight suit again; returned her impudent smile; began to readjust his togs. "If this be torture," he declaimed like an actor, "make the most of it."

"Up to the standards of your local ladies?"

"Oh yes," he said fervently, knowing it was only a small lie. "But I'm not sure I understand why you offered."

She squatted becomingly on her knees, brushing at his clothing. "You're very attractive," she said. "And mysterious. And if you'll help us, Locklear, I promise to plumb your mysteries as much as you like—and vice-versa."

"An offer I can't refuse, Grace. But I don't know how I can do more than I have already."

Her frown held little anger; more of perplexity. "But I've told you, my dear: we must have that kzin secret."

"And you didn't believe what I said."

Her secret smile again, teasing: "Really, darling, you must give me some credit. I *am* in the intelligence corps."

He did see a flash of irritation cross her face this time as he laughed. "Grace, this is crazy," he said, still grinning. "It may be absurd that the kzinti thought I was an agent, but it's true. I think the planet itself is a mind-boggling discovery, and I said so first thing off. Other than that, what can I say?"

"I'm sorry you're going to be this way about it," she said with the pout of a nubile teenager, then hitched up the sidearm on her belt as if to remind him of it.

She's sure something, he thought as they strode back to his clearing. *If I had any secret to hide, could she get it out of me with this kind of attention? Maybe—but she's all technique and no real passion. Exactly the girl you want to bring home to your friendly regimental combat team . . .*

Grace motioned him into the cabin without a word and, as Schmidt sent him into the room with Ruth and the old man, he saw both Gomulka and Stockton leave the cabin with Grace. *I don't think she has affairs of the heart,* he reflected with a wry smile. *Affairs of the glands beyond counting, but maybe no heart to lose. Or no character?*

He sat down near Ruth, who was sitting with Gimp's head in her lap, and sighed. "Ruth much smart about new woman. Locklear see now," he said and, gently, kissed the homely face.

The crew had a late lunch but brought none for their captives, and Locklear was taken to his judges in the afternoon. He saw hammocks slung in his room, evidence that the crew intended to stay awhile. Stockton, as usual, began as pleasantly as he could. "Locklear, since you're not on Agostinho's list of known intelligence assets in the Rim sectors, then maybe we've been peering at the wrong side of the coin."

"That's what I told the tabbies," Locklear said.

"Now we're getting somewhere. Actually, you're a kzin agent; right?"

Locklear stared, then tried not to laugh. "Oh, Jesus, Stockton! Why would they drop me here, in that case?"

Evidently, Stockton's pleasant side was loosely attached under trying circumstances. He flushed angrily. "You tell us."

"You can find out damned fast by turning me over to Interworld authorities," Locklear reminded him.

"And if you turn out to be a plugged nickel," Gomulka snarled, "you're home free and we're in deep shit. No, I don't think we will, little man. We'll do anything we have to do to get the facts out of you. If it takes shooting hostages, we will."

Locklear switched his gaze to the bedeviled Stockton and saw no help there. At this point, a few lies might help the gentles. "A real officer, are you? Shoot these poor savages? Go ahead, actually you might be doing me a favor. You can see they hate my guts! The only reason they didn't kill me today is that they think I'm one of you, and they're scared to. Every one you knock off, or chase off, is just one less who's out to tan my hide."

Gomulka, slyly: "So how'd you say you got that tabby ship?"

Locklear: "On Kzersatz. Call it grand theft, I don't give a damn." Knowing they would explore Kzersatz sooner or later, he said, "The tabbies probably thought I hightailed it for the Interworld fleet but I could barely fly the thing. I was lucky to get down here in one piece."

Stockton's chin jerked up. "Do you mean there's a kzin force right across those force walls?"

"There was; I took care of them myself."

Gomulka stood up now. "Sure you did. I never heard such jizm in twenty years of barracks brags.

Grace, you never did like a lot of hollering and blood. Go to the ship." Without a word, and with the same liquid gaze she would turn on Locklear— and perhaps on anyone else—she nodded and walked out.

As Gomulka reached for his captive, Locklear grabbed for the heavy toolbox. That little hand welder would ruin a man's entire afternoon. Gomulka nodded, and suddenly Locklear felt his arms gripped from behind by Schmidt's big hands. He brought both feet up, kicked hard against the table, and as the table flew into the faces of Stockton and Gomulka, Schmidt found himself propelled backward against the cabin wall.

Shouting, cursing, they overpowered Locklear at last, hauling the top of his flight suit down so that its arms could be tied into a sort of straitjacket. Breathing hard, Gomulka issued his final backhand slap toward Locklear's mouth. Locklear ducked, then spat into the big man's face.

Wiping spittle away with his sleeve, Gomulka muttered, "Curt, we gotta soften this guy up."

Stockton pointed to the scars on Locklear's upper body. "You know, I don't think he softens very well, David. Ask yourself whether you think it's useful, or whether you just want to do it."

It was another of those ideas Gomulka seemed to value greatly because he had so few of his own. "Well goddammit, what would you do?"

"Coercion may work, but not this kind." Studying the silent Locklear in the grip of three men, he came near smiling. "Maybe give him a comm set and drop him among the Neanderthals. When he's good and ready to talk, we rescue him."

A murmur among the men, and a snicker from Gazho. To prove he did have occasional ideas,

Gomulka replied, "Maybe. Or better, maybe drop him next door on Kzinkatz or whatever the fuck he calls it." His eyes slid slowly to Locklear.

To Locklear, who was licking a trickle of blood from his upper lip, the suggestion did not register for a count of two beats. When it did, he needed a third beat to make the right response. Eyes wide, he screamed.

"Yeah," said Nathan Gazho.

"Yeah, right," came the chorus.

Locklear struggled, but not too hard. "My God! They'll— They EAT people, Stockton!"

"Well, it looks like a voice vote, Curt," Gomulka drawled, very pleased with his idea, then turned to Locklear. "But that's democracy for you. You'll have a nice comm set and you can call us when you're ready. Just don't forget the story about the boy who cried 'wolf.' But when you call, Locklear—" the big sergeant's voice was low and almost pleasant "—be ready to deal."

Locklear felt a wild impulse, as Gomulka shoved him into the pinnace, to beg, "Please, Bre'r Fox, don't throw me in the briar patch!" He thrashed a bit and let his eyes roll convincingly until Parker, with a choke hold, pacified him half-unconscious.

If he had any doubts that the pinnace was orbit-rated, Locklear lost them as he watched Gomulka at work. Parker sat with the captive though Lee, beside Gomulka, faced a console. The three pirates negotiated a three-way bet on how much time would pass before Locklear begged to be picked up. His comm set, roughly shoved into his ear with its button switch, had fresh batteries but Lee reminded him again that they would be returning only once to bail him out. The pinnace, a lovely little craft, arced up to orbital height and, with only its transparent canopy between him and hard vac, Locklear found real fear added to his pretense. After pitchover, tiny bursts of light at the wingtips steadied the pinnace as it began its reentry over the saffron jungles of Kzersatz.

Because of its different schedule, the tiny programmed sunlet of Kzersatz was only an hour into its morning. "Keep one eye on your sweep screen," Gomulka said as the roar of deceleration died away.

"I am," Lee replied grimly. "Locklear, if we get jumped by a tabby ship I'll put a burst right into your guts, first thing."

As Locklear made a show of moaning and straining at his bonds, Gomulka banked the pinnace for its mapping sweep. Presently, Lee's infrared scanners flashed an overlay on his screen and Gomulka nodded, but finished the sweep. Then, by manual control, he slowed the little craft and brought it at a leisurely pace to the IR blips, a mile or so above the alien veldt. Lee brought the screen's video to high magnification.

Anse Parker saw what Locklear saw. "Only a few tabbies, huh? And you took care of 'em, huh? You son of a bitch!" He glared at the scene, where a dozen kzinti moved unaware amid half-submerged huts and cooking fires, and swatted Locklear across the back of his head with an open hand. "Looks like they've gone native," Parker went on. "Hey, Gomulka: they'll be candy for us."

"I noticed," Gomulka replied. "You know what? If we bag 'em now, we're helping this little shit. We can come back any time we like, maybe have ourselves a tabby-hunt."

"Yeah; show 'em what it's like," Lee snickered, "after they've had their manhunt."

Locklear groaned for effect. *A village ready-made in only a few months! Scarface didn't waste any time getting his own primitives out of stasis. I hope to God he doesn't show up looking glad to see me.* To avoid that possibility he pleaded, "Aren't you going to give me a running chance?"

"Sure we are," Gomulka laughed. "Tabbies will pick up your scent anyway. Be on you like flies on a turd." The pinnace flew on, unseen from far below, Lee bringing up the video now and then. Once he said, "Can't figure out what they're hunting in that field. If I didn't know kzinti were strict carnivores I'd say they were farming."

Locklear knew that primitive kzinti ate vegetables as well, and so did their meat animals; but he kept his silence. It hadn't even occurred to these piratical deserters that the kzinti below might be as prehistoric as Neanderthalers. Good; let them think they understood the kzinti! *But nobody knows 'em like I do*, he thought. It was an arrogance he would recall with bitterness very, very soon.

Gomulka set the pinnace down with practiced ease behind a stone escarpment and Parker, his gaze nervously sweeping the jungle, used his gun barrel to urge Locklear out of the craft.

Soichiro Lee's gentle smile did not match his final words: "If you manage to hide out here, just remember we'll pick up your little girlfriend before long. Probably a better piece of snatch than the Manaus machine," he went on, despite a sudden glare from Gomulka. "How long do you want us to use her, asshole? Think about it," he winked, and the canopy's "thunk" muffled the guffaws of Anse Parker.

Locklear raced away as the pinnace lifted, making it look good. They had tossed Bre'r Rabbit into his personal briar patch, never suspecting he might have friends here.

He was thankful that the village lay downhill as he began his one athletic specialty, long-distance jogging, because he could once again feel the synthetic gravity of Kzersatz tugging at his body. He judged that he was a two-hour trot from the village and paced himself carefully, walking and resting now and then. And planning.

As soon as Scarface learned the facts, they could set a trap for the returning pinnace. And then, with captives of his own, Locklear could negotiate with Stockton. It was clear by now that Curt Stockton considered himself a leader of virtue—because he was a man of ideas. David Gomulka was a man of action without many important ideas, the perfect model of a playground bully long after graduation.

And Stockton? He would've been the kind of clever kid who decided early that violence was an inferior way to do things, because he wasn't very good at it himself. Instead, he'd enlist a Gomulka to stand nearby while the clever kid tried to beat you up with words; debate you to death. And if that finally failed, he could always sigh, and walk away leaving the bully to do his dirty work, and imagine that his own hands were clean.

But Kzersatz was a whole 'nother playground, with different rules. Locklear smiled at the thought and jogged on.

An hour later he heard the beast crashing in panic through orange ferns before he saw it, and realized that it was pursued only when he spied a young male flashing with sinuous efficiency behind.

No one ever made friends with a kzin by interrupting its hunt, so Locklear stood motionless among palmferns and watched. The prey reminded him of a pygmy tyrannosaur, almost the height of a man but with teeth meant for grazing on foliage. The kzin bounded nearer, disdaining the *wtsai* knife at his belt, and screamed only as he leaped for the kill.

The prey's armored hide and thrashing tail made the struggle interesting, but the issue was never in doubt. A kzin warrior was trained to hunt, to kill, and to eat that kill, from kittenhood. The roars of the lizard dwindled to a hissing gurgle; the tail and the powerful legs stilled. Only after the kzin vented his victory scream and ripped into his prey did Locklear step into the clearing made by flattened ferns.

Hands up and empty, Locklear called in Kzin, "The kzin is a mighty hunter!" To speak in Kzin, one needed a good falsetto and plenty of spit. Locklear's command was fair, but the young kzin reacted as though the man had spouted fire and brimstone. He paused only long enough to snatch up his kill, a good hundred kilos, before bounding off at top speed.

Crestfallen, Locklear trotted toward the village again. He wondered now if Scarface and Kit, the mate Locklear had freed for him, had failed to speak of mankind to the ancient kzin tribe. In any case, they would surely respond to his use of their language until he could get Scarface's help. Perhaps the young male had simply raced away to bring the good news.

And perhaps, he decided a half-hour later, he himself was the biggest fool in Known Space or beyond it. They had ringed him before he knew it, padding silently through foliage the same mottled yellows and oranges as their fur. Then, almost simultaneously, he saw several great tigerish shapes disengage from their camouflage ahead of him, and heard the scream as one leapt upon him from behind.

Bowled over by the rush, feeling hot breath and fangs at his throat, Locklear moved only his eyes. His attacker might have been the same one he surprised while hunting, and he felt needle-tipped claws through his flight suit.

Then Locklear did the only things he could: kept his temper, swallowed his terror, and repeated his first greeting: "The kzin is a mighty hunter."

He saw, striding forward, an old kzin with ornate bandolier straps. The oldster called to the others, "It is true, the beast speaks the Hero's Tongue! It is as I prophesied." Then, to the young attacker, "Stand away at the ready," and Locklear felt like breathing again.

"I am Locklear, who first waked members of your clan from age-long sleep," he said in that ancient dialect he'd learned from Kit. "I come in friendship. May I rise?"

A contemptuous gesture and, as Locklear stood up, a worse remark. "Then you are the beast that lay with a palace *prret*, a courtesan. We have heard. You will win no friends here."

A cold tendril marched down Locklear's spine. "May I speak with my friends? The kzinti have things to fear, but I am not among them."

More laughter. "The Rockear beast thinks it is fearsome," said the young male, his ear-umbrellas twitching in merriment.

"I come to ask help, and to offer it," Locklear said evenly.

"The priesthood knows enough of your help.
Come," said the older one. And that is how
Locklear was marched into a village of prehistoric
kzinti, ringed by hostile predators twice his size.

His reception party was all-male, its members
staring at him in frank curiosity while prodding
him to the village. They finally left him in an open
area surrounded by huts with his hands tied, a
leather collar around his neck, the collar linked by
a short braided rope to a hefty stake. When he
squatted on the turf, he noticed the soil was torn
by hooves here and there. Dark stains and an
abattoir odor said the place was used for butchering animals. The curious gazes of passing females
said he was only a strange animal to them. The
disappearance of the males into the largest of the
semi-submerged huts suggested that he had furnished the village with something worth a town
meeting.

At last the meeting broke up, kzin males striding from the hut toward him, a half-dozen of the
oldest emerging last, each with a four-fingered
paw tucked into his bandolier belt. Prominent
scars across the breasts of these few were all exactly similar; some kind of self-torture ritual,
Locklear guessed. Last of all with the ritual scars
was the old one he'd spoken with, and this one
had *both* paws tucked into his belt. *Got it; the
higher your status, the less you need to keep your
hands ready, or to hurry.*

The old devil was enjoying all this ceremony,
and so were the other big shots. Standing in clearly-
separated rings behind them were the other males
with a few females, then the other females, evidently the entire tribe. Locklear spotted a few

kzinti whose expressions and ear-umbrellas said they were either sick or unhappy, but all played their obedient parts.

Standing before him, the oldster reached out and raked Locklear's face with what seemed to be only a ceremonial insult. It brought welts to his cheek anyway. The oldster spoke for all to hear. "You began the tribe's awakening, and for that we promise a quick kill."

"I waked several kzinti, who promised me honor," Locklear managed to say.

"Traitors? They have no friends here. So *you*— have no friends here," said the old kzin with pompous dignity. "This the priesthood has decided."

"You are the leader?"

"First among equals," said the high priest with a smirk that said he believed in no equals.

"While this tribe slept," Locklear said loudly, hoping to gain some support, "a mighty kzin warrior came here. I call him Scarface. I return in peace to see him, and to warn you that others who look like me may soon return. They wish you harm, but I do not. Would you take me to Scarface?"

He could not decipher the murmurs, but he knew amusement when he saw it. The high priest stepped forward, untied the rope, handed it to the nearest of the husky males who stood behind the priests. "He would see the mighty hunter who had new ideas," he said. "Take him to see that hero, so that he will fully appreciate the situation. Then bring him back to the ceremony post."

With that, the high priest turned his back and followed by the other priests, walked away. The dozens of other kzinti hurried off, carefully avoiding any backward glances. Locklear said, to the huge specimen tugging on his neck rope, "I cannot walk quickly with hands behind my back."

"Then you must learn," rumbled the big kzin, and lashed out with a foot that propelled Locklear forward. *I think he pulled that punch,* Locklear thought. *Kept his claws retracted, at least.* The kzin led him silently from the village and along a path until hidden by foliage. Then, "You are the Rockear," he said, slowing. "I am" (something as unpronounceable as most kzin names), he added, neither friendly nor unfriendly. He began untying Locklear's hands with, "I must kill you if you run, and I will. But I am no priest," he said, as if that explained his willingness to ease a captive's walking.

"You are a stalwart," Locklear said. "May I call you that?"

"As long as you can," the big kzin said, leading the way again. "I voted to my priest to let you live, and teach us. So did most heroes of my group."

Uh-huh; they have priests instead of senators. But this smells like the old American system before direct elections. "Your priest is not bound to vote as you say?" A derisive snort was his answer, and he persisted. "Do you vote your priests in?"

"Yes. For life," said Stalwart, explaining everything.

"So they pretend to listen, but they do as they like," Locklear said.

A grunt, perhaps of admission or of scorn. "It was always thus," said Stalwart, and found that Locklear could trot, now. Another half-hour found them moving across a broad veldt, and Locklear saw the scars of a grass fire before he realized he was in familiar surroundings. Stalwart led the way to a rise and then stopped, pointing toward the jungle. "There," he said, "is your scarfaced friend."

Locklear looked in vain, then back at Stalwart. "He must be blending in with the ferns. You people do that very—"

"The highest tree. What remains of him is there."

And then Locklear saw the flying creatures he had called "batowls," tiny mites at a distance of two hundred meters, picking at tatters of something that hung in a net from the highest tree in the region. "Oh, my God! Won't he die there?"

"He is dead already. He underwent the long ceremony," said Stalwart, "many days past, with wounds that killed slowly."

Locklear's glare was incriminating: "I suppose you voted against that, too?"

"That, and the sacrifice of the palace *prret* in days past," said the kzin.

Blinking away tears, for Scarface had truly been a cat of his word, Locklear said, "Those *prret*. One of them was Scarface's mate when I left. Is she—up there, too?"

For what it was worth, the big kzin could not meet his gaze. "Drowning is the dishonorable punishment for females," he said, pointing back toward Kzersatz's long shallow lake. "The priesthood never avoids tradition, and she lies beneath the water. Another *prret* with kittens was permitted to rejoin the tribe. She chose to be shunned instead. Now and then, we see her. It is treason to speak against the priesthood, and I will not."

Locklear squeezed his eyes shut; blinked; turned away from the hideous sight hanging from that distant tree as scavengers picked at its bones. "And I hoped to help your tribe! A pox on all your houses," he said to no one in particular. He did not speak to the kzin again, but they did not hurry as Stalwart led the way back to the village.

The only speaking Locklear did was to the comm set in his ear, shoving its pushbutton switch. The kzin looked back at him in curiosity once or twice, but now he was speaking Interworld, and perhaps Stalwart thought he was singing a death song.

In a way, it was true—though not a song of his own death, if he could help it. "Locklear calling the *Anthony Wayne*," he said, and paused.

He heard the voice of Grace Agostinho reply, "Recording."

"They've caught me already, and they intend to kill me. I don't much like you bastards, but at least you're human. I don't care how many of the male tabbies you bag; when they start torturing me I won't be any further use to you."

Again, Grace's voice replied in his ear: "Recording."

Now with a terrible suspicion, Locklear said, "Is anybody there? If you're monitoring me live, say 'monitoring.'"

His comm set, in Grace's voice, only said, "Recording."

Locklear flicked off the switch and began to walk even more slowly, until Stalwart tugged hard on the leash. Any kzin who cared to look, as they reentered the village, would have seen a little man bereft of hope. He did not complain when Stalwart retied his hands, nor even when another kzin marched him away and fairly flung him into a tiny hut near the edge of the village. Eventually they flung a bloody hunk of some recent kill into his hut, but it was raw and, with his hands tied behind him, he could not have held it to his mouth.

Nor could he toggle his comm set, assuming it would carry past the roof thatch. He had not said he would be in the village, and they would very likely kill him along with everybody else in the village when they came. *If* they came.

He felt as though he would drown in cold waves of despair. A vicious priesthood had killed his friends and, even if he escaped for a time, he would be hunted down by the galaxy's most pitiless hunters. And if his own kind rescued him, they might cheerfully beat him to death trying to learn a secret he had already divulged. And even the gentle Neanderthalers hated him, now.

Why not just give up? I don't know why, he admitted to himself, and began to search for something to help him fray the thongs at his wrists. He finally chose a rough-barked post, sitting down in front of it and staring toward the kzin male whose lower legs he could see beneath the door matting.

He rubbed until his wrists were as raw as that meat lying in the dust before him. Then he rubbed until his muscles refused to continue, his arms cramping horribly. By that time it was dark, and he kept falling into an exhausted, fitful sleep, starting to scratch at his bonds every time a cramp woke him. The fifth time he awoke, it was to the sounds of scratching again. And a soft, distant call outside, which his guard answered just as softly. It took Locklear a moment to realize that those scratching noises were not being made by *him*.

The scratching became louder, filling him with a dread of the unknown in the utter blackness of the Kzersatz night. Then he heard a scrabble of clods tumbling to the earthen floor. Low, urgent, in the fitz-rowr of a female kzin: "Rockear, quickly! Help widen this hole!"

He wanted to shout, remembering Boots, the new mother of two who had scorned her tribe; but he whispered hoarsely: "Boots?"

An even more familiar voice than that of Boots. "She is entertaining your guard. Hurry!"

"Kit! I can't, my hands are tied," he groaned. "Kit, they said you were drowned."

"Idiots," said the familiar voice, panting as she worked. A very faint glow preceded the indomitable Kit, who had a modern kzin beltpac and used its glowlamp for brief moments. Without slowing her frantic pace, she said softly, "They built a walkway into the lake and—dropped me from it. But my mate, your friend Scarface, knew what they intended. He told me to breathe—many times just before I fell. With all the stones—weighting me down, I simply walked on the bottom, between the pilings—and untied the stones beneath the planks near shore. Idiots," she said again, grunting as her fearsome claws ripped away another chunk of Kzersatz soil. Then, "Poor Rockear," she said, seeing him writhe toward her.

In another minute, with the glowlamp doused, Locklear heard the growling curses of Kit's passage into the hut. She'd said females were good tunnelers, but not until now had he realized just how good. The nearest cover must be a good ten meters away . . . "Jesus, don't bite my hand, Kit," he begged, feeling her fangs and the heat of her breath against his savaged wrists. A moment later he felt a flash of white-hot pain through his shoulders as his hands came free. He'd been cramped up so long it hurt to move freely. "Well, by God it'll just have to hurt," he said aloud to himself, and flexed his arms, groaning.

"I suppose you must hold to my tail," she said. He felt the long, wondrously luxuriant tail whisk across his chest and because it was totally dark, did as she told him. Nothing short of true and abiding friendship, he knew, would provoke her into such manhandling of her glorious, her sensual, her fundamental tail.

They scrambled past mounds of soft dirt until Locklear felt cool night air on his face. "You may quit insulting my tail now," Kit growled. "We must wait inside this tunnel awhile. You take this: I do not use it well."

He felt the cold competence of the object in his hand and exulted as he recognized it as a modern kzin sidearm. Crawling near with his face at her shoulder, he said, "How'd you know exactly where I was?"

"Your little long-talker, of course. We could hear you moaning and panting in there, and the magic tools of my mate located you."

But I didn't have it turned on. Ohhh-no; I didn't KNOW it was turned on! The goddamned thing is transmitting all the time . . . He decided to score one for Stockton's people, and dug the comm set from his ear. Still in the tunnel, it wouldn't transmit well until he moved outside. Crush it? Bury it? Instead, he snapped the magazine from the sidearm and, after removing its ammunition, found that the tiny comm set would fit inside. Completely enclosed by metal, the comm set would transmit no more until he chose.

He got all but three of the rounds back in the magazine, cursing every sound he made, and then moved next to Kit again. "They showed me what they did to Scarface. I can't tell you how sorry I am, Kit. He was my friend, and they will pay for it."

"Oh, yes, they will pay," she hissed softly. "Make no mistake, he is still your friend."

A thrill of energy raced from the base of his skull down his arms and legs. "You're telling me he's alive?"

As if to save her the trouble of a reply, a male kzin called softly from no more than three paces away: "Milady; do we have him?"

"Yes," Kit replied.

"Scarface! Thank God you're—"

"Not now," said the one-time warship commander. "Follow quietly."

Having slept near Kit for many weeks, Locklear recognized her steam-kettle hiss as a sufferer's sigh. "I know your nose is hopeless at following a spoor, Rockear. But try not to pull me completely apart this time." Again he felt that long bushy tail pass across his breast, but this time he tried to grip it more gently as they sped off into the night.

Sitting deep in a cave with rough furniture and booby-trapped tunnels, Locklear wolfed stew under the light of a kzin glowlamp. He had slightly scandalized Kit with a hug, then did the same to Boots as the young mother entered the cave without her kittens. The guard would never be trusted to guard anything again, said the towering Scarface, but that rescue tunnel was proof that a kzin had helped. Now they'd be looking for Boots, thinking she had done more than lure a guard thirty meters away.

Locklear told his tale of success, failure, and capture by human pirates as he finished eating, then asked for an update of the Kzersatz problem. Kit, it turned out, had warned Scarface against taking the priests from stasis but one of the devout and not entirely bright males they woke had done the deed anyway.

Scarface, with his small hidden cache of modern equipment, had expected to lead; had he not been Tzak-Commander, once upon a time? The priests had seemed to agree—long enough to make sure they could coerce enough followers. It seemed, said Scarface, that ancient kzin priests hadn't the slightest compunctions about lying, unlike modern kzinti. He had tried repeatedly to call Locklear with his all-band comm set, without success. Depending on long custom, demanding that tradition take precedence over new ways, the priests had engineered the capture of Scarface and Kit in a hook-net, the kind of cruel device that tore at the victim's flesh at the slightest movement.

Villagers had spent days in building that walkway out over a shallowly sloping lake, a labor of loathing for kzinti who hated to soak in water. Once it was extended to the point where the water was four meters deep, the rough-hewn dock made an obvious reminder of ceremonial murder to any female who might try, as Kit and Boots had done ages before, to liberate herself from the ritual prostitution of yore.

And then, as additional mental torture, they told their bound captives what to expect, and made Scarface watch as Kit was thrown into the lake. Boots, watching in horror from afar, had then watched the torture and disposal of Scarface. She was amazed when Kit appeared at her birthing bower, having seen her disappear with great stones into deep water. The next day, Kit had killed a big ruminant, climbing that tree at night to recover her mate and placing half of her kill in the net.

"My medkit did the rest," Scarface said, pointing to ugly scar tissue at several places on his big torso. "These scum have never seen anyone recover from deep body punctures. Antibiotics can be magic, if you stretch a point."

Locklear mused silently on their predicament for long minutes. Then: "Boots, you can't afford to hang around near the village anymore. You'll have to hide your kittens and—"

"They have my kittens," said Boots, with a glitter of pure hate in her eyes. "They will be cared for as long as I do not disturb the villagers."

"Who told you that?"

"The high priest," she said, mewling pitifully as she saw the glance of doubt pass between Locklear and Scarface. The priests were accomplished liars.

"We'd best get them back soon," Locklear suggested. "Are you sure this cave is secure?"

Scarface took him halfway out one tunnel and, using the glowlamp, showed him a trap of horrifying simplicity. It was a grav polarizer unit from one of the biggest cages, buried just beneath the tunnel floor with a switch hidden to one side. If you reached to the side carefully and turned the switch off, that hidden grav unit wouldn't hurl you against the roof of the tunnel as you walked over it. If you didn't, it did. Simple. Terrible. "I like it," Locklear smiled. "Any more tricks I'd better know before I plaster myself over your ceiling?"

There were, and Scarface showed them to him. "But the least energy expended, the least noise and alarm to do the job, the best. Instead of polarizers, we might bury some stasis units outside, perhaps at the entrance to their meeting hut. Then we catch those *kshat* priests, and use the lying scum for target practice."

"Good idea, and we may be able to improve on it. How many units here in the cave?"

That was the problem; two stasis units taken from cages were not enough. They needed more from the crypt, said Locklear.

"They destroyed that little airboat you left me, but I built a better one," Scarface said with a flicker of humor from his ears.

"So did I. Put a bunch of polarizers on it to push yourself around and ignored the sail, didn't you?" He saw Scarface's assent and winked.

"Two units might work if we trap the priests one by one," Scarface hazarded. "But they've been meddling in the crypt. We might have to fight our way in. And you . . ." he hesitated.

"And I have fought better kzinti before, and here I stand," Locklear said simply.

"That you do." They gripped hands, and then went back to set up their raid on the crypt. The night was almost done.

When surrendering, Scarface had told Locklear nothing of his equipment cache. With two sidearms he could have made life interesting for a man; interesting and short. But his word had been his bond, and now Locklear was damned glad to have the stuff.

They left the females to guard the cave. Flitting low across the veldt toward the stasis crypt with Scarface at his scooter controls, they planned their tactics. "I wonder why you didn't start shooting those priests the minute you were back on your feet," Locklear said over the whistle of breeze in their faces.

"The kittens," Scarface explained. "I might kill one or two priests before the cowards hid and sent innocent fools to be shot, but they are perfectly capable of hanging a kitten in the village until I gave myself up. And I did not dare raid the crypt for stasis units without a warrior to back me up."

"And I'll have to do," Locklear grinned.

"You will," Scarface grinned back; a typical kzin grin, all business, no pleasure.

They settled the scooter near the ice-rimmed force wall and moved according to plan, making haste slowly to avoid the slightest sound, the huge kzin's head swathed in a bandage of leaves that suggested a wound while—with luck—hiding his identity for a few crucial seconds.

Watching the kzin warrior's muscular body slide among weeds and rocks, Locklear realized that Scarface was still not fully recovered from his ordeal. *He made his move before he was ready because of me, and I'm not even a kzin. Wish I thought I could match that kind of commitment*, Locklear mused as he took his place in front of Scarface at the crypt entrance. His sidearm was in his hand. Scarface had sworn the priests had no idea what the weapon was and, with this kind of ploy, Locklear prayed he was right. Scarface gripped Locklear by the neck then, but gently, and they marched in together expecting to meet a guard just inside the entrance.

No guard. No sound at all—and then a distant hollow slam, as of a great box closing. They split up then, moving down each side corridor, returning to the main shaft silently, exploring side corri-

dors again. After four of these forays, they knew
that no one would be at their backs.

Locklear was peering into the fifth when, glancing back, he saw Scarface's gesture of caution.
Scuffing steps down the side passage, a mumble in
Kzin, then silence. Then Scarface resumed his
hold on his friend's neck and, after one mutual
glance of worry, shoved Locklear into the side
passage.

"Ho, see the beast I captured," Scarface called,
his voice booming in the wide passage, prompting
exclamations from two surprised kzin males.

Stasis cages lay in disarray, some open, some
with transparent tops ripped off. One kzin, with
the breast scars and bandoliers of a priest, hopped
off the cage he used as a seat, and placed a hand
on the butt of his sharp *wtsai*. The other bore
scabs on his breast and wore no bandolier. He had
been tinkering with the innards of a small stasis
cage, but whirled, jaw agape.

"It must have escaped after we left, yesterday,"
said the priest, looking at the "captive," then with
fresh curiosity at Scarface. "And who are—"

At that instant, Locklear saw what levitated,
spinning, inside one of the medium-sized cages;
spinning almost too fast to identify. But Locklear
knew what it had to be, and while the priest was
staring hard at Scarface, the little man lost control.

His cry was in Interworld, not Kzin: "You filthy
bastard!" Before the priest could react, a round-
house right with the massive barrel of a kzin
pistol took away both upper and lower incisors
from the left side of his mouth. Caught this suddenly, even a two-hundred kilo kzin could be
sent reeling from the blow, and as the priest reeled
to his right, Locklear kicked hard at his backside.

Scarface clubbed at the second kzin, the corridor ringing with snarls and zaps of warrior rage. Locklear did not even notice, leaping on the back of the fallen priest, hacking with his gun barrel until the *wtsai* flew from a smashed hand, kicking down with all his might against the back of the priest's head. The priest, at least twice Locklear's bulk, had lived a life much too soft, for far too long. He rolled over, eyes wide not in fear but in anger at this outrage from a puny beast. It is barely possible that fear might have worked.

The priest caught Locklear's boot in a mouthful of broken teeth, not seeing the sidearm as it swung at his temple. The thump was like an iron bar against a melon, the priest falling limp as suddenly as if some switch had been thrown.

Sobbing, Locklear dropped the pistol, grabbed handfuls of ear on each side, and pounded the priest's head against cruel obsidian until he felt a heavy grip on his shoulder.

"He is dead, Locklear. Save your strength," Scarface advised. As Locklear recovered his weapon and stumbled to his feet, he was shaking uncontrollably. "You must hate our kind more than I thought," Scarface added, studying Locklear oddly.

"He wasn't your kind. I would kill a man for the same crime," Locklear said in fury, glaring at the second kzin who squatted, bloody-faced, in a corner holding a forearm with an extra elbow in it. Then Locklear rushed to open the cage the priest had been watching.

The top levered back, and its occupant sank to the cage floor without moving. Scarface screamed his rage, turning toward the injured captive. "You experiment on tiny kittens? Shall we do the same to you now?"

Locklear, his tears flowing freely, lifted the tiny kzin kitten—a male—in hands that were tender, holding it to his breast. "It's breathing," he said. "A miracle, after getting the centrifuge treatment in a cage meant for something far bigger."

"Before I kill you, do something honorable," Scarface said to the wounded one. "Tell me where the other kitten is."

The captive pointed toward the end of the passage. "I am only an acolyte," he muttered. "I did not enjoy following orders."

Locklear sped along the cages and, at last, found Boot's female kitten revolving slowly in a cage of the proper size. He realized from the prominence of the tiny ribs that the kitten would cry for milk when it waked. *If* it waked. "Is she still alive?"

"Yes," the acolyte called back. "I am glad this happened. I can die with a less-troubled conscience."

After a hurried agreement and some rough questioning, they gave the acolyte a choice. He climbed into a cage hidden behind others at the end of another corridor and was soon revolving in stasis. The kittens went into one small cage. Working feverishly against the time when another enemy might walk into the crypt, they disassembled several more stasis cages and toted the working parts to the scooter, then added the kitten cage and, barely, levitated the scooter with its heavy load.

An hour later, Scarface bore the precious cage into the cave and Locklear, following with an armload of parts, heard the anguish of Boots. "They'll hear you from a hundred meters," he cautioned as Boots gathered the mewing, emaciated kittens in her arms.

They feared at first that her milk would no longer flow but presently, from where Boots had crept into the darkness, Kit returned. "They are suckling. Do not expect her to be much help from now on," Kit said.

Scarface checked the magazine of his sidearm. "One priest has paid. There is no reason why I cannot extract full payment from the others now," he said.

"Yes, there is," Locklear replied, his fingers flying with hand tools from the cache. "Before you can get 'em all, they'll send devout fools to be killed while they escape. You said so yourself. Scarface, I don't want innocent kzin blood on my hands! But after my old promise to Boots, I saw what that maniac was doing and—let's just say *my* honor was at stake." He knew that any modern kzin commander would understand that. Setting down the wiring tool, he shuddered and waited until he could speak without a tremor in his voice. "If you'll help me get the wiring rigged for these stasis units, we can hide them in the right spot and take the entire bloody priesthood in one pile."

"All at once? I should like to know how," said Kit, counting the few units that lay around them.

"Well, I'll tell you how," said Locklear, his eyes bright with fervor. They heard him out, and then their faces glowed with the same zeal.

When their traps lay ready for emplacement, they slept while Kit kept watch. Long after dark, as Boots lay nearby cradling her kittens, Kit waked the others and served a cold broth. "You take a terrible chance, flying in the dark," she reminded them.

"We will move slowly," Scarface promised, "and the village fires shed enough light for me to land.

Too bad about the senses of inferior species," he said, his ear umbrellas rising with his joke.

"How would you like a nice cold bath, tabby?" Locklear's question was mild, but it held an edge.

"Only monkeys *need* to bathe," said the kzin, still amused. Together they carried their hardware outside and, by the light of a glowlamp, loaded the scooter while Kit watched for any telltale glow of eyes in the distance.

After a hurried nuzzle from Kit, Scarface brought the scooter up swiftly, switching the glowlamp to its pinpoint setting and using it as seldom as possible. Their forward motion was so slow that, on the two occasions when they blundered into the tops of towering fernpalms, they jettisoned nothing more than soft curses. An hour later, Scarface maneuvered them over a light yellow strip that became a heavily trodden path and began to follow that path by brief glowlamp flashes. The village, they knew, would eventually come into view.

It was Locklear who said, "Off to your right."

"The village fires? I saw them minutes ago."

"Oh shut up, supercat," Locklear grumped. "So where's our drop zone?"

"Near," was the reply, and Locklear felt their little craft swing to the side. At the pace of a weed seed, the scooter wafted down until Scarface, with one leg hanging through the viewslot of his craft, spat a short, nasty phrase. One quick flash of the lamp guided him to a level landing spot and then, with admirable panache, Scarface let the scooter settle without a creak.

If they were surprised now, only Scarface could pilot his scooter with any hope of getting them both away. Locklear grabbed one of the devices they had prepared and, feeling his way with only his feet, walked until he felt a rise of turf. Then he retraced his steps, vented a heavy sigh, and began the emplacement.

Ten minutes later he felt his way back to the scooter, tapping twice on one of its planks to avoid getting his head bitten off by an all-too-ready Scarface. "So far, so good," Locklear judged.

"This had better work," Scarface muttered.

"Tell me about it," said the retreating Locklear, grunting with a pair of stasis toroids. After the stasis units were all in place, Locklear rested at the scooter before creeping off again, this time with the glowlamp and a very sloppy wiring harness.

When he returned for the last time, he virtually fell onto the scooter. "It's all there," he said, exhausted, rubbing wrists still raw from his brief captivity. Scarface found his bearings again, but it was another hour before he floated up an arroyo and then used the lamp for a landing light.

He bore the sleeping Locklear into the cave as a man might carry a child. Soon they both were snoring, and Locklear did not hear the sound that terrified the distant villagers in late morning.

Locklear's first hint that his plans were in shreds came with rough shaking by Scarface. "Wake up! The monkeys have declared war," were the first words he understood.

As they lay at the main cave entrance, they could see sweeps of the pinnace as it moved over the kzin village. Small energy beams lanced down several times, at targets too widely spaced to be the huts. "They're targeting whatever moves," Locklear ranted, pounding a fist on hard turf. "And I'll bet the priests are hiding!"

Scarface brought up his all-band set and let it

scan. In moments, the voice of David Gomulka grated from the speaker. ". . . Kill 'em all. Tell 'em, Locklear! And when they do let you go, you'd better be ready to talk; over."

"I can talk to 'em any time I like, you know," Locklear said to his friend. "The set they gave me may have a coded carrier wave."

"We must stop this terror raid," Scarface replied, "before they kill us all!"

Locklear stripped his sidearm magazine of its rounds and fingered the tiny ear set from its metal cage, screwing it into his ear. "Got me tied up," he said, trying to ignore the disgusted look from Scarface at this unseemly lie. "Are you receiving . . ."

"We'll home in on your signal," Gomulka cut in.

Locklear quickly shoved the tiny set back into the butt of his sidearm. "No, you won't," he muttered to himself. Turning to Scarface: "We've got to transmit from another place, or they'll triangulate on me."

Racing to the scooter, they fled to the arroyo and skimmed the veldt to another spot. Then, still moving, Locklear used the tiny set again. "Gomulka, they're moving me."

The sergeant, furiously: "Where the fuck—?"

Locklear: "If you're shooting, let the naked savages alone. The real tabbies are the ones with bandoliers, got it? Bag 'em if you can but the naked ones aren't combatants."

He put his little set away again but Scarface's unit, on "receive only," picked up the reply. "Your goddamn signal is shooting all over hell, Locklear. And whaddaya mean, not combatants? I've never had a chance to hunt tabbies like this. No little civilian shit is gonna tell us we can't teach 'em what it's like to be hunted! You got that, Locklear?"

They continued to monitor Gomulka, skating back near the cave until the scooter lay beneath spreading ferns. Fleeing into the safety of the cave, they agreed on a terrible necessity. "They intend to take ears and tails as trophies, or so they say," Locklear admitted. "You must find the most peaceable of your tribe, Boots, and bring them to the cave. They'll be cut down like so many vermin if you don't."

"No priests, and no acolytes," Scarface snarled. "Say nothing about us but you may warn them that no priest will leave this cave alive! That much, my honor requires."

"I understand," said Boots, whirling down one of the tunnels.

"And you and I," Scarface said to Locklear, "must lure that damned monkeyship away from this area. We cannot let them see kzinti streaming in here."

In early afternoon, the scooter slid along rocky highlands before settling beneath a stone overhang. "The best cover for snipers on Kzersatz, Locklear. I kept my cache here, and I know every cranny and clearing. We just may trap that monkeyship, if I am clever enough at primitive skills."

"You want to trap them here? Nothing simpler," said Locklear, bringing out his tiny comm set.

But it was not to be so simple.

Locklear, lying in the open on his back with one hand under saffron vines, watched the pinnace thrum overhead. The clearing, ringed by tall fernpalms, was big enough for the *Anthony Wayne*, almost capacious for a pinnace. Locklear raised one hand in greeting as he counted four heads inside the canopy: Gomulka, Lee, Gazho, and Schmidt. Then he let his head fall back in pretended exhaustion, and waited.

In vain. The pinnace settled ten meters away, its engines still above idle, and the canopy levered up; but the deserter crew had beam rifles trained on the surrounding foliage and did not accept the bait. "They may be back soon," Locklear shouted in Interworld. He could hear the faint savage ripping at vegetation nearby, and wondered if they heard it, too. "Hurry!"

"Tell us now, asshole," Gomulka boomed, his voice coming both from the earpiece and the pinnace. "The secret, *now*, or we leave you for the tabbies!"

Locklear licked his lips, buying seconds. "It's— It's some kind of drive. The Outsiders built it here," he groaned, wondering feverishly what the devil his tongue was leading him into. He noted that Gazho and Lee had turned toward him now, their eyes blazing with greed. Schmidt, however, was studying the tallest fernpalm, and suddenly fired a thin line of fire slashing into its top, which was already shuddering.

"Not good enough, Locklear," Gomulka called. "We've got great drives already. Tell us where it is."

"In a cavern. Other side of—valley," Locklear said, taking his time. "Nobody has an—instantaneous drive but Outsiders," he finished.

A whoop of delight, then, from Gomulka, one second before that fernpalm began to topple. Schmidt was already watching it, and screamed a warning in time for the pilot to see the slender forest giant begin its agonizingly slow fall. Gomulka hit the panic button.

Too late. The pinnace, darting forward with its canopy still up, rose to meet the spreading top of the tree Scarface had cut using claws and fangs alone. As the pinnace was borne to the ground, its canopy twisting off its hinges, the swish of foliage and squeal of metal filled the air. Locklear leaped aside, rolling away.

Among the yells of consternation, Gomulka's was loudest. "Schmidt, you dumb fuck!"

"It was him," Schmidt yelled, coming upright again to train his rifle on Locklear—who fired first. If that slug had hit squarely, Schmidt would have been dead meat but its passage along Schmidt's forearm left only a deep bloody crease.

Gomulka, every inch a warrior, let fly with his own sidearm though his nose was bleeding from the impact. But Locklear, now protected by another tree, returned the fire and saw a hole appear in the canopy next to the wide-staring eyes of Nathan Gazho.

When Scarface cut loose from thirty meters away, Gomulka made the right decision. Yelling commands, laying down a cover of fire first toward Locklear, then toward Scarface, he drove his team out of the immobile pinnace by sheer voice command while he peered past the armored lip of the cockpit.

Scarface's call, in Kzin, probably could not be understood by the others, but Locklear could not have agreed more. "Fight, run, fight again," came the snarling cry.

Five minutes later after racing downhill, Locklear dropped behind one end of a fallen log and grinned at Scarface, who lay at its other end. "Nice aim with that tree."

"I despise chewing vegetable matter," was the reply. "Do you think they can get that pinnace in operation again?"

"With safety interlocks? It won't move at more than a crawl until somebody repairs the—" but Locklear fell silent at a sudden gesture.

From uphill, a stealthy movement as Gomulka scuttled behind a hillock. Then to their right, another brief rush by Schmidt who held his rifle one-handed now. This advance, basic to any team using projectile weapons, would soon overrun their quarry. The big blond was in the act of dropping behind a fern when Scarface's round caught him squarely in the breast, the rifle flying away, and Locklear saw answering fire send tendrils of smoke from his log. He was only a flicker behind Scarface, firing blindly to force enemy heads down, as they bolted downhill again in good cover.

Twice more, during the next hour, they opened up at long range to slow Gomulka's team. At that range they had no success. Later, drawing nearer to the village, they lay behind stones at the lip of an arroyo. "With only three," Scarface said with satisfaction. "They are advancing more slowly."

"And we're wasting ammo," Locklear replied. "I have, uh, two eights and four rounds left. You?"

"Eight and seven. Not enough against beam rifles." The big kzin twisted, then, ear umbrellas cocked toward the village. He studied the sun's position, then came to some internal decision and handed over ten of his precious remaining rounds. "The brush in the arroyo's throat looks flimsy, Locklear, but I could crawl under its tops, so I know you can. Hold them up here, then retreat

under the brushtops in the arroyo and wait at its
mouth. With any luck I will reach you there."

The kzin warrior was already leaping toward
the village. Locklear cried softly. "Where are you
going?"

The reply was almost lost in the arroyo: "For
reinforcements."

The sun had crept far across the sky of Kzersatz
before Locklear saw movement again, and when
he did it was nearly too late. A stone descended
the arroyo, whacking another stone with the crack
of bowling balls; Locklear realized that someone
had already crossed the arroyo. Then he saw
Soichiro Lee ease his rifle into sight. Lee simply
had not spotted him.

Locklear took two-handed aim very slowly and
fired three rounds, full-auto. The first impact puffed
dirt into Lee's face so that Locklear did not see
the others clearly. It was enough that Lee's head
blossomed, snapping up and back so hard it jerked
his torso, and the rifle clattered into the arroyo.

The call of alarm from Gazho was so near it
spooked Locklear into firing blindly. Then he was
bounding into the arroyo's throat, sliding into chest-
high brush with spreading tops.

Late shadows were his friends as he waited,
hoping one of the men would go for the beam rifle
in plain sight. Now and then he sat up and lobbed
a stone into brush not far from Lee's body. Twice,
rifles scorched that brush. Locklear knew better
than to fire back without a sure target while pinned
in that ravine.

When they began sending heavy fire into the
throat of the arroyo, Locklear hoped they would
exhaust their plenums, but saw a shimmer of heat

and knew his cover could burn. He wriggled away downslope, past a trickle of water, careful to avoid shaking the brush. It was then that he heard the heavy reports of a kzin sidearm toward the village.

He nearly shot the rope-muscled kzin that sprang into the ravine before recognizing Scarface, but within a minute they had worked their way together. "Those kshat priests," Scarface panted, "have harangued a dozen others into chasing me. I killed one priest; the others are staying safely behind."

"So where are our reinforcements?"

"The dark will transform them."

"But we'll be caught between enemies," Locklear pointed out.

"Who will engage each other in darkness, a dozen fools against three monkeys."

"Two," Locklear corrected. But he saw the logic now, and when the sunlight winked out a few minutes later he was watching the stealthy movement of kzin acolytes along both lips of the arroyo.

Mouth close to Locklear's ear, Scarface said, "They will send someone up this watercourse. Move aside; my *wtsai* will deal with them quietly."

But when a military flare lit the upper reaches of the arroyo a few minutes later, they heard battle screams and suddenly, comically, two kzin warriors came bounding directly between Locklear and Scarface. Erect, heads above the brushtops, they leapt toward the action and were gone in a moment.

Following with one hand on a furry arm, Locklear stumbled blindly to the arroyo lip and sat down to watch. Spears and torches hurtled from one side of the upper ravine while thin energy bursts lanced out from the other. Blazing brush lent a flickering light as well, and at least three great kzin bodies surged across the arroyo toward their enemies.

"At times," Scarface said quietly as if to himself, "I think my species more valiant than stupid. But they do not even know their enemy, nor care."

"Same for those deserters," Locklear muttered, fascinated at the firefight his friend had provoked. "So how do we get back to the cave?"

"This way," Scarface said, tapping his nose, and set off with Locklear stumbling at his heels.

The cave seemed much smaller when crowded with a score of worried kzinti, but not for long. The moment they realized that Kit was missing, Scarface demanded to know why.

"Two acolytes entered," explained one male, and Locklear recognized him as the mild-tempered Stalwart. "They argued three idiots into helping take her back to the village before dark."

Locklear, in quiet fury: "No one stopped them?"

Stalwart pointed to bloody welts on his arms and neck, then at a female lying curled on a grassy pallet. "I had no help but her. She tried to offer herself instead."

And then Scarface saw that it was Boots who was hurt but nursing her kittens in silence, and no cave could have held his rage. Screaming, snarling, claws raking tails, he sent the entire pack of refugees pelting into the night, to return home as best they could. It was Locklear's idea to let Stalwart remain; he had, after all, shed his blood in their cause.

Scarface did not subside until he saw Locklear, with the kzin medkit, ministering to Boots. "A fine ally, but no expert in kzin medicine," he scolded, choosing different unguents.

Boots, shamed at having permitted acolytes in the cave, pointed out that the traps had been disarmed for the flow of refugees. "The priesthood will surely be back here soon," she added.

"Not before afternoon," Stalwart said. "They never mount ceremonies during darkness. If I am any judge, they will drown the beauteous *prret* at high noon."

Locklear: "Don't they ever learn?"

Boots: "No. They are the priesthood," she said as if explaining everything, and Stalwart agreed.

"All the same," Scarface said, "they might do a better job this time. You," he said to Stalwart; "could you get to the village and back here in darkness?"

"If I cannot, call me acolyte. You would learn what they intend for your mate?"

"Of course he must," Locklear said, walking with him toward the main entrance. "But call before you enter again. We are setting deadly traps for anyone who tries to return, and you may as well spread the word."

Stalwart moved off into darkness, sniffing the breeze, and Locklear went from place to place, switching on traps while Scarface tended Boots. This tender care from a kzin warrior might be explained as gratitude; even with her kittens, Boots had tried to substitute herself for Kit. Still, Locklear thought, there was more to it than that. He wondered about it until he fell asleep.

Twice during the night, they were roused by tremendous thumps and, once, a brief kzin snarl. Scarface returned each time licking blood from his arms. The second time he said to a bleary-eyed Locklear, "We can plug the entrances with corpses if these acolytes keep squashing themselves against our ceilings." The grav polarizer traps, it seemed, made excellent sentries.

Locklear did not know when Stalwart returned but, when he awoke, the young kzin was already speaking with Scarface. True to their rigid code, the priests fully intended to drown Kit again in a noon ceremony using heavier stones and, afterward, to lay siege to the cave.

"Let them; it will be empty," Scarface grunted. "Locklear, you have seen me pilot my little craft. I wonder . . ."

"Hardest part is getting around those deserters, if any," Locklear said. "I can cover a lot of ground when I'm fresh."

"Good. Can you navigate to where Boots had her birthing bower before noon?"

"If I can't, call me acolyte," Locklear said, smiling. He set off at a lope just after dawn, achingly alert. Anyone he met, now, would be a target.

After an hour, he was lost. He found his bearings from a promontory, loping longer, walking less, and was dizzy with fatigue when he climbed a low cliff to the overhang where Scarface had left his scooter. Breathing hard, he was lowering his rump to the scooter when the rifle butt whistled just over his head.

Nathan Gazho, who had located the scooter after scouring the area near the pinnace, felt fierce glee when he saw Locklear's approach. But he had not expected Locklear to drop so suddenly. He swung again as Locklear, almost as large as his opponent, darted in under the blow. Locklear grunted with the impact against his shoulder, caught the weapon by its barrel, and used it like a prybar with both hands though his left arm was growing numb. The rifle spun out of reach. As they struggled away from the ten-meter precipice, Gazho cursed—the first word by either man—and snatched his utility knife from its belt clasp, reeling back, his left forearm out. His crouch, the shifting of the knife, its extraordinary honed edge: marks of a man who had fought with knives before.

Locklear reached for the kzin sidearm but he had placed it in a left-hand pocket and now that hand was numb. Gazho darted forward in a swordsman's balestra, flicking the knife in a short arc as he passed. By that time Locklear had snatched his own *wtsai* from its sheath with his right hand. Gazho saw the long blade but did not flinch, and Locklear knew he was running out of time. Standing four paces away, he pump-faked twice as if to throw the knife. Gazho's protecting forearm flashed to the vertical at the same instant when Locklear leaped forward, hurling the *wtsai* as he squatted to grasp a stone of fist size.

Because Locklear was no knife-thrower, the weapon did not hit point-first; but the heavy handle caught Gazho squarely on the temple and, as he stumbled back, Locklear's stone splintered his jaw. Nathan Gazho's legs buckled and inertia carried him backward over the precipice, screaming.

Locklear heard the heavy thump as he was fumbling for his sidearm. From above, he could see the broken body twitching, and his single round from the sidearm was more kindness than revenge. Trembling, massaging his left arm, he collected his *wtsai* and the beam rifle before crawling onto the scooter. Not until he levitated the little craft and guided it ineptly down the mountainside did he notice the familiar fittings of the standard-issue rifle. It had been fully discharged during the firefight, thanks to Scarface's tactic.

Many weeks before—it seemed a geologic age by now—Locklear had found Boots' private bower by accident. The little cave was hidden behind a low waterfall near the mouth of a shallow ravine, and once he had located that ravine from the air it was only a matter of following it, keeping low enough to avoid being seen from the kzin village. The sun was almost directly overhead as Locklear approached the rendezvous. If he'd cut it too close . . .

Scarface waved him down near the falls and sprang onto the scooter before it could settle. "Let me fly it," he snarled, shoving Locklear aside in a way that suggested a kzin on the edge of self-control. The scooter lunged forward and, as he hung on, Locklear told of Gazho's death.

"It will not matter," Scarface replied as he piloted the scooter higher, squinting toward the village, "if my mate dies this day." Then his predator's eyesight picked out the horrifying details, and he began to gnash his teeth in uncontrollable fury.

When they were within a kilometer of the village, Locklear could see what had pushed his friend beyond sanity. While most of the villagers stood back as if to distance themselves from this pomp and circumstance, the remaining acolytes bore a bound, struggling burden toward the lakeshore. Behind them marched the bandoliered priests, arms waving beribboned lances. They were chanting, a cacophony like metal chaff thrown into a power transformer, and Locklear shuddered.

Even at top speed, they would not arrive until

that procession reached the walkway to deep water; and Kit, her limbs bound together with great stones for weights, would not be able to escape this time. "We'll have to go in after her," Locklear called into the wind.

"I cannot swim," cried Scarface, his eyes slitted.

"I can," said Locklear, taking great breaths to hoard oxygen. As he positioned himself for the leap, his friend began to fire his sidearm.

As the scooter swept lower and slower, one kzin priest crumpled. The rest saw the scooter and exhorted the acolytes forward. The hapless Kit was flung without further ceremony into deep water but, as he was leaping feet-first off the scooter, Locklear saw that she had spotted him. As he slammed into deep water, he could hear the full-automatic thunder of Scarface's weapon.

Misjudging his leap, Locklear let inertia carry him before striking out forward and down. His left arm was only at half-strength but the weight of his weapons helped carry him to the sandy bottom. Eyes open, he struggled to the one darker mass looming ahead.

But it was only a small boulder. Feeling the prickles of oxygen starvation across his back and scalp, he swiveled, kicking hard—and felt one foot strike something like fur. He wheeled, ignoring the demands of his lungs, wresting his *wtsai* out with one hand as he felt for cordage with the other. Three ferocious slices, and those cords were severed. He dropped the knife—the same weapon Kit herself had once dulled, then resharpened for him—and pushed off from the bottom in desperation.

He broke the surface, gasped twice, and saw a

wide-eyed priest fling a lance in his direction. By sheer dumb luck, it missed, and after a last deep inhalation Locklear kicked toward the bottom again.

The last thing a wise man would do is locate a drowning tigress in deep water, but that is what Locklear did. Kit, no swimmer, literally climbed up his sodden flightsuit, forcing him into an underwater somersault, fine sand stinging his eyes. The next moment he was struggling toward the light again, disoriented and panicky.

He broke the surface, swam to a piling at the end of the walkway, and tried to hyperventilate for another hopeless foray after Kit. Then, between gasps, he heard a spitting cough echo in the space between the water's surface and the underside of the walkway. "Kit!" He swam forward, seeing her frightened gaze and her formidable claws locked into those rough planks, and patted her shoulder. Above them, someone was raising kzin hell. "Stay here," he commanded, and kicked off toward the shallows.

He waded with his sidearm drawn. What he saw on the walkway was abundant proof that the priesthood truly did not seem to learn very fast.

Five bodies sprawled where they had been shot, bleeding on the planks near deep water, but more of them lay curled on the planks within a few paces of the shore, piled atop one another. One last acolyte stood on the walkway, staring over the curled bodies. He was staring at Scarface, who stood on dry land with his own long *wtsai* held before him, snarling a challenge with eyes that held the light of madness. Then, despite what he had seen happen a half-dozen times in moments, the acolyte screamed and leaped.

Losing consciousness in midair, the acolyte fell

heavily across his fellows and drew into a foetal crouch, as all the others had done when crossing the last six meters of planking toward shore. Those units Locklear had placed beneath the planks in darkness had kept three-ton herbivores in stasis, and worked even better on kzinti. They'd known damned well the priesthood would be using the walkway again sooner or later; but they'd had no idea it would be *this* soon.

Scarface did not seem entirely sane again until he saw Kit wading from the water. Then he clasped his mate to him, ignoring the wetness he so despised. Asked how he managed to trip the gang-switch, Scarface replied, "You had told me it was on the inside of that piling, and those idiots did not try to stop me from wading to it."

"I noticed you were wet," said Locklear, smiling. "Sorry about that."

"I shall be wetter with blood presently," Scarface said with a grim look toward the pile of inert sleepers.

Locklear, aghast, opened his mouth.

But Kit placed her hand over it. "Rockear, I know you, and I know my mate. It is not your way but this is Kzersatz. Did you see what they did to the captive they took last night?"

"Big man, short black hair? His name is Gomulka."

"His name is meat. What they left of him hangs from a post yonder."

"Oh my God," Locklear mumbled, swallowing hard. "But—look, just don't ask me to help execute anyone in stasis."

"Indeed." Scarface stood, stretched, and walked toward the piled bodies. "You may want to take a brief walk, Locklear," he said, picking up a discarded lance twice his length. "This is kzin business, not monkey business." But he did not understand why, as Locklear strode away, the little man was laughing ruefully at the choice of words.

Locklear's arm was well enough, after two days, to let him dive for his *wtsai* while kzinti villagers watched in curiosity—and perhaps in distaste. By that time they had buried their dead in a common plot and, with the help of Stalwart, begun to repair the pinnace's canopy holes and twisted hinges. The little hand-welder would have sped the job greatly but, Locklear promised, "We'll get it back. If we don't hit first, there'll be a stolen warship overhead with enough clout to fry us all."

Scarface had to agree. As the warrior who had overthrown the earlier regime, he now held not only the rights, but also the responsibilities of leading his people. Lounging on grassy beds in the village's meeting hut on the third night, they slurped hot stew and made plans. "Only the two of us can make that raid, you know," said the big kzin.

"I was thinking of volunteers," said Locklear, who knew very well that Scarface would honor his wish if he made it a demand.

"If we had time to train them," Scarface replied. "But that ship could be searching for the pinnace at any moment. Only you and I can pilot the pinnace so, if we are lost in battle, those volunteers will be stranded forever among hostile monk—hostiles," he amended. "Nor can they use modern weapons."

"Stalwart probably could, he's a natural mechanic. I know Kit can use a weapon—not that I want her along."

"For a better reason than you know," Scarface agreed, his ears winking across the fire at the somnolent Kit.

"He is trying to say I will soon bear his kittens, Rockear," Kit said. "And please do not take Boots' new mate away merely because he can work magics with his hands." She saw the surprise in Locklear's face. "How could you miss that? He fought those acolytes in the cave for Boots' sake."

"I, uh, guess I've been pretty busy," Locklear admitted.

"We will be busier if that warship strikes before we do," Scarface reminded him. "I suggest we go as soon as it is light."

Locklear sat bolt upright. "Damn! If they hadn't taken my wristcomp—I keep forgetting. The schedules of those little suns aren't in synch; it's probably daylight there now, and we can find out by idling the pinnace near the force walls. You can damned well see whether it's light there."

"I would rather go in darkness," Scarface complained, "if we could master those night-vision sensors in the pinnace."

"Maybe, in time. I flew the thing here to the village, didn't I?"

"In daylight, after a fashion," Scarface said in a friendly insult, and flicked his sidearm from its holster to check its magazine. "Would you like to fly it again, right now?"

Kit saw the little man fill his hand as he checked his own weapon, and marveled at a creature with the courage to show such puny teeth in such a feral grin. "I know you must go," she said as they turned toward the door, and nuzzled the throat of her mate. "But what do we do if you fail?"

"You expect enemies with the biggest ship you ever saw," Locklear said. "And you know how those stasis traps work. Just remember, those people have night sensors and they can burn you from a distance."

Scarface patted her firm belly once. "Take great care," he said, and strode into darkness.

The pinnace's controls were simple, and Locklear's only worry was the thin chorus of whistles: air, escaping from a canopy that was not quite perfectly sealed. He briefed Scarface yet again as their craft carried them over Newduvai, and piloted the pinnace so that its reentry thunder would roll gently, as far as possible from the *Anthony Wayne*.

It was late morning on Newduvai, and they could see the gleam of the *Wayne*'s hull from afar. Locklear slid the pinnace at a furtive pace, brushing spiny shrubs for the last few kilometers before landing in a small desert wadi. They pulled hinge pins from the canopy and hid them in the pinnace to make its theft tedious. Then, stuffing a roll of binder tape into his pocket, Locklear began to trot toward his clearing.

"I am a kitten again," Scarface rejoiced, fairly floating along in the reduced gravity of Newduvai. Then he slowed, nose twitching. "Not far," he warned.

Locklear nodded, moved cautiously ahead, and then sat behind a green thicket. Ahead lay the clearing with the warship and cabin, seeming little changed—but a heavy limb held the door shut as if to keep things in, not out. And Scarface noticed two mansized craters just outside the cabin's foundation logs. After ten minutes without sound or movement from the clearing, Scarface was ready to employ what he called the monkey ruse; not quite a lie, but certainly a misdirection.

"Patience," Locklear counseled. "I thought you tabbies were hunters."

"Hunters, yes; not skulkers."

"No wonder you lose wars," Locklear muttered. But after another half-hour in which they ghosted in deep cover around the clearing, he too was ready to move.

The massive kzin sighed, slid his *wtsai* to the rear and handed over his sidearm, then dutifully held his big pawlike hands out. Locklear wrapped the thin, bright red binder tape around his friend's wrists many times, then severed it with its special stylus. Scarface was certain he could bite it through until he tried. Then he was happy to let Locklear draw the stylus, with its chemical enabler, across the tape where the slit could not be seen. Then, hailing the clearing as he went, the little man drew his own *wtsai* and prodded his "prisoner" toward the cabin.

His neck crawling with premonition, Locklear stood five paces from the door and called again: "Hello, the cabin!"

From inside, several female voices and then only one, which he knew very well: "Locklear go soon soon!"

"Ruth says that many times," he replied, half amused, though he knew somehow that this time she feared for him. "New people keep gentles inside?"

Scarface, standing uneasily, had his ear umbrellas moving fore and aft. He mumbled something as, from inside, Ruth said, "Ruth teach new talk to gentles, get food. No teach, no food," she explained with vast economy.

"I'll see about that," he called and then, in Kzin, "what was that, Scarface?"

Low but urgent: "Behind us, fool."

Locklear turned. Not twenty paces away, Anse Parker was moving forward as silently as he could and now the hatchway of the *Anthony Wayne* yawned open. Parker's rifle hung from its sling but his service parabellum was leveled, and he was smirking. "If this don't beat all: my prisoner has a prisoner," he drawled.

For a frozen instant, Locklear feared the deserter had spied the *wtsai* hanging above Scarface's backside—but the kzin's tail was erect, hiding the weapon. "Where are the others?" Locklear asked.

"Around. Pacifyin' the natives in that tabby lifeboat," Parker replied. "I'll ask you the same question, asshole."

The parabellum was not wavering. Locklear stepped away from his friend, who faced Parker so that the wrist tape was obvious. "Gomulka's boys are in trouble. Promised me amnesty if I'd come for help, and I brought a hostage," Locklear said.

Parker's movements were not fast, but so casual that Locklear was taken by surprise. The parabellum's short barrel whipped across his face, splitting his lip, bowling him over. Parker stood over him, sneering. "Buncha shit. If that happened, you'd hide out. You can tell a better one than that."

Locklear privately realized that Parker was right. And then Parker himself, who had turned half away from Scarface, made a discovery of his own. He discovered that, without moving one step, a kzin could reach out a long way to stick the point of a *wtsai* against a man's throat. Parker froze.

"If you shoot me, you are deader than chivalry," Locklear said, propping himself up on an elbow. "Toss the pistol away."

Parker, cursing, did so, looking at Scarface, finding his chance as the kzin glanced toward the weapon. Parker shied away with a sidelong leap, snatching for his slung rifle. And ignoring the leg of Locklear who tripped him nicely.

As his rifle tumbled into grass, Parker rolled to his feet and began sprinting for the warship two hundred meters away. Scarface outran him easily, then stationed himself in front of the warship's hatch. Locklear could not hear Parker's words, but his gestures toward the *wtsai* were clear: there ain't no justice.

Scarface understood. With that kzin grin that so many humans failed to understand, he tossed the *wtsai* near Parker's feet in pure contempt. Parker grabbed the knife and saw his enemy's face, howled in fear, then raced into the forest, Scarface bounding lazily behind.

Locklear knocked the limb away from his cabin door and found Ruth inside with three others, all young females. He embraced the homely Ruth with great joy. The other young Neanderthalers disappeared from the clearing in seconds but Ruth walked off with Locklear. He had already seen the spider grenades that lay with sensors outspread just outside the cabin's walls. Two gentles had already died trying to dig their way out, she said.

He tried to prepare Ruth for his ally's appearance but, when Scarface reappeared with his *wtsai*, she needed time to adjust. "I don't see any blood," was Locklear's comment.

"The blood of cowards is distasteful," was the

kzin's wry response. "I believe you have my side-arm, friend Locklear."

They should have counted, said Locklear, on Stockton learning to fly the kzin lifeboat. But lacking heavy weapons, it might not complicate their capture strategy too much. As it happened, the capture was more absurd than complicated.

Stockton brought the lifeboat bumbling down in late afternoon almost in the same depressions the craft's jackpads had made previously, within fifty paces of the *Anthony Wayne*. He and the lissome Grace wore holstered pistols, stretching out their muscle kinks as they walked toward the bigger craft, unaware that they were being watched. "Anse; we're back," Stockton shouted. "Any word from Gomulka?"

Silence from the ship, though its hatch steps were down. Grace shrugged, then glanced at Locklear's cabin. "The door prop is down, Curt. He's trying to hump those animals again."

"Damn him," Stockton railed, and both turned toward the cabin. To Grace he complained, "If you were a better lay, he wouldn't always be— *good God!*"

The source of his alarm was a long blood-chilling, gut-wrenching scream. A kzin scream, the kind featured in horror holovision productions; and very, very near. "Battle stations, red alert, up ship," Stockton cried, bolting for the hatch.

Briefly, he had his pistol ready but had to grip it in his teeth as he reached for the hatch rails of the *Anthony Wayne*. For that one moment he almost resembled a piratical man of action, and that was the moment when he stopped, one foot on the top step, and Grace bumped her head against his rump as she fled up those steps.

"I don't think so," said Locklear softly. To Curt
Stockton, the muzzle of that alien sidearm so near
must have looked like a torpedo launcher. His
face drained of color, the commander allowed
Locklear to take the pistol from his trembling lips.
"And Grace," Locklear went on, because he could
not see her past Stockton's bulk, "I doubt if it's
your style anyway, but don't give your pistol a
second thought. That kzin you heard? Well, they're
out there behind you, but they aren't in here.
Toss your parabellum away and I'll let you in."

Late the next afternoon they finished walling up
the crypt on Newduvai, with a small work force of
willing hands recruited by Ruth. As the little group
of gentles filed away down the hillside, Scarface
nodded toward the rubble-choked entrance. "I
still believe we should have executed those two,
Locklear."

"I know you do. But they'll keep in stasis for as
long as the war lasts, and on Newduvai—well,
Ruth's people agree with me that there's been
enough killing." Locklear turned his back on the
crypt and Ruth moved to his side, still wary of the
huge alien whose speech sounded like the sizzle of
fat on a skewer.

"Your ways are strange," said the kzin, as they
walked toward the nearby pinnace. "I know something of Interworld beauty standards. As long as
you want that female lieutenant alive, it seems to
me you would keep her, um, available."

"Grace Agostinho's beauty is all on the outside.
And there's a girl hiding somewhere on Newduvai
that those deserters never did catch. In a few
years she'll be—well, you'll meet her someday."
Locklear put an arm around Ruth's waist and

grinned. "The truth is, Ruth thinks *I'm* pretty funny-looking, but some things you can learn to overlook."

At the clearing, Ruth hopped from the pinnace first. "Ruth will fix place nice, like before," she promised, and walked to the cabin.

"She's learning Interworld fast," Locklear said proudly. "Her telepathy helps—in a lot of ways. Scarface, do you realize that her people may be the most tremendous discovery of modern times? And the irony of it! The empathy these people share probably helped isolate them from the modern humans that came from their own gene pool. Yet their kind of empathy might be the only viable future for us." He sighed and stepped to the turf. "Sometimes I wonder whether I want to be found."

Standing beside the pinnace, they gazed at the *Anthony Wayne*. Scarface said, "With that warship, you could do the finding."

Locklear assessed the longing in the face of the big kzin. "I know how you feel about piloting, Scarface. But you must accept that I can't let you have any craft more advanced than your scooter back on Kzersatz."

"But—surely, the pinnace or my own lifeboat?"

"You see that?" Locklear pointed toward the forest.

Scarface looked dutifully away, then back, and when he saw the sidearm pointing at his breast, a look of terrible loss crossed his face. "I see that I will never understand you," he growled, clasping his hands behind his head. "And I see that you still doubt my honor."

Locklear forced him to lean against the pinnace, arms behind his back, and secured his hands with binder tape. "Sorry, but I have to do this," he said. "Now get back in the pinnace. I'm taking you to Kzersatz."

"But I would have—"

"Don't say it," Locklear demanded. "Don't tell me what you want, and don't remind me of your honor, goddammit! Look here, I *know* you don't lie. And what if the next ship here is another kzin ship? You won't lie to them either, your bloody honor won't let you. They'll find you sitting pretty on Kzersatz, right?"

Teetering off-balance as he climbed into the pinnace without using his arms, Scarface still glowered. But after a moment he admitted, "Correct."

"They won't court-martial you, Scarface. Because a lying, sneaking monkey pulled a gun on you, tied you up, and sent you back to prison. I'm telling you here and now, I see Kzersatz as a prison and every tabby on this planet will be locked up there for the duration of the war!" With that, Locklear sealed the canopy and made a quick check of the console readouts. He reached across to adjust the inertia-reel harness of his companion, then shrugged into his own. "You have no choice, and no tabby telepath can ever claim you did. *Now* do you understand?"

The big kzin was looking below as the forest dropped away, but Locklear could see his ears forming the kzin equivalent of a smile. "No wonder you win wars," said Scarface.

WILL *YOU* SURVIVE?

In addition to Dean Ing's powerful science fiction novels— *Systemic Shock, Wild Country, Blood of Eagles* and others—he has written cogently and inventively about the art of survival. **The Chernobyl Syndrome** is the result of his research into life after a possible nuclear exchange . . . because as our civilization gets bigger and better, we become more and more dependent on its products. What would *you* do if the machine stops—or blows up?

Some of the topics Dean Ing covers:
* How to *make* a getaway airplane
* Honing your "crisis skills"
* Fleeing the firestorm: escape tactics for city-dwellers
* How to build a homemade fallout meter
* Civil defense, American style
* "Microfarming"—survival in five acres
  And much, much more.

Also by Dean Ing, available through Baen Books:

ANASAZI
Why did the long-vanished Anasazi Indians retreat from their homes and gardens on the green mesa top to precarious cliffside cities? Were they afraid of someone—or some*thing*? "There's no evidence of warfare in the ruins of their earlier homes . . . but maybe the marauders they feared didn't wage war in the usual way," says Dean Ing. *Anasazi* postulates a race of alien beings who needed human bodies in order to survive on Earth—a race of aliens that *still* exists.

FIREFIGHT 2000
How do you integrate armies supplied with bayonets and ballistic missiles; citizens enjoying Volkswagens and Ferraris; cities drawing power from windmills and nuclear powerplants? Ing takes a look at these dichotomies, and more. This collection of fact and fiction serves as a metaphor for tomorrow: covering terror and hope, right guesses and wrong, high tech and thatched cottages.
